Danielle Steel

'Danielle's books always make me feel **strong, inspired and happy** – truly a page-turning experience' *Liz*

'She has a remarkable ability to write different stories at an **amazing pace**. Every time I pick up a book I know that I'm going to be taken through **highs and lows**' *Gillian*

'I feel like I've **travelled the world** through her descriptions of the places in her books' *Ann*

'Every book **gets you hooked** from page one' *Julie*

'Danielle Steel takes me to another place with her masterful story-telling … **Absolute reading pleasure** from the first page to the very last' *Holly*

'I have **drawn immense strength** from the characters in many of her books' *Sarika*

Daddy's Girls

Danielle Steel has been hailed as one of the world's most popular authors, with nearly a billion copies of her novels sold. Her recent international bestsellers include *Neighbours*, *The Affair* and *Finding Ashley*. She is also the author of *His Bright Light*, the story of her son Nick Traina's life and death; *A Gift of Hope*, a memoir of her work with the homeless; and the children's books *Pretty Minnie in Paris* and *Pretty Minnie in Hollywood*. Danielle divides her time between Paris and her home in northern California.

By Danielle Steel

Finding Ashley • The Affair • Neighbours • All That Glitters
Royal • Daddy's Girls • The Wedding Dress • The Numbers Game
Moral Compass • Spy • Child's Play • The Dark Side • Lost and Found
Blessing in Disguise • Silent Night • Turning Point • Beauchamp Hall
In His Father's Footsteps • The Good Fight • The Cast • Accidental Heroes
Fall From Grace • Past Perfect • Fairytale • The Right Time • The Duchess
Against All Odds • Dangerous Games • The Mistress • The Award
Rushing Waters • Magic • The Apartment • Property Of A Noblewoman
Blue • Precious Gifts • Undercover • Country • Prodigal Son • Pegasus
A Perfect Life • Power Play • Winners • First Sight • Until The End Of Time
The Sins Of The Mother • Friends Forever • Betrayal • Hotel Vendôme
Happy Birthday • 44 Charles Street • Legacy • Family Ties • Big Girl
Southern Lights • Matters Of The Heart • One Day At A Time
A Good Woman • Rogue • Honor Thyself • Amazing Grace • Bungalow 2
Sisters • H.R.H. • Coming Out • The House • Toxic Bachelors • Miracle
Impossible • Echoes • Second Chance • Ransom • Safe Harbour
Johnny Angel • Dating Game • Answered Prayers • Sunset In St. Tropez
The Cottage • The Kiss • Leap Of Faith • Lone Eagle • Journey
The House On Hope Street • The Wedding • Irresistible Forces
Granny Dan • Bittersweet • Mirror Image • The Klone And I
The Long Road Home • The Ghost • Special Delivery • The Ranch
Silent Honor • Malice • Five Days In Paris • Lightning • Wings • The Gift
Accident • Vanished • Mixed Blessings • Jewels • No Greater Love
Heartbeat • Message From Nam • Daddy • Star • Zoya • Kaleidoscope
Fine Things • Wanderlust • Secrets • Family Album • Full Circle • Changes
Thurston House • Crossings • Once In A Lifetime • A Perfect Stranger
Remembrance • Palomino • Love: Poems • The Ring • Loving
To Love Again • Summer's End • Season Of Passion • The Promise
Now And Forever • Passion's Promise • Going Home

Nonfiction
Expect a Miracle
Pure Joy: The Dogs We Love
A Gift of Hope: Helping the Homeless
His Bright Light: The Story of Nick Traina

For Children
Pretty Minnie in Hollywood
Pretty Minnie in Paris

Danielle Steel

DADDY'S GIRLS

PAN BOOKS

First published 2020 by Delacorte Press
an imprint of Random House
a division of Penguin Random House LLC, New York

First published in the UK 2020 by Macmillan

This paperback edition published 2021 by Pan Books
an imprint of Pan Macmillan
The Smithson, 6 Briset Street, London EC1M 5NR
EU representative: Macmillan Publishers Ireland Limited,
Mallard Lodge, Lansdowne Village, Dublin 4
Associated companies throughout the world
www.panmacmillan.com

ISBN 978-1-5098-7824-6

1 3 5 7 9 8 6 4 2

A CIP catalogue record for this book is available from the British Library.

Typeset in Charter ITC Std by Palimpsest Book Production Limited, Falkirk, Stirlingshire
Printed and bound by CPI Group (UK) Ltd, Croydon, CR0 4YY

MIX
Paper from
responsible sources
FSC® C116313

Visit **www.panmacmillan.com** to read more about all our books
and to buy them. You will also find features, author interviews and
news of any author events, and you can sign up for e-newsletters
so that you're always first to hear about our new releases.

To my wonderful children,
Beatrix, Trevor, Todd, Nick,
Samantha, Victoria, Vanessa,
Maxx, and Zara,

May our family and our love
for each other,
and mine for you,
give you comfort,
solace, strength, joy,
and make you wise and
loving.
Always!

       With all my love,
       Mom/d.s.

DADDY'S GIRLS

Chapter 1

The sky was just beginning to lighten and there were birds singing when Kate Tucker got up at four-thirty on a May morning, as she did every day. A tall, leggy blonde, she unwound herself from the sheets, and went to get a cup of coffee. Her days were long and started early, working on her father's ranch in the Santa Ynez Valley. They had moved there from Texas thirty-eight years before, when she was four years old. Her mother had died the year before, a few months after her youngest sister, Caroline, was born. Her father was a ranch hand. He had decided to come to California with his meager savings, his truck, and his three little girls, Kate, Gemma, who was a year younger than Kate, and Caroline, who was one.

Jimmy Tucker, JT, had heard about the Santa Ynez Valley, and it sounded like heaven to him. He had gotten a job on a modest but respected ranch, and had brought his experience and skill from Texas. He was only twenty-six years old then, and quickly proved his worth to the ranch owner who had given him a chance, and a cabin for him and his three little girls to live in. The foreman's wife ran her own daycare in town, and had given Jimmy a "family discount" for his girls. And her teenage daughters sometimes babysat for him when he had to work at night.

It had been rugged at first trying to make ends meet. There was never any money for anything extra. He got their clothes in the hand-me-down basket at their church, and some of the other ranch hands' wives gave him whatever their children had outgrown. He managed to feed and house his daughters, and worked hard at his job. He saved every penny he could, thinking of the future. Jimmy Tucker was a man with dreams, and the rancher he worked for thought he would go far. He had a fire in his belly like few men his boss had known.

Kate didn't remember the hard times in the beginning, and neither did her sisters. When the foreman retired four years after they'd arrived, JT was made foreman, at thirty, and ran the ranch. And when the owner died ten years later, he left a decent sized piece of land to Jimmy, which he had added to over the years. Now, at sixty-four, Jimmy owned ten thousand acres, and the most successful ranch in the Valley. They raised cattle, bred horses, and had a small dairy. And at forty-two, Kate helped him run it. She had grown up on a horse and in her father's shadow.

Jimmy couldn't imagine living anywhere else in the world, nor could Kate. She had everything she wanted right here, a beautiful place, a job she loved, and she liked working with her father, though he wasn't easy. He was larger than life, and had a powerful personality. He valued what she did for him, but rarely said so. He was a man of few words, but he knew how to run a ranch better than anyone in the county, and had taught her everything she knew. They had thirty-five employees on the ranch, who respected her just as they did JT.

Pleasing him was all-important to her, but earning his praise wasn't easy. He rarely acknowledged how hard she worked. She was an important part of his operation, and she knew it. She was a born country girl, unlike both her younger sisters, who had fled, Gemma at eighteen to L.A., and Caroline for college.

Caroline was a beautiful blonde, smaller than her two older sisters. She was thirty-nine, three years younger than Kate, married, and had two children. Neither Kate nor Gemma was married. Caroline had gone to UC Berkeley to get a teaching degree, and stayed on to get a master's in English literature. She'd started writing young adult books in grad school to make ends meet, while working as a teacher and a waitress. She made a respectable living now with her books.

It was the life Caroline had longed for growing up and her father and sisters had never understood. She had an unquenchable thirst for books, knowledge, and culture, none of which was available in the Valley, or not to the degree she wanted. She read everything she could lay hands on, while Kate had a natural instinct for horses and learned everything she could about the ranch. All Gemma wanted was to leave and go to Hollywood. They each had their own passions and Caroline's were totally foreign to her sisters. It set her apart from her family, and made her feel like a stranger in their midst from the time she was very young. She learned to read at five and had been a voracious reader ever since. She dreamed of doing and seeing the things she read about, and of writing herself.

Now at thirty-nine, she lived in Marin County outside San Francisco, with her husband, Peter, and their two children. She had met Peter at Berkeley when she was in college and he was in business school. He was five years older, from a family with money. Peter had grown up with all the cultural advantages she had missed. He had made a considerable fortune of his own in venture capital. Caroline and Peter were the typical successful Marin County couple. He drove a Porsche, she drove a Mercedes station wagon. They had a handsome house and two bright, nice kids who went to private schools. Their daughter, Morgan, was fifteen, and Billy was eleven. Caroline loved their life, her work, and their marriage.

She had snuck away while her father wasn't looking. Gemma, his middle child, had always been the star in his eyes, and Kate, the oldest, was the daughter he counted on to back him, and work with him on the ranch. Caroline never gave him a hard time about anything. He and Gemma fought constantly, but he loved and respected her all the more for it. While he and Gemma were battling, Caroline just quietly slipped away to the life she had fantasized about for years. She had everything she wanted now, a solid marriage, great kids, a pretty house. She was involved with the ballet, the film festival in Marin, the San Francisco Museum of Modern Art, and a career she enjoyed. She was still writing young adult books, and had won the coveted Printz Award, the most prestigious award for books for younger readers.

She had been starving for culture while she lived in the Valley, and all her hopes had come to fruition once she left Santa Ynez. She went back as rarely as possible, and occasionally felt guilty about it. She loved her father and sister, but found visiting the ranch oppressive. Just being there made her feel anxious. It was a déjà vu of her youth, which wasn't a happy memory for her. She had felt overlooked and out of place for all seventeen years she'd lived there until she left for college.

Peter was from New York and they visited his family more often than hers, although her kids thought it was fun to go to the ranch. Caroline loved going to New York, catching up on the latest museum exhibits, the opera, theater, and everything that the city offered. She took her children with her whenever possible.

They thought their maternal grandfather was a colorful person, full of charm, and a real cowboy. He had ridden in the rodeo when he was younger, and done well. He had even survived being gored by a bull in a roping contest, which fascinated her children. But they saw very little of him. Caroline, Peter, and the children usually had something else to do. She had quietly disconnected from her own family in every significant way over the years. It was just better for her, and Peter didn't press her about it. He wasn't fond of the ranch either, and he knew how much she hated going home, which gave him a valid excuse not to go there and to discourage her from going. She hadn't been back in three years.

In the early days of their relationship, Peter had teased Caroline mercilessly about growing up on a ranch. He called her a cowgirl, and referred to her "redneck origins" until she finally told him how it hurt her and got him to stop. It had taken years to win his parents' respect, and they made it obvious that they would have preferred it if he had married someone from their world. In time, they came to appreciate her value, and how much she loved their son. Their acceptance had been hard won.

Peter valued her intelligence, good judgment, sound advice, and solid values too. But in heated moments, the difference in how they had grown up still caused them to clash. She wasn't a New Yorker and didn't have the sophisticated upbringing he did, but she was a loving mother and a wonderful wife. The rare times he called her a cowgirl now were meant only to ruffle her feathers, not to wound her, although sometimes it still did anyway. She wasn't proud of her origins and still sorely felt the opportunities she had missed in Santa Ynez, with a father and two sisters who thought intellectual pursuits were a waste of time. She had more than made up for it as an adult.

Gemma didn't go home much more often than Caroline did. She had gone to L.A. as soon as she'd graduated from high school, without bothering with college. She was a striking, tall, beautiful, exotic-looking woman with dark hair and blue eyes. She'd done some modeling, paid for acting lessons herself, and started out with small parts on TV. At thirty-one, she had landed the starring role in a successful TV series, and was still firmly ensconced there. Now forty-one, she had had her eyes done, and enough Botox shots and fillers to look ten years younger than she was, with makeup and good lighting. She never seemed to age on the show or in real life. She was very decidedly a star, and lived that way, with a gorgeous house and pool in the Hollywood Hills, and a glamorous life. She had dated some of the best-known Hollywood bachelors, and fallen seriously in love once. Her romances were usually brief and tumultuous, and were reported in the tabloids. Her one serious love had left her for a more famous actress and broken her heart. She had kept things light ever since, never caring deeply for the men in her life. She was more dedicated to her career than to anything else. Her father loved reading about her, no matter what the papers said. Gemma could do no wrong in JT's eyes, though their battles were legendary and fierce. They were too much alike to get along, headstrong, stubborn, and determined to have their own way. Neither Gemma nor Kate had ever married, and Gemma claimed she didn't care. She was having too much fun to get tied down, once she got over her one and only broken heart. Kate worked too hard to meet a man and spend time with him. She was at her father's beck and call on the ranch day and night. If anything went wrong, he called her, at any hour.

Their father liked to say that he had a workhorse in Kate, Gemma was his star, and Caroline was the brain and suburban housewife, once she grew up. He never understood her life or her interests, and didn't try, but he was impressed by her husband's success, and he thought his grandchildren were great. They were smart and inquisitive and loved his stories when he occasionally saw them. He never went to San Francisco. He never left the Valley. He was always working. He loved it.

JT Tucker was a cowboy to the depths of his soul, and so was Kate. She worked hard to be the son he'd never had. She had lived up to all his expectations, even if he didn't acknowledge it often. She lived for one thing, to please him. Her life in the Santa Ynez Valley suited her to perfection. When she was younger, she assumed she'd marry, but as time went on, the men she dated fell by the wayside. They wanted more than she had to give. Her father and the ranch consumed all her energy and time. She was always canceling dates or standing men up to tend to a sick horse, help deliver a calf, or because her father insisted he needed her help with a project only she could do. It got harder and harder to explain, and eventually she stopped trying. She was married to the ranch now. Her father expected it and didn't realize what a sacrifice she'd made for him. It was what he expected of her. And she loved her father, the ranch, and the valley where they lived, with her whole heart and soul, more than she'd ever loved any man. The men in her life had gone on to marry other women, while her father continued to depend on her.

By six o'clock in the morning, she would be on a horse and stay there for most of the day, checking on their fences, watching what went on at the breeding barn, riding across the fields, helping to plan their livestock auctions. There was no aspect of their business that she wasn't involved in or knowledgeable about. It was a large operation, with bunkhouses for twenty-five of their thirty-five employees.

JT had no intention of retiring. He was a strong, vital man. He was a good father, as long as you did what he said, and agreed with him. Except for Gemma, who never did. He would never have tolerated the same behavior from Caroline or Kate. He had never hidden the fact that Gemma had been "Daddy's Girl" all her life, and still was. No one could match her looks or glamour when she showed up at the ranch. As much as it was foreign to him, he loved that she was a TV star. Despite the fact that Caroline was successful writing young adult books that were lucrative and admired, the value of what she did went right over his head. Writing for kids seemed irrelevant to him. But Caroline had never hungered for his praise, as Kate had. Instead she had sought freedom, and found it at Berkeley, and then in Marin County as a wife and mother. Peter and her kids were proud of her, that was enough. She always said that her father was a narcissist. Gemma didn't disagree with her. It was all about him.

None of them remembered their mother, although Kate thought she had some dim early memories from when she was three. She was never sure if she remembered her from the occasional mention of her, or the photograph of her that was in each of their bedrooms. The others weren't old enough when she died to have recollections of their mother, and their father didn't like talking about her. He never dwelled on the past. He tried valiantly to be both mother and father to his girls when they were growing up, and succeeded, some times better than others. Gemma gave him credit for that, but he had been more generous about spending time with her than with the others. She had been a gorgeous child. Kate was shyer, and avoided the spotlight, and Caroline simply didn't comment or speak up. She was almost always silent. She kept her opinions to herself. All she wanted now was to lead a good life and be the perfect wife and mother.

She supported Peter in everything he did, listened avidly to his plans and problems, and gave him sound advice. She tried to be the kind of mother she would have liked to have and didn't, because of her mother's death. She wondered about her parents' early life in Texas sometimes. Their father made no secret of the fact that they had been poor, and it had been a wild bet on his part to come to California with three little girls and no job lined up, but he had always managed to work things out, and provide for them. Handsomely, later on.

JT was an only child with no living family when they left Texas. He said the memories there were too painful for him once Scarlett died. He wanted a fresh start, and he got one for all of them. In California, he managed with the foreman's wife's daycare. He cooked for them himself when he got home at night. And the girls learned early to be self-sufficient and take care of each other. They had suffered at times from not having a mother, but he hadn't suffered from not having a wife. For a long time, his girls and his work were enough for him. He cooked breakfast for them every morning, bathed them, spent time with them whenever possible, and taught them all to ride.

Gemma was a capable rider but hadn't ridden in ten years, except briefly in movies and in ads. Caroline had been terrified of horses all her life. Only Kate had his natural talent for horses. She was as solid in the saddle as any cowboy on the ranch, and had ridden in the local rodeo herself when she was younger, and enjoyed it. She was too busy for the rodeo now, and she couldn't afford the time off if she got hurt. Her father had taught her to rope steers as a young girl, and she was good at that too. She had the eye and the timing, but she'd stayed off the broncos that he had always loved. Gemma called him a born show-off, to his face. No one else would have dared. One of Kate's biggest thrills was when she was the rodeo queen one year. It allowed her to demonstrate her riding skills, but be seen as a girl. Her father thought it was silly, but was proud of her anyway.

Kate had gone to college, because her high school teachers said she should. She'd gone to a state university, and hated it. Her father said it was a waste of time, and he needed her on the ranch. Kate missed her father, the ranch, and her sisters the whole time she was there. Gemma skipped college entirely and left for L.A. during Kate's sophomore year. Caroline had gone to Berkeley at the start of Kate's senior year. Kate couldn't wait to get home when she graduated, and never left again.

As the girls grew up, Jimmy had chosen the right female companion twenty-four years before. He was forty when they met. Juliette had grown up in the Camargue, where the wild horses were in France, in a small seaside town. Juliette Dubré was a young widow, thirty years old, who had lost her husband in a mountain climbing accident, and took a year off to try to recover. She had come to the Santa Ynez Valley on a whim, met Jimmy, and stayed. He was passionate about her, but they were discreet. He let her live in a small guesthouse on the ranch. She was a bright but quiet woman who enchanted him. She never engaged in battle with him, or challenged his sometimes outrageous, very male positions. She was subtle in her influence, and gentle in her ways with him. She was a beautiful young woman with a wild mane of red hair and green eyes. He had fallen in love with her, but never forced her on his children, and she stayed in the background, preferring to be their friend, rather than vying to be their mother. Several local women had been after Jimmy before that, but between the ranch and his daughters, he'd had little time to date, although he was considered a catch, as the ranch grew rapidly in its size and success. Juliette always waited for him quietly in the shadows. They spent hours together, talking, and over time she subtly introduced him to some of the cultural pursuits she enjoyed. She was a good rider too, and knew about horses, which he loved about her.

He didn't ask her to come and live with him in his house until Caroline, his youngest, left for college. After Kate graduated and returned, none of the girls were surprised to see Juliette living in the main house with him when they came home, and she was so gentle and discreet that none of them objected to her. She didn't crowd them or force herself on them. Kate was the closest to her because they saw more of each other living on the ranch. All of them were puzzled why he had never married her, but Juliette didn't seem to care and was satisfied with the arrangement they had.

She was ten years younger than Jimmy, fifty-four now, still beautiful, without artifice or makeup. Even in her mid-fifties there was an undeniably sexy quality to her, and a youthful style. She did the books at the ranch, and helped him run the livestock auctions, with Kate's help. But he was more inclined to give Juliette credit than his daughter, although Juliette always reminded JT of how hard Kate worked at everything she did for him. He took it for granted since the ranch would be hers one day too, and her sisters', though Gemma and Caroline wanted no part in the running of the ranch, or even being there. They had their own careers and were happy to be away from it. The ranch was Kate's career, her passion, her life and great love, to the exclusion of all else, most of the time. She had no opportunity for romance, and didn't seem to care. There weren't many options in the Valley and the boys she had gone to school with were all married and had families by now, in their early forties. The girls she had gone to school with had been married for years. Their friendships had fallen by the wayside, as they had less and less in common, once her old classmates had husbands and kids. Her more serious romances in college could never have lasted. She knew they had to end. The men she had dated would have tried to pull her away from the ranch, and she wouldn't let that happen.

Thad, their foreman, was like a brother to Kate, five years younger than she. They worked side by side much of the time. He was considered something of a player in the Valley, which she teased him about, especially when he looked like he'd had a long night, which happened often, especially after a particularly active weekend. He was classically tall, dark, and handsome, with dark brown hair and warm brown eyes, and looked like a poster of a cowboy. He even looked a little like her father had when he was younger. After nineteen years on the ranch, he seemed more like family than a mere employee, and he felt that way too.

Thad was the son JT had never had, and he treated him that way. He had come to work for a summer at eighteen, after seeing a notice for ranch hands on a bulletin board at the general store and feed store. He had called and had an interview, and after half an hour, JT was confident that Thad could handle the job well as a ranch hand, and maybe one day even as foreman. He lived in a cabin JT had let him build behind the barn. As the foreman, JT thought he deserved a better house now and had offered him one, but Thad insisted that his cabin was still adequate, even once he was foreman, since he was single at thirty-seven and only slept there. Like Kate, he was up before dawn, in one of the barns before six every morning, and outdoors, mostly on a horse, the rest of the time. He had the leathered skin of a cowboy, and Kate had a deep tan, which suited her. Gemma always warned her that her outdoor life would put twenty years on her one day. Kate didn't care. She never used the beauty products her sister sent her to preserve her youthful looks. Kate laughed when she got them, never opened the jars and bottles. She left them in the boxes they came in, languishing under the sink in her bathroom.

Kate's small house was hardly bigger than Thad's cabin, and she didn't mind either. Her father wanted to build her a better house, but she didn't want one. For the daughter of an important rancher, she was surprisingly modest. She and Thad enjoyed a warm friendship, which had built over many years while they worked together. She could have been jealous of him, because of the amount of attention he got from her father, but she respected Thad too. They worked well side by side, when they took on projects together. Thad was always willing to help her whenever he could.

After she had a piece of toast, half a banana, and a second cup of coffee, she showered and dressed, and walked into the barn at five-thirty A.M. to check on the horses. Everything looked fine. Thad had just come in when Kate got there, and they saddled up their respective horses, chatting about a fence near their grazing pastures that Thad said was down and she was going to look at. The fields were still green, but would be dry later in the summer, when fire often became a risk. There were professional firefighters nearby, and a large volunteer force of firemen who jumped in when needed. She knew all of them. She knew everyone in the Valley and they knew her. She was known as JT Tucker's daughter, more than as herself. She was an accessory to her father, which was how he liked it, with the attention on him, and she accepted it.

Her father came in as Kate tightened the saddle on her favorite horse, Bear, and the barn seemed instantly filled with JT's presence.

"What are you up to today?" he asked her, and smiled at Thad. They had a kind of unspoken understanding, born of two men who respected each other. JT understood men better than women and found them easier to be with, except for Juliette.

"I'm going to check on some fences Thad was just telling me about. Out past the south pasture," Kate told him.

"Why don't you let the ranch hands do that?" he said, pouring himself a cup of coffee from the pot she had just made.

"They say we need a new fence out there. I want to see it for myself. Saving you money, Dad," she teased him. She was scrupulous about watching their expenses, which he expected of her.

"I like that." He smiled at her and winked at Thad, and then went to saddle his own horse. He loved riding around the ranch, and keeping an eye on things himself. He had an eagle eye, and a sixth sense for anything that might be wrong. He wasn't a casual rancher or landowner, but a diligent, dedicated one, which was why the business was in such good shape. He delegated almost nothing, except to Thad and Kate, and their ranch hands were closely supervised. It had taken years for him to trust Thad to the extent he did, and he still questioned Kate about everything she did. He left nothing to chance and assumed nothing. He wanted to know about everything that went on, who had done it and why, and what it had cost him.

He was still a handsome man, tall and powerfully built with strong shoulders, long arms, and long legs. Kate and Gemma came by their height honestly, since both their parents were tall. Caroline was more delicate, and blond like Kate.

Thad followed Kate out of the barn on horseback. They rode down a familiar trail as the sun came up, and then took separate forks in the road. He had grown up in the state system, in foster care, south of L.A., and JT was the first important male influence he'd had in his life. He was deeply grateful to his patron for giving him a chance to shine. He had worked for him now for slightly more than half his life. He took none of the advantages he'd been given for granted. He'd gotten an education by taking college classes online, after a GED to give him the high school diploma he hadn't had time to get before he left school. Working on a ranch, around horses, had been his dream and he was good at it. It was natural instinct since he was an inner city kid and had had a hard life, for the first half of it. Both Kate and her father respected him for how far he'd come. He was a wholesome, honest, hardworking, ambitious guy, who gave as good as he got, and then some. He was loyal to a fault. He considered JT his mentor as well as his boss, and would have died before he let him down. Kate felt the same way about her father, so they had that in common.

The sun was bright as it came over the mountains and warmed them. It was going to be a beautiful day, and they were both looking forward to it.

"See you later," he said, as he rode off, his battered straw cowboy hat low over his eyes. Kate wore hers the same way, and it suited her with her blond hair tied back. She was wearing a checked shirt and jeans, and the well-worn cowboy boots she'd had for as long as she could remember. They were the staples of her wardrobe, and whenever Gemma invited her to L.A., Kate reminded her that she owned only one dress, which her sister said was pathetic.

"How do you expect to get laid if you dress like one of the ranch hands at your age?" Gemma chided her. "We're not twenty anymore. You have to make an effort, or you'll wind up a spinster forever," she teased.

"Is that what I am?" Kate laughed whenever Gemma said it. "A spinster?"

"Yeah, we both are." Gemma didn't seem to mind. She had an active sex life with some of the best-looking men in Hollywood, and wound up in the press with them regularly, much to her father's delight. She'd been out with many of the biggest stars, though seldom for second dates. There was a lot of movement and shuffling on the Hollywood dating scene, which Gemma seemed to like. Kate wouldn't have, and she had given up the idea of kids and marriage somewhere along the way. She was too busy working for her father, and told Gemma she didn't have the time, the wardrobe, or the inclination. "I'm going to drag you down to L.A. again one of these days," Gemma threatened her. Kate had a good time when she went, but she always felt like a fish out of water. Her sister's world couldn't have been more different from her own. They were each doing what they wanted. When she visited, she enjoyed watching Gemma on the set of her TV show, though. It still felt strange knowing that her sister was a star, and people asked for her autograph wherever she went. It was a popular show. Gemma's celebrity was nothing Kate had ever aspired to, but Gemma had had her nose plunged in movie magazines from the time she was twelve. Hollywood had always been her dream. The ranch was Kate's.

It took Kate half an hour to find the fence that had fallen. She took pictures of it with her phone, and sent them to Thad, so he could assign a detail to repair it. It was as bad as the men had reported. Then she gave Bear his head, and flew back to the barn at a gallop. She knew the property like her own hand, and could have ridden back blindfolded.

She was in good spirits when she got back to the barn, and her father rode in at the same time. He sat in the saddle for a minute, looking at her. He didn't notice her often, or how beautiful she was, or even mention it. She had a deep tan and her eyes were bright as he started to say something and she saw him wince, as though he was in pain suddenly. He pressed his chest with one hand, as she hopped off her horse and went to him.

"Are you okay, Dad?" she asked as she reached him, and he slumped forward, and then slid off his horse in her direction. She caught him, and lowered his powerful body to the ground. His eyes fluttered for a minute and then closed. He lay on the barn floor and she knelt beside him. She saw him stop breathing. She felt for his pulse and there was none. She gave him a few quick breaths mouth to mouth, and he still wasn't breathing as she shouted to one of the ranch hands to call 911, and told him to call Thad after that. Her father was lying completely still, and she gave him a few more puffs of air, felt his pulse, and there was still nothing. She started chest compressions then, as the ranch hands gathered around and watched her as she fought to save her father.

She kept up the steady rhythm of the breaths and chest compressions for what felt like hours before she heard sirens in the distance. As soon as she did, Thad ran in and knelt next to her.

"What happened?"

"I don't know. I think he had a heart attack," she said and continued CPR. The paramedics arrived in force then, and took over. The head paramedic was a man she'd gone to school with. Caroline had dated his younger brother in high school. He asked her for the details, as one of his men continued giving Jimmy CPR, and another took out a defibrillator. When the defibrillator instructed them to, they administered a shock, as Kate and Thad stood near, watching what was happening. Kate clutched Thad's hand. She could tell the defibrillator hadn't worked. They'd been working on him for an hour, when Kate's old schoolmate turned to her and shook his head. He stepped away from JT then and came over to her. They had done everything they could, and Kate and Thad had seen it. None of it had worked.

"I'm sorry, Kate. Sometimes you just can't bring them back. I think he went instantly. Did he have a history of heart problems?" She shook her head and had told them that in the beginning. It was just his time, with no warning. Kate looked as though she was in shock.

"How can that just happen? He was fine when I left him this morning."

"It's terrible to say, but sometimes it's better like that. He led a great life and was a terrific guy." They covered him then, put him on a gurney to take him to the ambulance outside, as the ranch hands stood staring, and Kate cried in Thad's arms. He was crying too.

"Oh my God, Thad . . . he was sixty-four years old, in perfect health." And now he was dead. Neither of them could believe it, as they stood there crying.

Juliette ran into the barn. She arrived just in time to see them carry Jimmy out on the stretcher, with his face covered, and she ran to him, uncovered him, and bent to kiss him. They put him in the ambulance then to take him to the hospital morgue, until Kate could recover enough to make arrangements.

Juliette looked like she'd been hit by a bomb. They all did. The two women hugged each other and stood crying, and then went back to JT's rambling ranch house, where Juliette lived with him. "I heard the sirens, and I thought someone got hurt. I never thought it was him," she said in her still heavy French accent.

Kate was so shaken she could barely speak. They walked into the house, and his belongings were everywhere, a pair of tall, mud-covered rubber boots that he'd worn the day before, his riding gloves on the table, a jacket he'd thrown over a chair. The three of them sat down at the kitchen table, staring at each other, unable to believe that he was gone. Thad poured them all coffee and Kate looked at him and Juliette bleakly.

"I have to call my sisters." She couldn't think of what to say.

"Give yourself a minute first," Thad said gently, and she nodded, but couldn't drink the coffee. Juliette lit a cigarette, and was as shattered as Kate. She had loved him for twenty-four years.

After they'd sat there for a while, Thad walked Kate to her house, and she sat down again and looked at him.

"I don't even know what to say to the employees. This feels like a bad dream and I'm going to wake up any minute." Only she knew she wouldn't. In a single instant, everything had changed, and her father would never wake up again. Thad stayed until she felt ready to call her sisters, and then he walked to his own cabin, with tears rolling down his cheeks, feeling as though his world had come to an end. What were they all going to do without Jimmy? It was unthinkable, unimaginable. As he walked into his cabin, he felt desperately sorry for Kate. For forty-two years, her whole life had been her father. That morning, in an instant, her world had changed, and so had his.

Chapter 2

Gemma was having lunch in her trailer on the set at the studio, her long legs stretched out, reading her lines for the next scene when her cellphone rang. She glanced at it, but wasn't going to answer, so as not to get distracted from the script. Her hair was in rollers, and she was wearing the bathrobe she always wore between scenes on the set. It had been a long morning shooting, and it was a hot day in L.A. She saw that the call was from her sister, and picked it up.

"Hi, cowgirl, how's life in the sticks?" Gemma teased her, as she always did. There was a long silence while Kate tried not to sob before she told her.

"Not so good." Kate's voice sounded like a stranger's to both of them. "Something just happened to Daddy." She hadn't called him that in years. She called him Dad now, or sometimes JT when referring to him, like everyone else, but never Daddy.

"Like what?" Gemma asked as she frowned.

Kate lost it then and started to cry. "He had a heart attack. He just died, Gem. They tried to revive him, and they couldn't. I gave him

CPR until the paramedics came. He was just gone, instantly. Dickie Jackson was the head of the paramedics. He was really nice about it. He said there was nothing they could do."

"Oh my God." Gemma didn't know what else to say. She didn't cry. She just stared into space, unable to believe what she'd just heard. "That can't be. He was fine. He's never sick." She tried to remember the last time she had talked to him, and couldn't. They never had much to say. Their father was a man of few words. He was better and more expressive face-to-face. He was a true Texan and a cowboy until the end.

"Can you come home?" Kate asked, sounding like a child. She felt as though her whole world had caved in. He was the center of her universe.

"Of course. I'll drive up tonight," she said quietly, and then hesitated. "I love you, Kate. Are you going to be okay?"

"I don't know," Kate said, feeling confused. "I love you too, Gem." They both knew that Gemma had been his shining star and his favorite, but it didn't matter now. They had all lost him, and all they had now was each other.

After they hung up, Gemma went to find the director to tell him what had happened and that she had to leave and they'd have to shoot around her for the next few days. They were going on hiatus soon anyway. He told her how sorry he was about her father. She thanked him and left the set a few minutes later in jeans and a T-shirt. She had to go home to pack a bag. She drove to the Hollywood Hills, not even sure where she was going. Everything around her was a blur. The father who had adored her was gone.

*   *   *

Kate called Caroline after that. She answered on speaker in the car. "Where are you?" Kate asked her youngest sister.

"Morgan forgot her lunch. I'm taking it to her at school. Why? Is something wrong?" Kate sounded odd, like she was sick or stoned or drunk, which she never was.

"Yeah," Kate said, choking on the words again. "It's Dad."

"What happened? Did he get hurt?" She didn't see her family often, but she loved them. She just didn't want to be with them all the time, or even very frequently. She had always felt out of place with them, she was the invisible person no one ever saw and never knew, and didn't try to. She was no match for her father or sisters. They were all stronger than she was. And so was Peter. Caroline had been meek all her life.

Kate told her what had happened, and Caroline pulled over off the freeway, and they both cried.

"Does Gemma know?" Caroline asked, feeling breathless. Whatever his failings, he was still her father.

"I just called her," Kate said, and it wasn't lost on Caroline that Kate had called Gemma first, and her last. It was always that way. She was the afterthought, even to their father. Even now. "She's coming home later." It would take her about three hours from L.A.

"I'll fly down with Peter and the kids tonight. I have to wait till he comes home from work. I'm sorry, Kate." Caroline said it as though he was Kate and Gemma's father, and not hers, and in some ways it was how she felt. Kate loved him, he loved Gemma, and she was always left out. It was why she had left so long ago and never gone back, except for very rare visits once every few years. She had asked herself, What difference would it make to them if she ran away and never came back? She had often pondered that question while she was growing up. And then she'd done it. Ran away and never came back to the ranch to live. She had never regretted it. And now she had to go home, and he was dead. She felt even worse when she realized it had been three months since she had called him. He never called her either, and now he never would again.

Kate was waiting in her house when Gemma arrived at six o'clock. She had wasted no time in L.A., and got on the freeway heading north as soon as she packed a bag. She found Kate sitting in her kitchen. She hadn't wanted to wait in their father's house, and intrude on Juliette. Kate had called her to see how she was and she didn't pick up. She was a very private person, and very French. She needed some time to recover from the shock and grieve on her own, and Kate respected that.

Kate and Gemma sat in Kate's kitchen and cried about their father again. They each realized that they were mourning entirely different men. The effusive, all-approving, all-forgiving father who thought Gemma could do no wrong, no matter how often she fought with him, or how vicious their fights were, and their words. And the father who had expected Kate to step up to the plate every time, back him in all things, second his decisions, and whom he forgot to praise except when someone reminded him, like Gemma or Thad or Juliette. They also knew that Caroline would be grieving an entirely other man, the father who had let her down and ignored her for her entire life. He loved her, but he didn't understand her, so he didn't try.

They were still talking when Thad picked up Caroline and her family at the airport. Her children had been inconsolable when she told them when they came home from school that their grandfather had died. No one had expected it. Peter was equally stunned when he got home and Caroline was packing. She hadn't wanted to call and tell him at the office. He had to pack in less than half an hour, and cancel his appointments for the coming days.

The three sisters hadn't spoken of it, but Caroline assumed that the funeral would be within the next few days. She didn't see any point to dragging it out, and she was sure her sisters wouldn't either. She hated the current trend of private family services, and then a memorial six months later. By then, she hoped to have put the grief behind her, and gotten on with living. What was the point of waiting? But she didn't know how Gemma and Kate would feel or what they would want.

They'd each had a glass of wine late that evening when they talked about it. Caroline and her family were staying in the guesthouse her father had built for her after she got married, hoping to inspire her to come home more, with Peter. But she never had. She had only used it a few times in the sixteen years since he built it. Gemma was staying in the guesthouse she occupied on her infrequent visits.

All three of them had gone to see Juliette that night, hugged her, and said how sorry they were. Her eyes were red-rimmed, and she couldn't stop crying. They left her after a few minutes to collect herself before they had to wade through the paperwork and formalities of "making the arrangements" the next day.

It sounded morbid to all three of them, and Juliette had said she was dreading it. She had no real right to make decisions, since they weren't married, but the girls wanted to include her. Their relationship had lasted longer and been warmer and happier than most marriages. If not a mother figure, she had always been a good friend to them, and never created problems with their father, or interfered with his relationship with them. If anything, she had always helped them, and reminded their father to make more effort with them, to understand them better. She had always been a good influence on him.

With a second bottle of wine, back in Kate's kitchen, they started telling funny stories about him, and reminiscing about their childhood. Caroline had the least to contribute, since she had spent the least possible amount of time with him, intentionally. Listening to them now, she wondered if she had missed something. She didn't know the man they were describing, and her memories of him were entirely different from Kate's and Gemma's. But Kate had worked with him as an adult for the last twenty years, and Gemma could do no wrong. He worshipped her. Caroline had been a ghost in his life. He had never sought to try to bridge the gap between them. She couldn't even explain now why she hadn't been to the ranch in the past three years. She was busy with the children, she and Peter entertained his most important clients, and they traveled with the children on school vacations. There was never time to come home and see her father.

"You ran away from him, Caro," Gemma said quietly, seeing the questions in her sister's eyes, and Caroline nodded. She didn't deny it.

"I know I did. But he never tried to find me, or even know me."

"Maybe that was your job and not his," Gemma said softly, "once you grew up. But I was no better. I haven't been home in nearly a year. It's hard to come home sometimes, and I got tired of fighting with him."

"We all did," Kate chimed in.

"You never fought with him," Gemma corrected her. "That was my role. All you ever did was please him, or try to." That was Kate's place in the family. The pleaser and peacemaker. It surprised her that

Gemma sounded harsh about it. In a way, her relationship with their father had been the easiest of all. They were workmates and colleagues as well as father and daughter.

After they finished the second bottle of wine, they went back to their respective cottages, Caroline in the barely used guesthouse, where Peter and her children were sound asleep, and Gemma to the guesthouse she was familiar with. Kate was in her own cottage, but nothing felt right anymore, not even her father's house with his belongings everywhere.

As they left Kate's cottage, Gemma turned to look at her sisters. "We're orphans now, aren't we? No mother and no father." They couldn't mourn a mother they had never known and didn't remember, only the idea of her, but their father was all too real, and they knew exactly who and what they were mourning.

"I don't think they call it 'orphans' at our age. We're grown-ups. We're supposed to be standing on our own two feet, with children of our own. Caro's the only one who's managed to do that. I was his willing slave, and you were always his favorite. That doesn't make us orphans," Kate said firmly. She didn't like what Gemma said.

"I was always Daddy's Girl. He called me that, he even said it to other people," Gemma said sadly.

"I guess we all have to grow up now," Kate said, but she wasn't at all sure how to do it. Who was going to run the ranch now? She knew the others would expect her to do it, but it couldn't possibly be the same without her father to guide her, even if he didn't recognize her contributions. She realized now that she had let her father run her world. And there was no one to do it now.

* * *

Their visit to the mortuary the next day was more depressing than any of them had expected. They were suddenly faced with painful decisions. Cremation or burial? If cremated, would they put the urn into the ground or divide up his ashes between the three of them and Juliette? And where would they bury him, if they did, at the cemetery or on the ranch? Would they have a large church service, or private family interment? Someone had to write the obituary. Caroline said she'd do it, since she was the writer among them, so she was the obvious choice.

They decided to hold a proper funeral, and put an announcement in the local paper, since his life had been there for nearly forty years, and he was respected in the community. They needed to pick a photograph for the program. Kate said she'd order the flowers, and Gemma said she'd choose the music. Juliette made only a few minor requests, and was relieved when they decided not to have an open casket, but to have him cremated. They were going to divide his ashes among them. Caroline and Kate were going to scatter them at the ranch, Gemma wanted to take her share with her to scatter in the ocean near L.A., and Juliette said she was going to pick a handsome box and keep them in the house with her. They thought it might be a French tradition, but didn't know and didn't ask.

They left the funeral home feeling drained, and went to meet Peter and Caroline's children. They had been to visit a nearby miniature horse farm to keep them distracted. Then they went back to the ranch for lunch, and Juliette cooked for them in her kitchen. She served pâté she'd made herself that their father loved, a big salad, some cold chicken she bought on the way home, and two bottles of wine that Peter opened for her. Everything Juliette did always came out seeming French, no matter how many years she'd been there.

They went out for dinner that night, to a small Italian restaurant, and every five minutes someone came to the table to extend their condolences. They were exhausted by the time they went home.

Two days later, the service was dignified and simple, the way their father would have liked it. The church was filled to the rafters with all the people who had admired and respected him, and many who barely knew him. At the funeral, Juliette sat next to Jimmy's daughters in the front pew with Peter, Morgan, and Billy. Thad and the senior ranch hands sat in the pew right behind them. There were faces from the past and the present.

Jimmy's lawyer was there. They all knew him and he said on the way out of the church that he would drop off a copy of the will for each of them that afternoon. Their father had discussed it with Kate when he'd last brought it up to date, and they expected no surprises. He was leaving the ranch and any money he had divided equally among the three of them. They had decisions to make about that too. They could maintain their joint ownership, if they wished, or if any of the girls didn't want their share of the ranch, they could sell it to the others. His only wish was that they keep it in the family. But neither Gemma nor Caroline used it, and they had no idea what to do about it. They weren't planning to discuss it that weekend. Four days before, he'd been vital and alive, and now they were faced with reading his will, and whether or not to divide up the property and how to do it.

"We should go through his safe in the office before you two leave," Kate said on their way back to the house, where they knew several hundred people would be waiting for them to pay their respects to the family. Gemma had called a caterer in Santa Barbara to handle it, and provide a bar and buffet, and none of them were looking forward to it.

"Do you think there's anything important in the safe?" Caroline didn't look eager to deal with it. The funeral had been hard enough, and she had agreed to stay for a few days, to go through her father's personal effects with them. Peter was going to take the children back to San Francisco the day after the funeral. Since she and Gemma came so rarely, Kate wanted to take advantage of the opportunity of having them there, and they reluctantly agreed to go through his safe in the office, and some of his personal effects at the house.

In the end, hundreds of people came and went all afternoon. Peter stood on the receiving line with them, somberly greeting the guests, and speaking softly to Caroline, and occasionally his sisters-in-law. Afterward, they were too emotionally drained to deal with their father's safe, and put it off to do the next morning.

Looking exhausted, all three sisters met in their father's office at ten o'clock the next morning, after Peter and the children had gone. They hadn't even read the copies of their father's will by then, and were in no rush to do it. The lawyer had dropped off copies for Juliette and Thad too, which suggested that he had left them bequests, which seemed appropriate in Juliette's case, to honor the twenty-four years they had spent together. And Thad had been devoted to him for nineteen years, and was almost like a son in JT's eyes.

Kate knew the combination of the huge safe by heart, and opened it easily. There were stacks of recent ledgers relating to different aspects of their business. She was surprised to find an envelope with fifty thousand dollars in it. It was unusual for him to keep that much cash on hand. Kate put it on the desk, along with everything she pulled out of the safe. It all related to the business. At the very back, she found a thick manila envelope with her father's handwriting. It said "Scarlett" on it, their mother. Kate wondered if there were sentimental papers in it, maybe letters from her, or photographs, or her death certificate. Both Gemma and Caroline noticed the envelope as Kate set it down, and they spotted their mother's name.

"Do we really want to go through that?" Gemma asked, looking uncomfortable. "Isn't one death enough to deal with?" Caroline looked as though she agreed with her, but said nothing.

"We might as well do it now," Kate said, and removed the yellowed tape that sealed it. There were several smaller envelopes inside. One looked like a letter and was addressed to him in an unfamiliar hand, and there was a file of court documents, which Kate opened and started to flip through, and then looked up at her sisters.

"What is it?" Caroline glanced over at her, startled by the look on her sister's face. It was obviously something she hadn't expected.

"Did Dad ever say anything to you about their being divorced before Mom died?" Kate asked in barely more than a whisper.

"Of course not," Gemma answered. "They weren't divorced. They were married when she died. What is that?"

Without a word, she handed the file to Gemma, who flipped through several pages, and then handed the file to Caroline with a look of amazement. "Shit, Kate, why didn't he tell us?" Gemma said, shocked.

"I don't know," Kate said.

"He never told me either," Caroline whispered, staring at both of them.

There was a divorce decree from the state of Texas, dissolving the marriage of James Edward Tucker and Scarlett Jane Carson Tucker. "They must have gotten divorced right before she died. Maybe he didn't want to spoil our illusions about them, or he was embarrassed. There was a stigma attached to divorce then," Kate said as she continued to glance through the papers, and then stopped at another yellowed sheet of paper, and handed it to them. It was even more shocking than the first one. Caroline looked over Gemma's shoulder as she read it. Then both of them stared at Kate. It was a relinquishment of custody and parental rights by Scarlett Tucker. She had given up all right to them, even to visitation.

"Oh my God, why would she do that?" Caroline said, profoundly unnerved by it. With children of her own, she couldn't imagine her mother giving them up. In a separate envelope there was a canceled check to Scarlett for three thousand dollars, on the same date as the relinquishment papers were signed.

"Do you think he paid her to give us up?" Gemma looked stricken.

"I have no idea," Kate said, dumbstruck. "He never told me any of this. All I know is what you know. She died, he said he was heartbroken, and a year later we moved out here. He never liked talking about her."

"Do you think she sold us to him for three thousand dollars?" Gemma asked them both, and Kate winced.

"That's a hell of a way to put it. There must be some explanation. Dad wouldn't have lied to us. He may not have told us the whole story, but he wouldn't lie. And three thousand dollars was a lot of money to him then, probably all he had saved up. That was a lot for him to pay her. So it must have been important to both of them."

"Is her death certificate in there too?" Caroline wanted to know. Kate went through all the papers again, but it wasn't.

"She must have died after she signed these papers, because this is eleven months before we moved to California."

Gemma looked at them both then, with a thunderstruck expression, and almost didn't dare say what she was thinking. "What if she didn't die? What if she's alive somewhere? What if she's been alive all this time, and he told us she was dead?" Suddenly, she was suspicious of him, more so than her sisters.

"Dad wouldn't do that," Kate defended him immediately. "There's got to be an explanation. I wonder if he ever said something to Juliette about it." They went through the file again and the only significant documents were the divorce decree and the relinquishment of Scarlett's three children. They opened and read the letter then, it was from their mother to Jimmy, telling him how sorry she was, and that in spite of the papers she had signed, she hoped to see the children soon. She had written the letter a few days later, and must have died almost immediately after. Gemma's suggestion that she hadn't died was just too outlandish to consider. A man like him would never have told his children that their mother was dead if she wasn't. They all agreed that he wouldn't do that. But there was a terrible nagging feeling in Kate's stomach. He hadn't told them about the divorce and the relinquishment of her rights either. And what if Gemma was right, and their mother had sold him custody for three thousand dollars, a thousand for each of them? Selling the custody of children was illegal, but nothing on the check indicated why he had paid her the money. Only the timing of it had made them wonder.

Kate carefully put the yellowed papers back in the envelope, and decided to take them with her to her house. She wanted to read them again carefully. Maybe they had missed something. It was a mystery she wanted to solve quickly, to put their minds at rest. What they'd found raised questions for each of them about their father.

"Let's do an internet search and see what turns up," Gemma suggested, after Kate locked the safe and they left the office.

"Why? I'm sure she's dead," Caroline said in a whisper. She didn't want to know. It was just too painful questioning their mother's death, while trying to adjust to their father's.

They walked to Kate's house. Her computer was sitting on her desk. She turned it on, and without consulting her sisters, she typed in her mother's name for a national search of her whereabouts, or death records.

"This is crazy," Gemma said, as Caroline walked away and stared out the window. She was exhausted from the emotions of the past few days, and now they had added their mother's death to it. All she wanted to do was go home to Peter and her children. Coming to the ranch always made her unhappy, especially this time. The father who had always put her in last place was gone. It was never going to get better now, he was never going to "fix" it. She wasn't a star, and she didn't run the ranch for him or do his bidding, so for him she had never existed. Even when she was a child, he always overlooked her, because she was bookish and a good student, which Kate and Gemma weren't. They were more like him. Bright, but with a more limited scope of interest. Gemma only cared about her Hollywood life, and Kate the ranch. Caroline cared about art and literature and history and other intellectual pursuits in a broader world.

When Caroline turned around, she saw Kate staring at her computer screen, and Gemma gave a sharp gasp, when she saw it too.

"Holy shit, that's not possible." But her name and date of birth matched up. It was clearly the right person. She had given up the name Tucker, and was back to using her maiden name, Scarlett Jane Carson. A profile showed up on the screen, with a photograph of an attractive older woman with white hair.

"What does it say?" Caroline asked them both. She was on the other side of the computer. "Is she dead?" She hoped she was, she didn't want to have to deal with a monumental lie on top of everything else, and a mother who had abandoned them thirty-nine years ago and given them up, not died, as their father had always told them.

"No. Dad lied to us," Kate said in a strangled voice. "She's alive, and living in Santa Barbara." Less than an hour away. How long had she been there? For all these years? Less? They had lost their father suddenly, and now their mother had returned from the grave. Caroline bowed her head with a devastated look, as Kate and Gemma stared at each other.

"I want to go see her," Gemma said immediately.

"I don't." Caroline was adamant. "Whatever the reason was she gave us up is their business. I don't want to know. And I don't want to see her. We don't know her. She's been dead to us for thirty-nine years, whether it was true or not."

"You don't have to see her," Kate said quietly, trying to calm them both. She wanted to slow Gemma down, and reassure her youngest sister, who looked badly shaken.

"What about you?" Gemma asked Kate.

"I don't know," Kate said, staring at her computer screen again, and then at her sister. "I honestly don't know what I want to do. I need some time to digest this."

"Then I'll go alone," Gemma said in a strong voice. "I want to know why she gave us up, and why she never saw us again. Did she sell us? Did he pay her off? And why did he tell us she was dead, when she isn't?" They were important questions, and in her heart of hearts, Kate wanted to know too. She just didn't know if she could face the mother she had never known and had mourned all her life, on the heels of losing her father too.

They asked Juliette that afternoon if she knew anything about it, and she said she didn't. They believed her. Their father didn't share everything with her. And the answers to their questions had died with their father, and if they wanted answers, they had no choice. They would have to go and see their mother. For right now, it was more than any of them felt ready to deal with. The fact that they might have a living mother was shocking news to all of them. It made a liar of their father, and if true, they had been deprived of a mother by someone's choice, either his or hers. She hadn't been stricken by an early death, as they had always believed. Had she given them up willingly, or had he forced her to? The answer was important to each of them, even as adults. Was she a drug addict, a terrible person, a criminal? And why had he hidden it from them? To protect the memory of their mother, or to cover some foul deed of his own?

Caroline knew better than either of them that no woman walks away from three small children easily, unless she has no choice. What it told her was that none of them knew their father as well as they thought they did. Gemma's hero, and the man Kate had given up her life for, to serve and protect, was the same man who had dismissed Caroline all her life because she was different from him. If this was true, he had a cruel side to him too.

Caroline had always thought him controlling and domineering. He knew how to manipulate all of them, and even Juliette, who loved him so deeply. He got them all to do what he wanted, supposedly for their own good. Had he taken the children from Scarlett, a young, innocent girl in Texas, who was probably no match for his strength and willfulness? They had each paid a price for not having a mother. Their lives would have been so different if she'd been there. Caroline could remember easily all the times she'd missed having a mother growing up, and fantasized about her. Girl Scouts, dressing for prom, becoming a woman with only Kate to explain it to her. And not being the son her father wanted or wanting to ride in the rodeo like Kate. It had taken years of therapy to find herself after she married, and even while she was in college. Now it turned out that their mother was alive all along? Was she a derelict of some kind? It took Caroline's breath away just thinking about it. She and Gemma went for a walk that afternoon, before starting an inventory of their father's belongings, which was painful enough, without adding this to it. Kate went back to their father's house to see Juliette again. She was trying to make sense of it too.

Juliette was wearing jeans and an old black sweater when she opened the door to Kate. She looked like she'd lost weight in the last few days, and she'd been thin enough before. Her mane of red hair, which she sometimes wore in a braid or a bun, was loose, and made her look a little wild when she let Kate in. She was intrinsically feminine and sexy, and very French, although she'd been in the States for twenty-four years. She spoke English well now, but had never lost her accent. She offered Kate coffee or wine, and had a glass of red wine in her hand. She wasn't a heavy drinker, but she liked good wine, especially at a time like this. From one moment to the next, the bottom had fallen out of her world.

"Hello, Kate, come and sit down. It sounds like you found some big surprises in the safe. It's strange. I always wondered about your mother, but Jimmy wouldn't talk about her. He didn't even say how she died. Only that she broke his heart when she died, and he couldn't stay in Texas, so he came here. But I never suspected she was alive. You were so young when you moved here. What woman leaves three babies that age?"

"Maybe she was crazy or on drugs and he was trying to protect us," Kate said, looking pensive. She preferred to think the best of him, especially now that he was gone. "Are you doing okay?"

Juliette shrugged in answer in her very Gallic way. "Not so okay," she admitted. "He was too young to die. And he was so strong. I don't understand. Life is so fragile. What about you? What will you do now about the ranch? Will you sell it?"

"Never," Kate answered immediately. "I've got Thad to help me . . . and you." She smiled at the woman who had been a friend but not a mother to her. Juliette was more of a woman than anything, and had no maternal instincts, and said so. She had never wanted children with him, although she loved him passionately, and hadn't pretended to be a mother to his. She and Jimmy's daughters were just good friends. Maybe it was why they got along with her. She never tried to displace the memory of the mother they fantasized about and had never known. Jimmy liked that about her too. She wasn't someone who interfered, or imposed her will on him. She went with the flow, and had survived a loss of her own. She had been very much in love with the husband who had died in France when she was twenty-nine. She shared a more mature love with Jimmy, and a deep physical passion that had lasted until the end.

Juliette had read her copy of the will that morning, and Jimmy had left her a very respectable amount of money, without leaving his daughters wanting. He always said that he was land rich, and cash poor. He sank all his profits back into the ranch, which was how he had grown it into such a lucrative operation, with Juliette's help, managing the money he made. She was smart about it, and had worked as an accountant in France. The same principles applied, although the ranch was a new experience for her. But she had given Jimmy solid advice that had served him well.

In addition to the money he had left her, he had given her the use of his house on the ranch for as long as she wished to live there. It was a handsome gift. She had family in France, but had made her life in the States with him, and hadn't gone home in years. Her home on the ranch was secure, unless Kate sold it, which she was free to do, but she had no desire to sell. She wanted to preserve the empire her father built. And she had never wanted to live anywhere else.

"What are you going to do about your mother? Are you going to contact her?" Juliette asked, curious, lighting a cigarette. Occasionally, her brother still sent her the brand she had smoked in France. They were pungent and seemed a part of her, along with the subtle, musky perfume she wore.

"I don't know," Kate said. "Gemma wants to see her. Caroline doesn't. I haven't made my mind up. The idea that we still have a mother is a major shock. There has to be a good reason why Dad never told us. He wouldn't have lied to us if there wasn't. And she gave us up."

"He wouldn't want the competition," Juliette said in her soft voice. She knew him well. "Perhaps he wanted you to himself." He was a selfish man and she knew it, but loved him anyway. She had no illusions about him, and loved him as he was, which was the strength of their relationship. She made no excuses for him, to the world, or to herself. Jimmy always had to be in control. Kate knew it too. It was at the root of Gemma's battles with him. She refused to let him control her. So did Caroline, but she had tiptoed away. Gemma regularly slammed the door in her father's face and stopped talking to him, and it only made him love her more, for the sheer guts of it. They were cut from the same cloth. Kate always tried to find a peaceful compromise, and gave in to him more often than she liked. But now she had the ranch to run the way she wanted. She hadn't figured out what that meant yet, and for the moment, there was nothing she wanted to change, except maybe to enlarge their livestock auctions, which Juliette had been suggesting for several years. It was one of the biggest moneymakers in their business, and people came from all over the state, and as far away as Wyoming, Montana, and Texas. Kate had a lot to deal with now, without her father making all the decisions. It was both exciting and frightening. She hadn't thought his time would come so soon. No one had expected it, and Juliette hadn't either.

"What do you think you're going to do now?" Kate asked her, although none of them had had time to figure it out yet.

"Maybe I'll go to visit my brother this summer. I haven't been back to France in ten years. It would be nice to see him." Their parents were gone, and he owned the family home she had grown up in. He used it in the summer. She felt no deep attachment to it anymore, except that it was familiar. Her brother was a judge in Paris, his children were grown, and he was divorced, and had suggested that she come over now that Jimmy was gone. He had never been interested in her roots in France, had never visited, and had engulfed her in his life on the ranch. He hardly ever went to see Gemma in L.A. either, nor Caroline in Marin at all. His life was here, and so was Kate's. Tucked in the Santa Ynez Valley. It was easy to forget that there was a broader world. To Jimmy, this was the world, the only one that mattered or that he cared about, and he was king in his world.

"We were going to start the inventory this afternoon," Kate said to Juliette hesitantly, "if that's okay with you. I don't know when the girls will be back, and I'd rather do it when they're here. The estate taxes would be due in nine months, and we'll have to get an appraisal." She wanted to know if there was anything her sisters wanted, but there was nothing of great value in her father's home. It was all comfortable furniture of little worth. It was warm and cozy, with well-worn pieces he had had for years, and neither he nor Juliette paid much attention to the décor. Their life was mostly outdoors.

"The girls can have whatever they want," Juliette said easily. She wasn't attached to material things, and Jimmy hadn't been either, although their home was friendly and welcoming. Kate glimpsed a hat stand in the hall, with her father's battered hats on it, and it tugged at her heart a few minutes later when she hugged Juliette and left. She found her sisters back at her house, making a salad for lunch.

They had been reading the will and noticed that their father had left Thad a very generous bequest, in honor of Thad's long years of dedication to him. It would allow him to buy a house somewhere if he wanted, or make an investment in a small ranch of his own. As with the bequest to Juliette, both Caroline and Gemma thought it was fair, and didn't begrudge it to him. Kate was happy for him, and knew he deserved it. He had been her father's right-hand man for nineteen years, and had helped him improve and grow the ranch in countless ways.

"What about you guys?" Kate asked them over lunch, before they went to their father's house to start the inventory. "We own the ranch together now. How do you feel about that?"

"Fine, as long as I don't have to live here, and you run it," Gemma stated clearly. It would be a major windfall for all three of them if they sold the ranch. The ten thousand acres their father had accumulated over the years were worth a fortune now. And their livestock auctions were very lucrative. But neither of them was desperate for money. Only Kate had neither husband nor career, all she had were her years of service to her father on the ranch. "You could buy us out, if either of us ever want to sell," Gemma said, smiling.

"If I have the money," Kate reminded them. "Dad always plowed everything we made back into the business, or used it to buy more land," she said. "Dad invested in bonds," which was how Juliette and Thad would probably get their bequests. "We never have a lot of loose cash, except from the auctions. I'd have to sell bonds and some of the land to buy you out," and she would hate to do that.

"I'll have to talk to Peter about it," Caroline said vaguely. She consulted him for all decisions, even the contracts for her books. Kate always thought that she had traded their controlling father for her husband, but would never say it to her. She just hoped that Peter would never push Caroline to sell her share, and want Kate to come up with the money for some other hot investment, and impact the ranch to do it. He had no great loyalty to her family or the ranch, and had never liked her father. He expected his wife's first loyalty to be to him once they were married, and it was.

"You should come down with the kids now," Kate suggested. "You never use the house Dad built for you." It stood empty all the time, and had for years. "All it needs is a little furniture. You could furnish it in a day at Ikea. You don't need anything fancy here." They had expensive modern furniture in Marin, and had used a decorator to achieve the right look to impress their guests with how much they'd spent, particularly on art. Peter had a showy side to him that Caroline didn't, and had grown up with fine things.

Gemma's home in L.A. was filled with French antiques that reflected her taste. Life was simpler on the ranch. Jimmy had never liked showing off, and used the old Texan expression "All hat and no cattle" to describe people who did, but Peter had the income to back it up, and so did Gemma with her starring role on the show. She even got to keep her character's expensive designer wardrobe per her contract, was always dressed to the teeth in L.A., and got a new sports car every year. She said she needed it for her image. Kate had no image to keep up. She had a ranch to run.

"It depresses me to come here," Caroline said about using the house on the ranch. And Kate knew that Peter wasn't a big fan of their father. They were two powerful male egos colliding, with Caroline trapped in the middle, squeezed by both. But that would be different now, with their father gone. Kate wondered if it would make Caroline more independent and freer, or more dependent on Peter.

"It would be fun for your kids to spend time here," Kate said gently.

"Maybe," Caroline said noncommittally, as they cleared away the dishes, and headed for their father's house a few minutes later. Kate made notes for the inventory. Gemma wanted one small cowboy painting as a souvenir. She had always loved it. Caroline said she didn't want anything. It was all part of an unhappy memory for her, of her childhood in a place she hated where she didn't fit in.

"You need to go through his papers here," Juliette reminded Kate before they left. "And his clothes. I can't do it. It will make me too sad." Just hearing her say it made his absence suddenly all too real, to be giving away his things.

"You should just give it all to Goodwill," Gemma said. The very thought of it tore at Kate's heart, all the familiar well-worn plaid shirts, his vests, his battered cowboy hats, his roping chaps he'd worn at the rodeo. She wanted it all to be there forever. More than anything she wanted him back.

"Do you two want to come for a weekend and go through his things with me? There's a lot of our old childhood stuff too in the back barn. We could go through it at the same time."

"Mostly yearbooks and Barbie dolls," Gemma said with a wry grin. "I guess we could come for a weekend," she said hesitantly, and Caroline nodded but didn't comment. She didn't really want to unearth those memories and remember the past. "Maybe we could go to Santa Barbara and check out our mother then," Gemma suggested.

"Should we call her first?" Kate asked her, and Gemma shook her head.

"Let's not. Let's surprise her. Maybe we can get a look at her, and decide if we want to connect," Gemma said cautiously, and Kate nodded. It seemed like a good idea to her.

"Count me out for that," Caroline said firmly. She was adamant about not seeing her. "What would you say to her? 'Why did you give us up?'"

"Yeah, that's the whole point, isn't it?" Gemma answered. "Why did she? We can't ask Dad now, and he lied to us about it for our whole lives. She's the only one who can tell us. I want to know. Don't you?" She looked from Caroline to Kate, and Kate nodded. She did want to know, and they couldn't confront their father. But she did think it was a good idea to approach with caution, and see what she looked like. Kate was burning with curiosity now, and so was Gemma. "Maybe I'll come back in a few weeks when we're on hiatus. I don't know why, but now that the place belongs to us, it's a little more appealing. And we don't have to deal with Dad when we come here." Caroline nodded agreement, but she wasn't sure it was enough to make her come back anytime soon. They were going to Aspen for most of the summer.

Kate and Gemma didn't have those constraints. Gemma had the show to film every week, but they were off every year in June and July, and part of August, which gave the cast a chance to do other things, or just play and relax. Gemma hadn't done other projects in at least five years. She made more than enough money on the show to meet her needs, and she usually went to Europe in the summer, and rented a house in Italy or Saint Tropez. Sometimes she chartered a yacht and took friends, but she hadn't made her summer plans yet. Kate never went away, although Gemma invited her, but the ranch was a living, breathing entity, and needed her every day, now more than ever. She didn't see how she could get away. She never did.

The three sisters had dinner together that night, and tried to figure out a weekend they could spend together to go through their father's papers and personal effects. It was going to be painful, but it had to be done, and Kate didn't want to do it alone, so she pressed them to join her. They finally settled on a date in early June, and then Caroline went back to the half-empty house she had hardly ever used, and Gemma to the small guesthouse where she always stayed. The three sisters hugged each other before they left, and Kate clung to each of them for a minute, wishing they had more time with each other. There was comfort in being together no matter how differently they viewed their father, and how differently he had treated them when he was alive. Despite their divergent views of him, he had loved them, and Kate thought he had been a good father. The one mystery they wanted to solve now was what had really happened with their mother, and what the truth was. Kate was sure there was an explanation for it. Caroline and Gemma weren't as sure. It was an enormous lie to have told them.

It had been a strange few days with their father's death, his funeral, and the discovery they had made about their mother, which gave rise to a thousand questions about the past.

Caroline was leaving early the next morning, and had arranged for a car to pick her up to take her to the airport for the flight to San Francisco. Gemma had to be on the set at seven A.M. in Burbank and had to start the drive at four, so they said goodbye that night.

Gemma and Caroline headed down the path together in the dark, as Kate called after them in the starry moonlit night, "I love you guys!" They turned and waved at her, as she watched them disappear and gently closed the door. There weren't three more different women on the planet, but they were sisters and they loved each other, and as Kate thought about their father, she was sure that whatever his mistakes, he had loved them too. Now she had the ranch to run, and his legacy to carry on for him. She missed him more than her sisters would, since she saw him every day. She hoped that whatever they discovered about their mother wouldn't shatter their illusions about him forever, and destroy their ties to each other. She needed them. They were the only family she had. And whether they knew it or not, they needed her. They each brought their own strengths to the table and complemented each other.

Chapter 3

Kate got up the next morning at four, just as Gemma was driving off the ranch. She heard the car drive by as she woke up.

She followed her morning routine, and was in the barn at five-thirty. She saw her father's hat on a peg on the wall, and it hit her again that he was gone. For a minute, she had forgotten and was expecting to see him. It was a shock to realize that she never would again. She looked pale and stunned a minute later when Thad walked into the barn.

"You okay?" he asked, worried about her. She had a lot on her shoulders now, and it had been a hard few days.

"Yeah." She nodded. "It just hit me again."

"It keeps happening to me too. It doesn't feel real yet," he said, as he poured coffee into a mug and handed it to her. There would be decisions to make now, and all of them would rest on her, even if he was there to help her. The ultimate responsibility was hers. "I wanted to tell you what it meant that your father left me . . ." He stumbled over the words. ". . . what he did. He didn't need to do that. I never expected it." She smiled at him. He was a good man, and she was glad to have him there, more than ever now, to run the ranch with her.

"I'm glad he did. Are you going to buy a decent house now? Or a ranch?" The cabin he lived in was so small he hardly had room to move around in it, but always said it was enough for him, until he got married and had kids, and he was in no rush for that. He had plenty of fun on his time off the way things were.

"I don't need a house, or a ranch," he said, sipping his coffee. "I've got this ranch to keep me busy, and I don't need a bigger house. Are you going to start using his office?" She had a smaller one next to her father's, and could have used more space for everything she kept there, but she shook her head.

"Not yet." It would have hurt too much to take over his desk. It would mean that he was really gone, and she wasn't ready to face that.

"Do you want to ride out and check the north pastures with me?" he offered, and she nodded. It would be a relief to get back to work, and get her mind off her father, the funeral, and their discovery about their mother. She didn't want to think about anything, just ride with Thad, as they always did.

They left the barn, and took a familiar path, until they were cantering across the fields as the sun came up in a brilliant pink and purple sky, and she started to feel alive again.

"Are your sisters okay with sharing the ranch?" he asked her when they slowed down.

"It's fine for now," she said with a sigh. "Neither of them is interested in it. I have to beg them to come here."

"I figured they might want to sell their share."

"They might eventually, but for now they don't need the money, so nothing's going to change," she reassured him.

"What if they decide to cash out, and want you to buy their shares? That's a bundle of cash you'll have to come up with." He knew their financial status, and that her father never kept much liquidity and often used cash to buy more land. A sudden request from her sisters might come at a bad time for her.

"Then I'll have to sell some land to pay them, I guess," she said. "I'll figure it out when it happens, if it ever does." She wasn't going to worry about it now, since she didn't have to.

He hesitated for a moment, and then decided to speak up. "If that ever happens, I'd pay you for the land. I can't give you enough to pay both of them. But if one of them wants to sell, I've got some money saved up, and with what your father just left me, I think I could manage."

"To buy a third of the ranch?" She looked surprised, and impressed.

"I've been saving for a long time. I've been wanting to buy a piece of your dad's land since I got here. I think I could do it now, thanks to him. Just keep it in mind, in case one of them wants to sell and you're short at the time. I'd like nothing better than to own part of all this. We could still run it together, if you want. It doesn't have to be a big change."

"Thanks, Thad. It might make a big difference if the time comes. They're not in any hurry now, thank God. I figure Caroline will be the first one to bail, if her husband thinks she should. But we're in good shape for now. Let's keep it that way." She smiled at him and they picked up the pace again. She was glad to know that if she had to pay off one of her sisters, she could sell some land to him if she wanted to. She thought her father would have liked that too. And if both her sisters wanted to sell at the same time, Thad's buying out one of them would make it easier for Kate.

It was a beautiful morning, the sun was warm on their faces, and the pain of the last few days started to ease. The land around them belonged to her, as far as the eye could see. Whatever else he had done, her father had left her an incredible gift, and she was grateful to him.

Gemma dropped off her bag at her house on her way to work. She hadn't hit traffic on the freeway, and she had time to change, and picked up coffee on the way to work. She hadn't studied her lines, but she knew she'd be able to do it in her trailer. The director had sent her a text that she wasn't going to be in a scene until after lunch, and she remembered her lines with ease.

She was on set by seven-thirty, only half an hour late, got her hair colored, and was in her trailer with the latest version of the script by ten-thirty. It felt good to be back to work. It was always hard going to the ranch, and this time particularly, although it was good being with Caroline and Kate. As different as they were, they shared something special. Her mind wandered to their discovery about their mother while she was studying her lines, and she wondered how that would turn out. She wanted to go to Santa Barbara with Kate, since Caroline wouldn't go. Caroline never liked confronting the hard situations, always bowed out, and let them do the dirty work. She wanted to know what had happened as much as they did, she just didn't want to have to see her mother or confront her. Gemma wasn't afraid of it, although this was possibly the most important confrontation they'd ever had. It was no small thing to have given up custody of three young children. Nor for their father to have pretended that their mother was dead. If he were still alive, Gemma would have been at his throat, wanting answers, and an explanation of the massive lie. Her sisters could always count on her for that, but no more. All they had to do now was find their mother, and hear it from her, if she was willing to see them, and tell them the truth. Gemma wondered what kind of woman she was. Giving up three very young children didn't speak well for her.

The producer came to see her before lunch to find out how she was. He expressed his sympathy about her father, and said he was glad that she was back. The director came in a little while later. They were shooting back-to-back the scenes that she had missed while she was away. She would be on set all of the next day. But she was happy to be back in her real life. Whenever she went to the ranch, it reminded her of how trapped she had felt when she was young. All she had wanted to do was get the hell out. She always felt as though her life had begun when she left and went to L.A. Even starving there in the early years had been better than being on the ranch. She always felt as though she had been switched at birth and didn't belong there. The last thing she wanted was to be a hick. She was a city girl to her very core. She knew Caroline felt that way too. Only Kate loved life on the ranch, and must have had an overdose of her father's Texan blood. She was a cowboy just like him. She smiled thinking about it and went back to work.

She worked hard for the next two days to catch up, and on Friday afternoon, the director let them break early. They had covered a lot of ground that week, and the producer was coming on set to have a word with them. Usually, a general meeting with the producer meant some unpleasant change on set. It was rarely good news, but there had been no recent rumors, and everyone hoped it would be some ordinary announcement, maybe a big name actor joining the show, a better time slot than the one they had, which would have been hard to improve, or an important new sponsor. Everyone was in a good mood when the producer and executive producer showed up. The executive producer waited for silence on the set. They hardly ever saw him. He was the money guy, dealing with investors, insurance, and the overall planning of the show. They were in their tenth season, and everything was pretty well set. He had two other major shows on the air, one of which had just debuted in the fall and was a huge hit.

"Well, we have good and bad news for you." Two of the actors on the show had been nominated for Emmys. Gemma had been nominated in the past but hadn't won at first. She had won one in their third season. And the show had won a Golden Globe Award from the foreign press several times. "We've had a record year for our tenth season, thanks to all of you." He smiled at them. "And the show is still solid. We've been debating this for a long time, trying to figure out the life span of the show, and at what point we should elegantly fold up our tents and go home, before we start to slide. We've been discussing it with our wonderful writers for months." He paused. "As much as we hate to do it, our decision is that we've really done it. We've stretched as far as we can go. We want to go out on a high, not when people start switching to other channels when we come on. So the bad news is that when we wrap in June, that's going to be it. The show is over. But the good news is that you'll be free to pursue all the other projects that I know many of you are itching to do, feature films, other series, Broadway shows. I know several of you are ready to spread your wings, and now you can.

"For those of us who have settled into a comfortable routine here, including me, this is a good kick in the butt to get us going and become more creative again, and reinvent ourselves. We've had a great run, folks, and now it's time to take a final bow, and leave the stage." There was dead silence on the set when he finished, and then an explosion of chatter and exclamations as everyone started talking at once. Their contracts would determine how they got paid, but none of the contracts had showed up yet for the new season, and this was obviously why. The show was over, and they only had a few weeks of shooting left before the hiatus, and this time it would be permanent. The show was over. They didn't want to wait to be canceled by the network one day. They wanted to leave on a high, and for a minute, Gemma was too shocked to speak to the actors standing next to her.

"Fuck," her co-star said to her, "and they call that good news? I have three ex-wives and five kids to support. Shit. I never saw that coming." He looked panicked.

"Neither did I," Gemma said, "and I only have me to support, which is bad enough." In the past ten years, she had grown comfortable in a lifestyle that she couldn't manage without the show, and thinking it would go on forever, she hadn't saved a penny, and lived a life of first-class travel to luxury hotels at fabulous destinations, drove a Bentley sports car, spent a fortune on jewelry, expensive restaurants, and had a heavy mortgage on her house. It was a major shock, and would take some serious figuring to slim down her overhead. Everything but her mortgage would have to go. She didn't want to lose her house. She had to call her agent immediately to find work. Hopefully she'd be in major demand for another show. She'd only done minor things on the side for the last decade, a perfume campaign, a hair products line, an occasional appearance on a movie made for TV, and one in a feature film. She didn't need the work and didn't have the time, and she liked playing hard during the hiatus, frequently in Europe. She hadn't had to seriously look for a job in ten years.

She left the set quickly after the announcement, and didn't stick around. She called her agent when she got home, and he came right on the line. He spoke even before she did.

"I know. I just heard. I'm going to have a dozen calls by five P.M. I didn't expect that at all."

"Neither did I. Our ratings are through the roof," Gemma said, still in shock, and a little angry now. It seemed so unfair. And it was going to turn her whole life upside down, in a very unpleasant way.

"We should have suspected it. Abrams always closes his shows on a high, and this one really outlived all the predictions for it, and the projections. But ten years is ten years. Who knows, maybe he's right. And I'd rather be looking for work for you after a hit, than after a show that went down the tubes, so there's something to be said for that."

"How fast do you think you can find me work?" Gemma asked, sounding worried. It was no surprise to her agent. All his clients did the same thing. They lived high on the hog when they were on a hit show, but had nothing to live on if the show closed.

"I'll have to get out my crystal ball. I don't know, Gemma. There are several new shows starting in the fall, but they've already got their stars lined up. I can definitely get you some appearances, but a starring role isn't going to fall into our lap overnight. You know the reality here. You were thirty or thirty-one when you started on the show. You're over forty now. You look fabulous and you don't look your age, but work for a female over forty is not the same thing as for a thirty-year-old. It's the ugly truth."

"Are you telling me I'm over the hill?" she almost shrieked at him.

"No, but I'm telling you that there's more work out there for a thirty-year-old than for a forty-year-old. That can't come as a surprise to you. There's work, but not as much of it, and a lot of forty-five-year-old actresses are scrambling for those parts." She almost cried when he said it, but wouldn't let herself.

"Well, I need work. I have a hefty mortgage on my house."

"So does all of Hollywood. I have to look up your contract, but I think you get a three-month severance if they fold the show. Maybe four, I'll check."

"Jerry, that will get me through the summer, and after that I'm screwed."

"Don't panic yet. You're a gorgeous woman with a big name. We'll get you something, maybe enough appearances to tide you over for a season, and then you can jump on a new show. They're doing great series out of England right now too. I'll see what we can drum up there. Take it easy, Gemma, your career isn't over. This is just a rough patch. It happens to everyone, and the show was bound to close at some point." But she hadn't planned for this at all. She lived lavishly from paycheck to paycheck, and had almost nothing in the bank. Her father had warned her about that. She never listened to him.

She poured herself a stiff drink after they hung up, and spent the rest of the night figuring out her expenses, the ones she couldn't avoid like her mortgage, what she paid her maid, although she could fire her, her car payments, and now she wouldn't have the freebies she got on a show, like wardrobe and hair, which cost a fortune, and all the perks that went with a starring role. She was being catapulted back to real life. As much as she hated to hear it, he was right. At forty-one, she wasn't going to have the wealth of parts to pick from that she had had at thirty-one. Work started to dry up at forty, and actresses her age, really talented ones with big names, were begging for parts.

She was panicked, and she didn't have her father to fall back on now. Before her part on the show, he had bailed her out several times, and even paid her mortgage for a year on the condo she had before her house. She didn't have him to turn to now, and she could hardly ask Kate to support her. She didn't even know that their father had helped Gemma repeatedly for several years until she landed the starring role. It was their secret, and now she had her back to the wall. She could sell her house if she had to, but she didn't want to do that. She'd give up the Bentley immediately, and hope they would let her out of the lease, but there would probably be a stiff penalty. She had a ridiculously expensive tennis club membership she didn't need, and a fancy famous trainer she paid five thousand a month to, who came every day. It occurred to her that she could rent her house out for the summer, furnished, and charge a fortune for it, if she really had to. But if she did that, where would she stay? She had the chilling thought that she could stay at the ranch for the summer, but that sounded like a fate worse than death. She could hardly make it through a weekend there, let alone an entire summer. She'd rather rent a studio apartment if she had to, but that was expensive too.

She had to rethink it all now, and re-examine everything she did. No more designer clothes on Rodeo, on a whim, or two-thousand-dollar alligator shoes. For the past ten years she had been living a part, like the one on TV, that suited her, but now the party was over, and she had to scramble in all directions to survive. She had never been so panicked in her life, because she had gotten so used to all those luxuries that seemed entirely normal to her now, but she could no longer pay for them.

By the next morning when she got to the set, she looked like she'd been dragged behind a bus by her teeth for a week, but everyone else on the set looked the same. There were only a very few actors who either lived simply, or had put money away. Most of them were like her, riding a wave, with the illusion that it would never hit the beach. It just had. She felt as though she had been run up on the rocks, and no one else on the show looked much better. They were worried about alimony, child support, rent, mortgages, private school for their kids, ex-wives, current wives, expensive girlfriends, and all the things they loved to do, from fancy restaurants to facials, trainers, shrinks, vacations, hotels, Ferraris. Gemma was not alone in her panic and misery, but that didn't make it any better. The atmosphere on the set was agonizingly tense, and the only time anyone came to life was when they were on camera, but even their performances were impacted by how upset they were by the news of the day before. Their lifestyles and futures were on the line, and everyone was calling either their agent or their shrink or both. Her panic over her situation obscured her grief over her father for the moment, which was something of a relief.

Gemma had no intention of telling her sisters what had happened. They'd hear about it soon enough, but Kate called her to see how she was doing, and she could hear something in her sister's voice.

"Something wrong?" She had an uncanny sense of her sisters, which made it hard to hide from her.

"No, of course not. Just a long week on the set. I had a lot of scenes to catch up on, and well, you know, Dad . . ." She tried to blame her tone on him to get Kate off the scent. But she didn't sound sad, she sounded panicked and anxious. In fact, she was so scared, she hadn't thought of him in several days, except to lament the fact that he couldn't bail her out this time, as he had in the past. He always came through for her, after a brief lecture about saving her money for a rainy day. But she was a star, and he knew she needed to maintain a lifestyle. She was Daddy's Girl. He would have been horrified if he'd known what that added up to. She spent more on makeup and her trainer than most people did on rent, not to mention facials. She had a woman fly in from New York to give her facials, with a gentle electric shock machine for two thousand dollars a pop, plus her airfare and hotel. And she hadn't thought twice about spending it until now. She flew first class everywhere, or chartered planes for the life of a star.

"I just wanted to remind you that you're coming up to go through Dad's things. I think it's hard on Juliette to have it all sitting there. It'll be nice for her if we can go through it, keep what we want, and give the rest away. We still have his papers to go through. And we agreed to do it before Caroline goes to Aspen for the summer. They've rented a house there. And you're probably going away too. Are you chartering a boat this year?" Her sisters' lives were on another planet from Kate's, but she didn't begrudge it to them. It was what they did, while she worked on the ranch, which was the life she had led, and wanted, for twenty years. She had raced home from college to do it, so now she couldn't complain, and didn't.

When Kate asked Gemma about the boat, she felt sick momentarily, remembering what she had spent on it. Seven hundred thousand dollars for a week, which had seemed like nothing to her. But it had been fabulous, and she had invited ten friends to go with her. They'd gone to Monaco, Corsica, and Sardinia.

"No, not this year," she said, trying to sound casual. "I haven't figured out my plans yet. I might stick around L.A. and do some work."

"Why don't you spend the summer here?" Kate suggested. "You can drive down to L.A. if you need to, for a day of work, or a couple of days. You have a house here, you might as well use it."

"It's a thought," Gemma said bleakly. She could suddenly see herself living there, trapped in the Valley again, as though the last ten years had never happened. It made her want to cry, thinking about it.

"I remember that we agreed to go through his things." Gemma sighed and couldn't come up with a good excuse not to be there. She really wasn't in the mood to do it now. She had bigger worries.

"Make sure Caroline can still do it too, so we can get it over with." As long as they would be in the Valley again, she wanted to do their detective work in Santa Barbara, and check out their mother, if they had time. But they'd be busy going through their father's things. It was a depressing project. Caroline wasn't enthused about it either when Kate called her. She knew she had promised to do it, but she dreaded going back so soon. And their recent discovery about their mother had really upset her.

"Do we have to do it now?" Caroline complained.

"It's like pulling teeth getting you two to come here, and I think it's hard on Juliette having his clothes and papers all over the place. It feels like he's going to walk in any minute. She's been very respectful, and she wants us to do it. I think we should. Do you want to bring the kids?"

"I'll ask them. They may have plans, and I have to see what Peter wants to do. I'll ask them tonight, and call you tomorrow to confirm." Kate hung up, feeling frustrated. Getting her sisters to commit to a weekend in the Valley was like dragging a dead buffalo across the floor.

Caroline brought it up at dinner that night, and Morgan and Billy were lukewarm about it. Morgan thought there might be a party at a friend's, and Billy wanted to play tennis at their club. But Caroline was touched when Peter said he thought they should go. He told the children that they should be supportive of their mother, and reminded them that they'd have fun, and could go riding. They'd enjoyed their recent weekend there, despite the funeral.

"Do you want to come too?" Caroline smiled at him, grateful for the help. She'd rather take the kids than go alone. They grounded her.

"I can't. I have to work. We're in the middle of a big deal. I was going to tell you." He looked regretful. "Why don't the three of you go?" The children grudgingly agreed, and Caroline called Kate in the morning, and said she could make it, and was going to bring the kids.

"Thad can take them riding while we sort things out," Kate said, pleased. She was looking forward to spending another weekend with them, despite their sad mission, putting their father's things away.

Caroline and her children were going to fly in on Friday, and Gemma was going to drive up from L.A.

"I'll have to rent a car," she said, sounding distracted.

"Something wrong with yours?" Kate sounded surprised.

"It's so ridiculously expensive, and it's really too much car for me, it's more of a guy's car. I turned it in, and I'm trying to decide what I want now." Gemma sounded breezy about it.

"How about a Rolls?" Kate teased her, and Gemma sounded vague.

"Yeah. Maybe. See you soon," she said, and hung up quickly. She had to call the bank to see if she could get a line of credit. She was trying to lease a less expensive car. And she needed to call her agent to see if he had any leads for work. Her life was a constant merry-go-round of terror now, trying to reduce her expenses, cancel things, and find work. Her agent had checked her contract. She was getting four months' severance and could keep the wardrobe from the season, as she always did. All of which meant that by the end of September, she would have no money left, and no work. She had to do something about it, because there was no Daddy to bail her out this time. Daddy's Girl was up the creek, and her life was down the tubes.

Chapter 4

On the weekend Gemma and Caroline had agreed to come to the ranch, both of them arrived on Friday night shortly before dinner. One of the ranch hands picked up Caroline and her children at the airport, and Gemma arrived in a small rented Ford. Kate had a simple meal set out for them at her house, and she'd gone to their cottages herself to make sure that everything was in order. Juliette had agreed to join them for dinner.

Morgan and Billy couldn't wait to go riding with Thad the next day. Juliette surprised the girls by telling them that she had decided to go home for the summer. She was returning to France for the first time in ten years, planning to visit friends in Bordeaux and Provence, and her brother in Paris, then go to their old house in the Camargue with him. It was going to be a big change from the ranch, but she felt she needed a change of scene. It was lonely for her there without Jimmy. She hadn't expected his sudden death to hit her as hard as it did.

"I'll try not to screw up the books while you're gone," Kate said, smiling at her. Juliette had brought two bottles of good French wine to dinner, which she shared with the three sisters. It was a fine French Bordeaux that their father had loved too. Juliette had taught him about French wines, and he had become very knowledgeable, and had some excellent vintages stocked in his cellar.

"You should take some," she told Kate. "It will take me the rest of my life to drink it. Your father liked buying in large quantities." He liked doing everything bigger, better, and more than anyone else. It was part of his giant personality. And in many ways, Gemma was a lot like him, although he hadn't been a spendthrift like her, and was careful with money.

She hadn't intended to tell them, but after her second glass of wine, Gemma told them that the show had been canceled. There was shocked silence at the table for a moment, and no one knew what to say. Then Kate recovered herself.

"I'm sorry, Gem. It must be incredibly disappointing."

"It is," Gemma admitted. "I could see it if our ratings had gone down, but they're stronger than ever. But that's the way our executive producer likes to do it. Go out on a high, and leave them laughing." Gemma looked as if she was close to crying, and Caroline reached over and patted her hand.

"At least you've had ten great years on the show. You'll probably get on a new show very soon," she encouraged her. Morgan and Billy had left the table and were watching TV in Kate's bedroom. She had just treated herself to a new TV.

"Apparently not," Gemma countered. "According to my agent, over forty, I'm screwed."

"That's ridiculous. You don't look your age," Kate said, outraged. "I'm a year older than you are, and I look ten years older."

"I keep telling you, Kate, sunscreen and moisturizer!" Gemma scolded her and Kate laughed.

"I know, I know." But Kate was still beautiful too. Gemma looked incredibly youthful. Kate was right about that. "Is this going to have a big impact on you?" Kate asked her gently.

"Impact? No. Knock me flat on my ass, yes, definitely. I've been living a little too lavishly. It gets to be a bad habit. And the studios and production companies spoil you. You can have damn near everything you want when you're on a successful show, and then suddenly it's over. The clock strikes midnight, the show turns to dust, and you're Cinderella, and Neiman's takes back the glass slipper. I'll be okay, I guess, but I need to cut back pretty dramatically. I'm thinking about renting my house out for the summer. It will help fill the coffers a little. There's a lot that I can do without."

"If you rent your house, you can stay here for the summer," Kate said warmly. "Hell, you can stay here whenever you want, you own the ranch now too. We all do. And you have a house here. You could commute to L.A. when you need to, for meetings and auditions."

"I hope I don't have to," Gemma said. "My agent says the new shows are pretty well set for next season, so it might be a slim winter, till they come up with new shows next spring. But he doesn't think I'll get a lead part at my age. The part I had was tailor-made for me, but I was thirty when they cast me. That makes a big difference."

"That's disgusting," Caroline said.

"I have to admit, it's been kind of a shock. None of us on the show were expecting it. It's been a shit few weeks, between Dad and the show getting canceled."

"It always works like that," Kate said with a sigh. "Bad things come in bunches."

"So do good things," Caroline said optimistically. But Gemma thought that it was easy for her to say, with a husband who was a partner in a venture capital firm, and family money. Their life was totally secure. It wasn't as visibly luxurious as Gemma's, but they could do whatever they wanted. Private school for the kids, and they were thinking of buying a house in Aspen. Peter flew around on a corporate jet and made a ton of money. Caroline had nothing to worry about. She could write her young adult books when she felt like it. She didn't have to worry about her future, her age, or a mortgage.

"Well, you can come home whenever you want to, or need to," Kate said simply. Gemma hated to think of it as home again. It seemed like a giant twenty-year step backward if she were to wind up back in the Santa Ynez Valley. She'd played hard for the last ten years and spent a lot of money. She cringed every time she thought of it now. She wished she had listened to her father and saved some, but she thought the show, and the gravy train, would go on forever. Now the ride was over. And in four months, she'd have no income.

She stayed and had another glass of wine with Kate after Caroline and her children went back to her cottage, and Juliette had left to go to bed. She wasn't leaving for France until July, so she had another month on the ranch, to help Kate with the books and prepare for their summer auction in July. They had a Thoroughbred auction then too, as well as their livestock auctions, which usually brought in a lot of money.

"I didn't think I'd have to do it, but if I can't find work, I may have to sell you and Caroline my share of the ranch in the not-too-distant future. When Dad died, I thought I was secure, and now I'm ass over tits on the ground, and the money will run out eventually." Very soon in fact. September was only three months away.

"Thad said he might be interested if you or Caroline decides to sell your share of the ranch. With the money Dad left him, and his savings, he thinks he could manage it."

"That would be interesting. How would you feel about his owning a third of the ranch?" She knew how possessive Kate and their father were about it, and how proud he was of owning ten thousand acres, after starting from nothing.

"I'd rather hang on to all of it, like Dad, and keep it in the family. But if you need the money soon, I'd have a hard time coming up with it in a hurry. I might be able to buy half your share, and Thad could buy the other half. Then I wouldn't be giving up so much, and I wouldn't have to sell bonds. I don't think Caroline will buy it from you. She's more likely to sell too, to free up the money. Neither of you comes here much, although I wish you would. Anyway, let me know how it's going, and if there's anything I can do to help."

"Dad always used to help me when I got in a jam," she said in a small voice. She had never admitted it to her sisters before.

"Yeah, I kind of thought he did. Daddy's Girl, and all that."

"He hasn't had to for a long time. I made great money on the show, and blew it all," she admitted. "Art, furniture, the house, trips, chartering yachts, flying private. It's amazing how fast it goes." Instead, their father had bought Thoroughbreds for his breeding operation, and pastureland for his livestock, which always seemed less glamorous to Gemma. "I guess I was really stupid. I'll sell the house if I have to," but it was mortgaged to the hilt so she wasn't going to get as much from it as she should have. "I'd hate to do it, but if I have to, I will. That would tide me over for a while. Don't say anything to Thad yet."

"I won't," Kate promised. She could see that her sister looked shell-shocked. "Have you thought any more about contacting our mother?" Kate asked her.

"Not really. I've been going crazy trying to figure out what to get rid of, ever since I heard the show was canceled." They were wrapping in a week. The end had come quickly. "We probably won't have time this trip anyway. Maybe this summer?" Kate nodded. She half wanted to rush into it, and meet her and get the straight story, and she was half afraid to. Caroline still didn't want to see their mother at all.

"Dad was an odd guy. I think he always had secrets. There was only so much he wanted anyone to know. He almost never talked about his youth in Texas, except that he grew up dirt poor, and came out here with nothing except three little girls and a truck full of diapers. It took him a year to tell us he was serious about Juliette, and he didn't tell us she'd moved in with him till we came home for Christmas, so who knows what really happened between him and our mother. If we hadn't found that envelope, we'd never have known. He probably intended to destroy it, and forgot to," she said, and Kate agreed. He would have had a fit if he'd thought they were contemplating looking up their mother and meeting her, since he had claimed she'd been dead for the last thirty-nine years.

Gemma left a little while later, to go back to her cottage. The three of them met the next day at the main house. Juliette had strong coffee and homemade croissants waiting, and then she went to the office, to let them do what they wanted. She had already taken the things that were meaningful to her, and had given Kate a list of them, some books, two paintings she and Jimmy had bought together, an antique silver samovar Juliette had given him, the things she'd bought for the house, and the rack of cowboy hats he wore every day. Jimmy had no possessions of great value, except the ranch itself.

They went through his clothes, his desk, his papers. Kate boxed up what they needed to send to the office. They packed up his clothes for Juliette so she didn't have to, and the girls took a few things they had given him or made for him, including the ceramics Caroline had made for him in camp. She was surprised that he still had them. They did the inventory that the lawyer wanted for the appraisal. The only things of any value were those Juliette had had sent from France, a rug of her grandmother's, a small desk, some horn chairs. The girls only took things that were of sentimental value to them. They didn't want to disrupt his house. It was Juliette's home now too.

They drove into town for lunch afterward, and ate at a cowboy bar their father had liked. It reminded them of him, and they had always liked it too.

"I never thought he'd die so young," Gemma said softly halfway through lunch.

"Neither did I," Kate agreed with her. It still seemed unreal to all of them, especially here on the ranch, where they were used to seeing him walking around, riding his horse, or coming out of the barn, talking to Thad. The ranch seemed empty now without him. Kate was happy that Caroline's children were enjoying being there. They added new life to the place, and another generation. Thad was keeping them busy on horses all day long, and had them mucking out stalls, and hooking up milking machines in the dairy.

"If you came more often, you could write here," Kate suggested.

It's a good place to walk and think, and get back in touch with your-self."

"Is that what you do here?" Gemma asked her and Kate laughed.

"No, I work my ass off. It'll be different now without Dad," she said. "I'll have to work even harder and so will Thad. He already is," and so was she, but she enjoyed it.

"Yeah, maybe you'll get to do things your way, for a change," Gemma commented. "Is there anything you want to do, now that he's not looking over your shoulder telling you that everything you do is wrong?" Gemma always got right to the point, without frills.

"He came around eventually. It just took some talking to him," Kate said gently, still making excuses for him, as she always did. She rarely criticized their father.

"He only came around if it suited him. I've never known anyone more headstrong, stubborn, and self-centered, except maybe me," Gemma said, and all three of them laughed. There was some truth to it. "I always think I'm right too."

"I wish I did. I always think everyone else knows better than I do, like you two," Caroline said wistfully. She was the meekest of the three of them, and yet she had gone after what she wanted too, fear-lessly, and with determination, but quietly. She just had to get away from the ranch and her father to do it.

"We don't know any better than you do," Gemma assured her. "In fact, you're smarter and better educated. You have a master's de-gree," she reminded her. "What's Peter up to these days? I hardly spoke to him at the funeral." Peter was never overly chatty with Car-oline's sisters, but Gemma usually managed to draw him out.

"He's working on a big deal. He'll only be with us for a week in

Aspen. He has to go back to San Francisco. The kids don't know yet, he just told me. They're going to be disappointed. Billy loves to go fishing with him. So I guess I'll be the one going fishing, and putting the worms on the hooks," she said with a grimace and her sisters smiled at her. She really was the perfect mother; and now their own mother had turned up. She had been far from perfect if she'd given up her parental rights and abandoned them. What she'd done was worse than dying, and Gemma and Kate wanted to know about it, and how she justified it. Caroline said it didn't matter. Whatever the reason, she hadn't been around for them, and it was too late for her to make up for it now. She particularly had hated growing up without a mother, which was why she was so devoted to her kids and would do anything for them, and for Peter.

They left the restaurant and went back to the ranch, and the kids were just coming out of the barn with Thad. They'd had a long, full day and they were tired. They were city kids, and not used to all the fresh air and exercise. He had worn them out since early morning. He smiled at Kate when he saw her.

"They're going to sleep well tonight," he said, and she laughed. "We've been riding most of the day. They won't be able to walk tomorrow," he told Caroline, and she laughed too. She had known Thad since he'd come to the ranch at eighteen, when she was twenty. She'd had a crush on him for about five minutes, and then she got involved with Jock Thompson the summer of her junior year in college. They broke up at the end of the summer when she went back to Berkeley, and by Christmas when she came home, Jock had gotten a local girl pregnant and married her.

The girls reminisced about their teenage romances that night over dinner and laughed about them. Gemma had had a million boy-friends and flirted with everyone. Caroline had had two or three seri-ous boyfriends in high school. And Kate had dated the captain of the football team at the local high school until she left for college. He'd gone to college in the East and never came back to California, then his family had moved away, and she'd lost track of him.

"So who are you dating now?" Gemma asked Kate. She hadn't heard about a man in Kate's life in a long time.

"There's no one to date around here," she said matter-of-factly, "and I'd probably fall asleep if anyone took me to dinner. I get up at four-thirty in the morning." She had substituted work on the ranch for re-lationships for many years. Her father had kept her too busy to date.

"There must be someone," Caroline chimed in.

"Not that I know of. The boys we grew up with have kids in col-lege. Some of them are grandfathers. Now there's a scary thought. They either left to work somewhere else, went to college and never came back, or married their high school sweethearts, and have been married for twenty-four years by now, since I went to school with them," Kate said and didn't seem to care.

"Jesus, that's depressing," Gemma commented. "You should get out of here."

"I don't want to. I like it here. I'm running this place for the three of us now. Before I was running it for Dad."

"Isn't there a cute cowboy around or something?" Gemma asked, sorry for her older sister. It seemed like a sad life to her, but Kate was happy.

"I'll have to sign up for the rodeo again," she said, laughing, "and find me a guy who rides the broncos, or ropes steers." She was de-scribing their father. The idea of marrying anyone they'd gone to high school with sounded pathetic to all three of them, but it was what most people did. It was a far cry from Gemma's glamorous life in L.A., or Caroline's suburban life in Marin. But this was the life Kate had chosen, at first to please her father, and now it pleased her. She was happy here, as hard as that was for them to understand. Gemma had never settled down either, after one very serious romance that went sour, and after that, countless meaningless affairs. Gemma wasn't desperate to marry either. All she wanted now was a good part, money in the bank, and her career back on track.

The three of them had a nice weekend together, and Caroline's children loved it. Caroline and Gemma left on Sunday afternoon. Gemma had a week of shooting left before they wrapped the show, and she had to figure out what to do now. Caroline said she'd think about bringing the kids back for a few days before they left for Aspen, if she and Peter didn't have too much to do. She wanted to spend time with him before Aspen, but he had already warned her that he had a heavy work schedule all summer. With Peter, his work always came first, but they always got closer when they spent time together. He wasn't good at expressing emotions, but underneath his cool exterior and serious work ethic, she knew he loved her, and their marriage was solid after seventeen years.

He was at the office when she came home on Sunday, he texted her that he'd be home in a few hours, and suggested that she and the kids go out to dinner in Mill Valley, which they did. It was nice to be back in their suburban life, which seemed a million miles from the Santa Ynez Valley, much to her relief. Everything about their life in Marin was home to her now, not the ranch.

* * *

Thad dropped by to see Kate that night. She had a few of her father's things put aside for him, some jackets, his roping gear, and his rodeo chaps which Thad had wanted.

"Thank you for being so nice to the kids," she said with a smile.

"I enjoyed them. They're so bright. Morgan says she wants to be a writer or a lawyer, and Billy wants to be a soccer star or an entrepreneur. I couldn't even pronounce that word at his age." They both knew he had options that Thad had never dreamed of. But like her father, she could easily see Thad having his own ranch one day. He had that kind of determination and drive and was willing to work hard. He was as bright as her father, which was why they had gotten along so well. Jimmy had seen that in him at eighteen, when he was just a kid. "They're nice children."

"They are," Kate agreed. "And Caroline's a great mom." She didn't tell him about Gemma's financial difficulties. She didn't want to get his hopes up. Gemma wasn't ready to sell her share of the ranch. She would only do it in extremis, out of respect for their dad, and she would probably have a starring role in another show in a few months, and she'd be making big money again. She was resourceful, and Kate wasn't worried about her, yet.

"Do you want to go into town for dinner?" he asked her. It was quiet after her sisters left, and they did that sometimes, went out for a burger, to talk about what they were doing on the ranch. He had an active dating life with the local girls, and he only invited Kate to dinner when he didn't have more exciting plans. He was a busy guy. It was easy to understand. He was a good-looking man, and had a gentlemanly style with women. It was an old-fashioned way of treating women that some cowboys had. Her father had treated Juliette that way, except that he was more domineering. Thad was more modern than that, but his relationships never lasted long, since he didn't want to get tied down. He never misled them, and described himself as not being a "commitment kind of guy," except to the ranch. She suspected it came from the way he'd grown up, being bounced from one foster home to the next, until he was old enough to be emancipated at sixteen. Now he was careful never to get too attached.

They talked about ranch business all through dinner. He insisted on paying the check, and then he drove her home.

"Are you doing okay, Kate?" he asked when they stopped in front of her house. "I know it's different without your dad." She had been missing him terribly and suspected that Thad was too.

"He could be such a pain in the ass sometimes," she said with a wistful smile. "But there was nobody like him."

"You know, he didn't say it much, but he admired you. He said you'd do a great job with the ranch one day, and he was right. You can do everything he did. You can make this place grow even bigger, if you want to."

"I'd like to try," she said, touched by what he'd told her about her father admiring her. It was news to her.

"I'd like to help you. JT didn't want to go past a certain point. He didn't want it to get any bigger than he could manage, he knew his limits, which was one of his strengths. But there are some things we could modernize to get better results. We should sit down sometime and talk about it."

"I'd like that." She had the feeling that he wanted to be a manager, and not just an employee or a foreman, and she had no doubt that he was capable of it.

"Thank you for giving me the chance, Kate." Just as her father had kept her in her place, he had kept Thad in his. There was no question about who ran the ranch when JT was alive, but there was room for growth now, and change. Kate was open to it, and so was Thad. "I hope I get to buy a piece of the operation one day." She realized that if he didn't, he'd start a ranch of his own. He had the money to do that now, but he was waiting to see if the opportunity came up with her, and it might. It was too soon to know. Her father had just died and she didn't know if her sisters were going to sell their shares eventually and want her to buy them out.

She got out of his truck then, and he walked her to the door.

"Are you going to be moving into the big house?" he asked her, curious, and she shook her head.

"That's for Juliette. I don't need it. I'm fine here." She knew it would be hers one day. She was in no rush. Like her father, she was more interested in the land, and the functioning of her ranch, than her home. She always said that she didn't have that gene. She left that to her sisters. She was more like her dad. And she knew Thad was the same way, in his tiny cabin, that he said was all he needed. Even if he was the foreman, he wasn't interested in the trimmings, just in the job he did. And the job was the bond between them.

"You know, he taught us well." He stood smiling at her on her porch.

She smiled back. "I think he did. We're going to do a good job of it here," she said with a warm look. "Thanks, Thad." She leaned up and kissed his cheek, which surprised him, and then she opened the door and walked into her house. It had been a nice evening, and she knew they were going to do good work together. A minute later, he drove away. And he was smiling too.

Chapter 5

Gemma's descent into hell was almost complete in the next week. They had the final show to film, everyone on the set was tense. Her agent had drummed up no work for her, not even makeshift money jobs, or appearances on other shows. He told her it might take a few months. Hollywood was dead in the summer, so things might not pick up until the fall. She was hit with an avalanche of bills for items she had forgotten she'd bought or money she'd spent for services. It seemed like her overhead was out of control, and she was paying close attention now. She realized that she was paying six thousand dollars a month to her gardener, who hardly ever showed up, and never got it right when he did. She had forgotten that she'd had her fence painted for ten thousand dollars. It seemed like every time she turned around, someone was gouging her, and she had been letting it happen for months, or even years.

In a moment of panic, she called a realtor and put her house on the market to rent for the summer. Two days later, a well-known actor came to see it and loved it, and agreed to rent it for three months. She had to be out in a week, but he was willing to pay a fortune, while he was filming on location in L.A. He was supposedly a quiet sort, and he was going to be living there alone. His wife and kids were at their house in Montana for the summer, so there wouldn't be much wear and tear on her place. She hated to move out, but she needed the money. She priced some studio apartments after that for herself, and they were ridiculously overpriced, so suddenly she didn't know where to live in L.A.

They wrapped the series, everyone sobbed when they said good-bye, the technicians, the actors, the producers. She was depressed when she drove home, in the small Japanese car she was leasing that was even cheaper than the Ford. Everything about her life was depressing. Overnight she felt like a has-been, and wondered if she'd ever work again. It felt like she wouldn't. There were people she liked to hang out with, but she didn't call them. She was ashamed to be out of work. In Hollywood you were a pariah, and no one, once you weren't on a show. She had forgotten what that was like, in the past ten years.

Kate called her the night they wrapped the show. "How's it going?" she said cheerfully. She'd had a good day with Thad, planning the next auction. They were selling more livestock than usual, and had sent out a huge mailing, which had been his idea.

"Don't ask. I'm looking for a studio apartment. They're insanely expensive."

"Why don't you just stay here?" Kate suggested again. "It's free. You have a house, and you can drive to L.A. when you need to." Gemma hated the thought, but she didn't have any other options. She had to be out in three days for the actor who had rented it, and wanted to have the carpets cleaned before he arrived.

"Maybe for a few weeks. If I find a decent studio, I can come back. It really feels like rewinding the film, though, to some of the worst days of my life, when all I wanted to do was get out of there."

"It's temporary, Gem, it's not forever. Just until you find work, and get a few jobs under your belt, or a part on another show."

"I hope so. If I wind up back in the Valley for good, I think I'll shoot myself."

"No, you won't. You'll be working again by the fall."

"Tell my agent that. He acts like I'm a hundred years old. Maybe I should get my eyes done again while I have the time. And a boob job. I swear, they're an inch lower than they were last year. Maybe he's right."

"You don't need your eyes done, or a boob job. I know twenty-year-olds who would kill to have a body like yours."

"Well, for five thousand a month to my trainer, six thousand to my gym, two thousand to my Pilates class, and another three to my fancy yoga coach, they can have this body. Surgery would be cheaper," she said, and her sister laughed. "My trainer and my yoga coach have their own TV shows."

"Jesus, that's a lot of money to look as good as you do. I'm glad I live up here. So what do you think? Do you want to come up for a while?"

"Not really. I'd rather cut my liver out with an ice pick. But I don't have much choice, for the moment. Maybe I'll stay at the ranch for a month."

"You can stay for as long as you want," Kate said warmly. "It would be nice to have you here, even for a while. I'm hoping Caroline will come down for a few days before they go to Aspen. I think the kids get out of school this week." Kate was busy with the upcoming auction, but she liked the idea of her sisters staying at the ranch. Juliette was leaving soon too. Now that her father was gone, Kate would have no one to talk to at night. Thad had a new flame, so it was going to be a lonely summer, although Thad's romances never lasted long. He said this one was different, but they always were. She was twenty-two, a waitress at a local bar. He always managed to find someone new.

"I'll let you know," Gemma said, sounding distracted, and they hung up a few minutes later. Kate called Caroline after that, to see if she wanted to come down. She didn't sound enthused either, and told Peter about it when she hung up.

"Maybe you should," he said gently. "Your sister works like a dog on that ranch. And with your father gone, it all rests on her. You're a part owner there now too. It might be nice for her to have some support and company. It's a lonely life for her." It was the first time Peter had been that sympathetic to Kate, and she was touched. He made Caroline feel guilty for not seeing her more often, but she had just been there with the kids, and for her father's funeral only weeks before.

"She loves that life. I don't think she's lonely. But I do think she works too hard. If she was lonely, she'd try to meet a guy, and she doesn't. All she does is work."

"You're a good distraction for her with the kids. And they seem to love it down there," Peter reminded her, and leaned over and kissed her. She really didn't want to leave him.

"You don't mind my going?" She didn't like deserting him, especially to go to the ranch, which she didn't enjoy anyway. But she'd had a nice weekend there with her sisters, and Morgan and Billy had loved it. She was looking forward to the weeks they were going to spend in Aspen at the house they rented, although Peter had said he was going to have trouble getting away. He was planning to spend a week or two with them, and to come out for as many weekends as he could, if his big deal went well. She'd heard the house they'd rented was fabulous. A friend of theirs had rented it for his family last year. Peter always provided wonderful vacations for them. She just hoped he'd be able to enjoy it with them. He was working late every night on his deal.

Caroline still felt guilty leaving him alone in Marin, just to go see her sisters. She hadn't seen them this much in years, although it had been nice spending time with them and reconnecting. It was different at the ranch now without her father there. He wasn't an overbearing presence, showing off, and telling everyone what to do. She could never understand how Kate had stood working for him for all these years, but now at least she could run it the way she wanted, after twenty years of doing his bidding, and having to do everything his way, although Kate had never complained. In Caroline's opinion, she was a saint and had more than paid her dues.

With a heavy heart, Gemma packed some summer clothes to take to the Valley, put several racks and suitcases in storage, emptied some closets and locked others, had the carpet cleaners in, and was ready for her tenant on the appointed day. She hated to leave her house, and leave L.A. even for a month. But she would have been on hiatus and away anyway. Her agent had no work for her, and no auditions, and at least at the ranch, she wouldn't be spending any money. It was a way to save for a month, with her funds running out at a rapid rate. Caroline had called her and was going to the ranch for a week with her kids, so they would all be there together. A month seemed like an eternity to Gemma, and Kate was trying to get her to stay longer. But all she could think about for now was one month, and she'd see how she felt at the end of it. If she was crawling out of her skin, or morbidly depressed, she was going back to L.A., whether she had work or not. A studio apartment somewhere in L.A. might be less depressing than the ranch, which was always a painful déjà vu for her.

Gemma left her house with a rented van full of bags of the clothes she was bringing to the ranch, including clothes she might need for auditions, her exercise equipment, her favorite cappuccino machine, and everything she could take with her. The rent she was getting for her house would more than cover her mortgage so she would be saving some money for three months, though less if she went back and rented an apartment in L.A.

She arrived at the ranch looking like a refugee on the run. Kate showed up to welcome her, as Gemma was hauling bags out of the car and dragging them into the guesthouse she always used when she was there.

"Good lord, what is all this stuff?" Kate asked, laughing at her. She was carrying barbells into the living room, her mountain bike was leaning against the wall on the porch.

"I just brought the bare necessities," Gemma said, looking exhausted and stressed. "I thought the house was bigger. I think it shrank."

"I think you've grown. How many bags did you bring?"

"How many closets are there?"

Kate looked worried. "Three, I think. Maybe four." She helped Gemma with her bags, and within minutes, they had created a mess of boxes and suitcases in every room. There was hardly any furniture, just the bare minimum in the bedroom, a bed and a chest, a couch, a coffee table and two chairs in the living room, and no TV, but Gemma had brought one, just in case, and her computer. The little guesthouse had never been properly furnished since she almost never used it, and as she looked around, she wanted to cry. She was ready to pack up and leave. "Why don't you come down to my place for a glass of wine?" Kate suggested. "I'll come back with you later and help you unpack. Thad is bringing me some papers to sign." Gemma followed her out of the cottage, and got into Kate's truck. They drove down the hill to Kate's house, which was only slightly bigger. She opened a bottle of wine and handed Gemma a glass. Kate was smiling at her sister, who looked flustered and upset. "And to think I used to share a room with you."

"I didn't have as much stuff then." But she'd always had more than her sister, and her closets had been stuffed. Kate had never had Gemma's interest in clothes, and still didn't. Juliette showed up a few minutes later and greeted Gemma with a warm hug. And then Thad arrived with the papers for Kate to sign, and they disappeared into the kitchen.

"You can stay at my house if you want," Juliette offered. "I'm leaving soon."

"No, I'm going to make it work. I just need to figure it out," Gemma said, looking distracted, already missing her house in L.A., and sorry that she'd rented it. She hated being broke. She wasn't yet, but would be soon. Renting her house had been the right thing to do. But she wasn't sure that coming to the ranch was. Even with her father gone, she could feel his presence there, and her memories of his dominating all of them were strong.

Kate and Thad walked back into the room with the signed papers, and he chatted with Gemma for a few minutes and offered to lend a hand if she needed it, but she insisted she was fine. When she finished her wine, she walked back up the hill, determined to solve the puzzle of where to put her stuff. Kate offered to come up, but Gemma wanted to do it herself. She wrestled with bags and boxes and garment bags for the rest of the night, but she managed to get it all in. There was a tiny second bedroom, which she turned into a closet with rolling racks she had brought. She packed them in as tightly as she could. And she put her empty suitcases on the porch to put in Kate's garage the next day. She put her barbells there too, since it was warm enough to exercise outside. She sat down on the couch and made a list of everything she needed to make it feel like home, and she knew exactly what she wanted to do.

Kate showed up the next morning at nine. She'd been working for three hours by then, and was impressed that Gemma had managed to put everything away. She even had shoe racks set up between the rolling racks in the tiny room.

"You're a magician," Kate said with admiration. "I can never figure out where to put two shirts and a pair of jeans."

"I'm good with wardrobe changes." Gemma grinned at her. She felt less panicked than she had the day before. She had a list of things she wanted to get from town. She had called a number she had used before in L.A. for things she knew she couldn't get in the Valley. They had promised to deliver the next day.

"If you need furniture, we've got some leftovers in the barn," Kate said helpfully. "Thad can bring it over for you."

"I'm all set," she said, and took off half an hour later, and waved as she drove by Juliette leaving her house to go to the office. She wanted to get the books in good order before she left for France and had found a bookkeeper to help Kate while she was gone.

Gemma was back from town in two hours, and stopped in to see Kate in her office. She looked busy, with ledgers all over her desk, and a pencil stuck in her hair, which was pulled back in a braid.

"Do you know they have a nail salon in town now?" she said, looking pleased, and Kate laughed, and glanced down at her own, which were cut short. She hadn't worn nail polish since her teens, when Gemma used to do her nails for her.

"I'm thrilled to hear it," she teased her sister. But she was relieved to see her in good spirits, and not looking as though she was ready to run, as she had the night before. She hadn't even bothered to eat dinner while she unpacked. She was determined to make the guesthouse feel like home, as best she could.

"They have a new shoe store, which is a little sketchy, and the hardware store is pretty good," Gemma reported. "The drugstore has some decent magazines for a change. Civilization has hit the Valley." And three people had recognized her and asked for her autograph, which made her feel like a star again. The last few weeks in L.A. had been so depressing, once everyone knew that the show was going off the air. Nothing made an actor feel worse than being out of work. But she was a big star here, and everywhere she went, people smiled and knew who she was. She had even run into a girl she'd gone to school with, with her three teenagers in tow. Gemma was shocked by how old she looked.

Kate was a star in her own right here too, as the owner of the biggest ranch in the Valley. But no one asked for her autograph, and she didn't need them to. Gemma did. Kate understood that about her. Gemma needed the validation that she existed and was important, and people cared. Kate had lived in her father's shadow all her life, and was used to it and didn't mind. All she needed to know was that she was doing a good job. Thad said she was, more than her father ever had.

"Well, I won't keep you from work," Gemma said, and started to walk out of her office. "When is Caroline arriving?"

"Tomorrow," Kate said, amused by her sister. She'd seen more of her in the last month than she had in years, but she enjoyed it. She was reminded of their differences, the same ones they'd had as kids growing up. As Daddy's Girl, Gemma had been the star. Caroline had been invisible, and the star student. And Kate had been the peacemaker and the pleaser. She wanted everyone to be happy, especially her father, and to get along. She had gone on to serve him as an adult, to be his support team, his backstage person behind the scenes, the one who did all the work and never got the credit, as long as he was happy.

And now here they were as grown-ups. Caroline deferred to her husband for every move she made and every decision. She respected his career, his success, and how smart he was. And Peter was proud of her books. She had a successful writing career she never talked about, she was always discreet and modest about herself. She lived below the radar, and always put the spotlight on Peter. Caroline didn't like it when people noticed her too much. And meanwhile, Gemma was signing autographs in the Santa Ynez Valley, after her show was canceled, and needed the attention desperately. The two sisters couldn't have been more different.

The only thing changed now for Kate was that she was no longer the understudy, the invisible assistant. She was running the whole show, and for once she wasn't pleasing anyone but herself. It was brand new to her, since her father's sudden death, and more than a little scary, but she was in the driver's seat now, and much to her own amazement, she liked it. She had finally come into her own at forty-two. She missed her father terribly, but she didn't miss being his minion or his slave, or the person he ignored while he took credit for what she did, and just assumed she would continue doing it forever, and she probably would have. But fate had intervened and freed the slaves. She was no longer working for her father, after twenty years of it. She was working for herself. At Juliette's suggestion, she had increased her meager salary by a small amount. She could have taken more, and Juliette thought she should, but like her father, she didn't like taking too much money out of the ranch, and she said she didn't need it.

Thad thought she was doing a great job, but even if she wasn't, she was following her own intelligence and her instincts, and her own ideas. She hoped she was doing a good job of it, but if not, she was going to make her own mistakes too. It was her turn now, she was ready, and it felt good. Her father had always treated her like a slightly lesser being, as though her opinions were not quite valid, her voice didn't need to be heard. He was in charge at all times, and she was a lowly foot soldier. And suddenly she was running the whole show, and managing very nicely. Thad was helping her, but she was making the decisions, and willing to be accountable for them. She was actually enjoying it. She was smiling thinking about it as Thad walked into the office and saw the pleased look on her face. She was sitting at her father's desk because she'd been looking for something.

"It's nice to see you smiling," he said, "and sitting in that chair." She was only in her father's chair for a moment, and suddenly realized that he wasn't going to walk in and give her hell for sitting there.

"I was just in here for a minute," she explained to Thad and he shook his head.

"Maybe you should move into this office. It would give you more space and a bigger desk," he said. But it was also symbolic. She was the boss now. And this was the boss's office.

"Maybe I will," she said, and smiled at him. There was a new confidence about her that Thad could see growing day by day.

Kate moved into her father's office that afternoon. A few people looked startled when they saw her do it, but it felt right to her. Thad came by at the end of the day, to drop off an expense sheet, he gave her a thumbs-up, and she laughed at him. She felt giddy with excitement. She liked the feeling of sitting there. She had earned it.

The following day, Kate ran home at lunchtime to make herself something to eat. She looked up the hill and saw a truck delivering furniture to Gemma's cottage. She wondered what she'd ordered, went inside to make a sandwich, and took it up the hill to eat while she visited her, and was stunned when she walked in the front door. There were bright modern paintings on the walls, a vivid red couch that added punch to the room, big plants in handsome cachepots in two of the room's corners, end tables, a small round dining table with brass chairs, and a Moroccan rug on the floor with a straw background and red embroidery. The room looked suddenly exotic and fun and stylish, like something you'd see in a magazine, and wished you lived there. When she peeked into the bedroom, it was cotton candy pink with a big plastic chair and pink night tables with a matching chest and a small round pink rug. The whole room looked like a candy box, and Gemma came out of the bathroom carrying a large pink plastic poodle and saw her sister.

"What do you think?" She looked enormously pleased with herself.

"It's fantastic! I love it! Where did you find all this great stuff?" It was feminine and modern and young, and Gemma looked a little sheepish.

"I had it staged. I called them yesterday. It was so depressing the way it was. I've used them for parties before. I picked everything online. It's all rented. And when I get tired of it, I can change it, or send it all back. Or buy it if I make some money."

"Does it cost a fortune?" Kate had never seen anything like it before, but you had to have Gemma's eye to pick the right things and make it work.

"It's not cheap, but it's worth it. Instant happiness, instead of dreary old furniture, or buying things you'll get tired of anyway." Kate looked around, admiring the effect, and they went to sit in the kitchen, which was all red and white now, and there was a small red lacquer table big enough for the two of them. They'd even put in a small red refrigerator, which fit the space perfectly.

"Forget acting. You should be a decorator. I should have you stage my place, but I wouldn't know what to do with all my grungy old furniture." She'd used the leftovers from the ranch hands' bunkhouse and it looked it. Gemma was delighted with her new décor, and the two of them sat and talked while Kate ate her sandwich before she went back to the office.

Caroline loved it too when she arrived that afternoon, and Gemma suggested she do the same in her cottage, which was bigger than Gemma's and had three bedrooms.

"Actually, the kids and I are going to Ikea tomorrow to see what we can do." None of the cottages had ever been fully furnished or decorated, because neither of the girls had ever used them except for a night once every year or two, or less often in Caroline's case. But suddenly the cottages had become useful, and they wanted to make them livable. Caroline had promised to let Morgan pick the furniture for her bedroom, and at Ikea they couldn't go too far wrong or do too much damage.

It was beginning to feel like home, or a fun second home for all of them. Juliette came to take a look too when Kate told her about it, and she loved the effect. She knew that Jimmy wouldn't have liked it. It wouldn't have looked like a ranch to him, but it was what the place needed, and what they needed to feel at home there, a youthful feminine touch, which expressed their personalities. Juliette smiled all the way back to her house after she saw it. She liked having the girls there, and the children. She was almost sorry she was going to France for the summer. She liked being there with them. And Jimmy would have liked seeing his girls there too. It was Kate who was bringing them together, and getting them back to the ranch, and that was the whole point. It was a family operation and they owned it jointly now, with Kate running it, and the benefit of everything her father had taught her.

"Change is in the air," Thad said as he walked past her house, after helping Gemma install a light fixture she had bought at the hardware store.

"My father would have hated it," Kate said to Thad and they both laughed.

"Leave it to Gemma to have the cottage 'staged,' and have it looking like a feature in a decorating magazine. She's got an eye, though," he said admiringly.

"She painted our room purple and orange once. Our father almost killed us. He made her repaint it white. She looked like a snowman when she finished. He wouldn't let me help her."

"He's not here anymore," Thad said gently. "You can paint the place any color you want." It was good to be reminded, and she nodded, as he walked back to his own tiny house behind the barn.

Her sisters had brought light into her life, and Kate realized that she needed it. They all did. It was a new regime, and she was going to have fun with it, just like Gemma had done with the cottage. It was exactly what they needed, a woman's touch, because she was running the ranch now, not their father. He had finally lost control of them, and sadly, he had to die to do it.

Chapter 6

It took Gemma and Caroline a few days to settle in. Gemma loved the new décor in her cottage, and managed to fit everything in, although it was barely bigger than a dollhouse, but she enjoyed spending time there when she wasn't with her sisters or outdoors. And Caroline's trip to Ikea with Morgan was fruitful. Caroline had an eye for design too, and following Gemma's example, she went a little wild, picking things she liked. Morgan got the lavender bedroom she'd wanted, and they'd picked a cowboy theme for Billy. Caroline didn't know how much time they'd be spending there, probably not much, but the rooms looked comfortable and inviting, fresh and new when they'd finished. They borrowed a truck from the ranch to bring everything home. The dilemma was assembling the furniture once they brought it back, but Thad and the kids pitched in and figured it out, Gemma lent a hand, and by that afternoon, like magic, the little guesthouse was decorated. They even had rugs and curtains. Kate was vastly impressed with the effect both her sisters had achieved, and Morgan said she liked it better than her bedroom at home. They had bought new pots and pans too, and bright colored china and glasses, towels, and large framed photographs to put on the walls. Gemma's little cottage was fancier, but Caroline's had a good look too, and they had fun doing it.

Thad was making himself available to both girls, and was impressed with what they had achieved in a short time. The day after Caroline arrived, all three sisters and Morgan and Billy went out to dinner, and went bowling afterward. Caroline acknowledged that it had been a good idea to spend some time at the ranch before they went to Aspen.

"I used to hate coming here," she admitted, as the kids bowled and they waited for their turn. It still reminded her of her father, but with a space of their own to retreat to, it no longer gave her that oppressive feeling. He had taken up every inch of space wherever he was, not only physically, but psychologically. She always felt like she couldn't breathe when she was around him. "It feels better now," she admitted to her sisters, although her children said they missed him. She was embarrassed to admit that she didn't.

Billy had loved the idea that he had a real cowboy as a grandfather, in contrast to Peter's very East Coast intellectual parents. Peter's was the kind of family Caroline had always wanted. His father was a publisher and his mother had been a political journalist before she retired. They had a house in Maine where she and Peter took the kids for a week every year at the end of August, and spent time with his sister and her three children. She was a physics professor at Harvard, and like Peter, her husband was in high-tech finance.

Their childhoods had been very different from Caroline's, and at first she had felt like trailer trash when she was around them. Born in Texas, and raised on a ranch in Southern California, she didn't

have the same highbrow background they did. Jimmy had been uncomfortable around Peter's parents when they met at the wedding,
which Peter and Caroline had insisted on having in San Francisco,
where their friends were. It was a small affair at a stuffy club that
was affiliated with Peter's father's club in New York. Jimmy had worn
cowboy boots and a Stetson with a suit to the wedding, and at
twenty-two, Caroline had nearly died of embarrassment, compared
to the well-tailored dark blue suits of Peter's family and guests from
New York, and Boston, where his mother was from.

But the marriage had worked well, despite their different back-
grounds. Caroline deferred to Peter for most big decisions and even
small ones. Their children went to the best private schools, and after
the first few years, Peter stopped teasing her about what he called
her redneck background. He had been impressed by the ranch, although they seldom went, and acknowledged that her father was an
interesting man, and not nearly as simple and modest as he pretended to be. He was a powerhouse, and had an extraordinarily good
grip on the concepts of finance, and had made some very successful
investments with little advice from anyone, just using his own instincts. The two men had never become friends, and Peter had never
warmed to him but acknowledged that he was worthy of respect.
Jimmy was a smart, straightforward man from a simple background
who had made a huge success of his ranch, without the benefit of
Harvard Business School or the East Coast establishment Peter had
grown up in. Whether one liked him or not, Peter gave him credit for
what he had achieved. Peter always respected financial success.

It had taken his parents longer to warm up to Caroline, but they
finally had and admired her steady success with her young adult
books. Her publisher father-in-law was particularly impressed by

them, once she won the Printz Award, and started making real money for them. Young adult books were very much in demand. Material success was important to Peter and his family, it was their yardstick of someone's merits, and determined whether or not they liked people. Peter emphasized those same values to their children and Caroline didn't agree. But it was how Peter had been brought up. And in spite of Peter's materialistic views about money, he was a good and attentive father and loved his children. And he was attentive to Caroline too, although he wasn't demonstrative or overly emotional around other people. He was warmer with her in private.

It was their third night at the ranch when Kate broached a delicate subject. They'd had dinner at her house, which Caroline and Gemma cooked, and the children had gone back to Caroline's house to play videogames on their new TV. They were enjoying the freedom of being on the ranch, able to go wherever they wanted to. Kate had given them both bikes to ride, and Thad was proving to be an excellent babysitter, assigning them chores, and riding with them whenever possible, or taking them in his truck when he had some task to perform at the far reaches of the ranch.

"I was thinking we might take a ride down to Santa Barbara." Kate opened the subject with caution, knowing it was a sensitive issue for Caroline, and for them all.

"Am I correct in assuming you don't just have shopping in mind?" Gemma inquired, as she poured them all another round of wine. Kate had purposely waited until they'd had dinner, and at least a glass of wine, so they'd be more relaxed. She saw Caroline stiffen when she nodded. Their father had been dead for six weeks, and in some ways, it seemed like a long time, and in others, it felt as though his funeral had been yesterday. There were already noticeable changes in their reactions to the ranch, without his powerful presence. Neither of Kate's sisters had ever been willing to spend a week there since they'd left. They never lasted more than a few days when their father was alive.

"I just think we should follow up on what we discovered. We can't spend the rest of our lives knowing that our mother is alive, fifty miles away, and not finding out more about her, and why we never knew she was alive," Kate said calmly.

"We never knew because our father obviously lied to us," Gemma said bluntly. She was angry at him about it.

"I'd like to know why he lied. Maybe she's some awful derelict and he was protecting us from her our entire lives. Maybe she's a drug addict or a criminal of some kind. But if she is, I want to know," Kate said. "I think we should know. Or at least I want to. I would have checked it out sooner, when we found out right after Dad died, but I wanted to wait for you two. It affects all three of us, it didn't feel right to just rush into it without you."

"God knows what she is. We may have her on our necks forever after this, trying to bilk us for money. That could be part of why he steered clear of her. Something big must have happened for her to give up custody, and relinquish her parental rights," Gemma said, wondering.

"Maybe he forced her to do that," Caroline said in a soft voice, having a lesser opinion of her father than either of her sisters. "But whoever she is, I don't want to know her. She wasn't here when it counted, and I don't think we need the headache now of a brand-new mystery mother in our forties."

"You're only thirty-nine," Gemma reminded her. "And according to my latest bio, I'm only thirty-five, thank you," and then she turned serious. "Dad may have been tough, but he was an honest, honorable guy. He wouldn't have 'forced' her to do anything. He never 'forced' us, even though he had strong opinions. He may have been responding to a bad situation out of necessity."

"He *pressured* us into doing what *he* wanted. That's as good as forcing us. He wanted everything his way, Gemma, and you know it," Caroline countered.

"You never stood up to him, that's why he pushed you around. You had to go toe to toe with him, he respected that." Caroline was a small person, with a meek personality, especially in her youth. She had spent most of her childhood afraid of him, terrified sometimes, although he'd never laid a hand on any of them. But one look, his voice, his clear commands were enough to send Caroline scurrying into the bushes.

"You're the only one who ever stood up to him," she said to Gemma and glanced at Kate, who had never opposed him either, and always did his bidding, "and you're the only one he would take it from."

"I never gave him any choice," Gemma said matter-of-factly and knew that what Caroline had said was true. It was the advantage of being his favorite. He put up with a lot more from Gemma than he had from the others. They had never gotten away with what she did, and they all knew it.

"Well, this isn't about him, it's about our mother," Kate reminded them. "And about us."

"Of course it's about him," Gemma interrupted her. "It's about what the hell happened to make her disappear from our lives. They were divorced and we never knew it, and she's been living in Santa Barbara for God knows how long, after he told us she was dead for the last thirty-nine years. I'd like to know what the hell happened, who and what she is, and why he lied to us for our entire lives."

"That's what I want to know too," Kate agreed, and they could see Caroline shut down just talking about it.

"Well, I don't. So you two can go. Count me out. If you're going to Santa Barbara for that, I'll stay here. You can tell me about it later," she said, and took a long sip of wine. Kate noticed that her hand was shaking. The thought of it affected her deeply, just as the memories of their father did. He still upset her even now.

"Why do you get to go underground?" Gemma confronted her. "You let us do the dirty work of going to see her and you stay home? How does that seem right to you? You want to be a no-show as usual," Gemma said harshly, annoyed about it. "This isn't easy for us either."

"I'm not a no-show. I just don't need to open Pandora's box and see what's inside. She's obviously not a good person if they got divorced and she abandoned us, and signed away her rights."

"And how do you feel about Dad? How good was he to lie to us for all these years? I'd rather have known that I had a bad mother, even if she was in prison for murder, than to think I had no mother and she was dead. Maybe he needed to keep her away from us as kids, but he could have told us the truth as adults, and he never did. If he weren't dead, and Kate hadn't gone through his safe, we wouldn't even know about her now, and we have a right to. Don't you want to know about her for your kids? She's part of their gene pool, and ours. What kind of woman is she? Why did she give up her rights to three kids? You weren't even a child then, you were an infant. How the hell could she walk away from all of us? And what did he have on her if he made her do that? I think I'd rather know if I'm related to a murderer, wouldn't you?" Caroline couldn't even imagine Peter's reaction, if that was the case. It had taken years for him to swallow her being the daughter of a cowboy, let alone of a murderess. He had finally let go of her humble origins and now she would be adding to it, if she told him. And she had finally earned her snobbish parents-in-law's respect. She didn't want to jeopardize that either.

"I think it's pretty unlikely," Kate said to calm them both, "that she's a murderer. Maybe just a bad mother." The discussion was getting heated, and she could see that Caroline was feeling cornered, which was how discussions between the three of them often ended up. Caroline was no match for Gemma, just as she hadn't been for their father. Kate didn't want her packing up and going back to San Francisco because Gemma badgered her, which was the way Caroline handled unpleasantness. She ran. "Look, Caroline doesn't have to go. This is a free choice. Why don't you and I go, and look around on an exploring mission," she said to Gemma. "We might not see her or find her. She may have moved. She might not want to see us," Kate said calmly, as Gemma nodded.

"Are we going to call and ask to see her?" Gemma inquired. Kate had been debating about that herself.

"I'd rather not. Why don't we just drive by her house and get a feeling for where and how she lives? We can always call her if we want to, and ask to see her. If she looks like a total mess, or is falling down drunk in the street, we may not want to see her, and let it go at that. That would at least explain why Dad kept her out of our lives. Or maybe she kept herself out of our lives. Maybe she didn't want to see us, and Dad was trying to protect us from that rejection. I know he wasn't an easy person, but this can't be *all* Dad's fault. She has to have played a part in it too. Maybe she abused us, or neglected us, or just didn't want to see us for all these years. She could have shown up by now. That's all I really want to know. What happened and why did she leave? And why did she never come back later? Why he lied is his part of the equation, and he's not here to tell us. Maybe we can figure it out ourselves from her side of the story, and then we'll feel better about it now that we know about her. I'd never have gone looking for her. It never occurred to me to check it out, or doubt what he told us. Now that we know there's a discrepancy, and she's less than an hour from here, I want to go and find out what I can," Kate said.

"So do I," Gemma said, nodding at Kate. She agreed with everything she'd said. Caroline didn't.

"Well, I don't have that kind of curiosity. She wasn't here, and I don't need her anymore, so I'd rather let sleeping dogs lie."

"And let us do the dirty work," Gemma reproached her again, and Caroline stood up.

"You don't need to do anything for me, Gemma. I don't need to know about her, and don't even want to. If it's what you need, fine. But leave me out of it. And if you decide to meet her, don't bother to include me. I won't go." She had made herself clear and Kate respected it, and didn't want to push her. She could see that her younger sister was way out of her comfort zone, and they were crossing her boundaries, and Kate didn't want to do that and make her feel ganged up on. Gemma had a powerful personality, like their father, and Kate didn't want to add to its impact on Caroline. As always, she was the peacemaker, and enjoyed that role, which suited her personality.

"That's fine, Caro. Don't stress about it. Gem and I will go, and fill you in later, IF you want us to." She turned to Gemma then. "What about tomorrow?" Gemma nodded agreement. "We can leave around ten?"

"Works for me. I have nothing to do here." The dinner lasted a few more minutes, and then Caroline left, with the excuse of checking on her children at her house. Gemma stayed to help Kate put the dishes in the machine.

"Wow, she is sensitive. I forget how fragile she is sometimes." Gemma looked surprised.

"So did Dad. He didn't know how to handle her, so he ignored her. I'm not sure what was worse, bullying her, or ignoring her. He never knew how to handle people like her."

"I don't think I do either," Gemma admitted. "She just crawls right into her shell, and refuses to engage."

"It's who she is. I think Peter is more like Dad than she realizes. He makes most of her decisions for her, and she lets him. But she's stubborn once she makes up her mind." Gemma nodded agreement. It was the opposite personality from hers and her father's. Kate was kind of a hybrid between the two. She wasn't forceful, but she had her own opinions, and confronted things head-on, but in a gentle way. Caroline had been in hiding for most of her life. And Peter's early criticism of her hadn't helped. He loved her, but had been vocal about not liking where she came from, and his parents had added to it. They had wanted their only son to marry a debutante. Caroline was smart and loving, but not that.

"Are you nervous about tomorrow?" Gemma asked her. Kate thought about it and then nodded.

"Yeah, I am. What if she turns out to be a weirdo or a creep, or a really terrible person?" Kate responded.

"That would be sad, but at least we'll know. Now that we've found her, I'm dying of curiosity. We don't need her anymore, but she's still our mother. I wish she'd turned up a long time ago. I could have used a mother then. Having just a father wasn't enough. He tried to cover all the bases, but he was all guy, and pure testosterone, and Juliette didn't really get deeply involved with him until we were in college. It was too late by then, and she was careful not to step on Dad's toes and get too engaged. It was smart of her, because he wouldn't have liked it if she had, but it didn't do much for us. I'm past needing a mother now, unless she's fabulously wealthy and would like to pay off all my debts." Kate grinned. She worried about Gemma and the pinch she was in.

"How's that going?" Kate asked her.

"Okay. The rent I'm getting for the house will pay my mortgage, but I've got a lot of debts, more than I realized. I'm going to need to take all the money jobs I can get for a while, to try and make up for the show getting canceled. I hate to do it, but I may need you to buy out my share of the ranch by the fall." Kate nodded. She didn't like it, but she wasn't surprised. Gemma needed money, and soon, if she didn't find another big job. She had an expensive lifestyle, and wasn't shy about running into debt. Their father had complained about it to Kate before.

"Thad said he'd be willing to buy it if it comes to that," Kate reminded her.

"How do you feel about that?" Gemma asked her.

"I'd rather not," Kate said, "but I probably wouldn't have the money fast enough to help you out. We don't have that much liquidity. As Dad said, land rich and cash poor. If you want to cash out, I'd have to sell off some land to someone. It might as well be Thad, who has the best interests of the ranch at heart, and won't encroach on us, or try to steal more."

"I hate to do that to you." Gemma felt badly about it but she had no choice. "We'll see how things look in September. There's almost no work in summer. Everything's pretty dead."

"Good, then you can relax here." Kate smiled at her. They had finished cleaning up the kitchen by then. "I like having you here, Gem," she said warmly and Gemma hugged her. "I'll pick you up at ten tomorrow, and we'll head out."

"Too bad Caroline doesn't want to come too."

"She doesn't need to," Kate said easily. "You and I should be able to handle one mother between us." Kate grinned and Gemma laughed.

"Hell, yeah. We handled Dad, didn't we? The human tornado. Shit, our mother will be a piece of cake," she said, and Kate laughed, as Gemma left. Tomorrow was going to be an interesting day, meeting the mother who had supposedly been dead for thirty-nine years. And now she was alive.

Chapter 7

Kate got all her morning chores done, and spent an hour in the office, returning calls, sending emails, and signing expense reports, before she got in her truck to pick Gemma up. When Kate got there, Gemma was standing on her porch in black designer shorts, a white T-shirt, and Italian sandals that laced up to her knee. She looked ten feet tall and very stylish, as she slung a white bag over her shoulder and ran down her porch steps and got in the truck. Her shining dark brown hair was tied in a neat knot, and her blue eyes were the color of the summer sky, as she put on dark glasses that Kate suspected cost more than the bag on her shoulder. Gemma always looked fabulous and spent a fortune to do it, which was part of why she was in debt now.

Kate was wearing jeans and a plaid work shirt. She'd ridden for two hours that morning with Thad, while they talked ranch business and checked the livestock. She had on battered cowboy boots she'd had for at least fifteen years, and one of her father's straw Stetsons she'd grabbed from a peg in the barn, since she'd forgotten her own at home.

"Do we look like stereotypes or what?" Gemma laughed, looking them both over. "The cowgirl and the Hollywood slut."

"Not slut, 'star,'" Kate corrected her. "Can I have your autograph?"

"I charge for that nowadays," Gemma said, as they both saw Caroline run out of her house, waving her arms. She was wearing a denim skirt and espadrilles and a crisp white shirt. Kate stopped the truck to talk to her.

"Something wrong?"

"No, I decided to come. Thad said he'd watch the kids," she said, as she opened the door and hopped into the backseat of the truck. Kate and Gemma exchanged a glance and didn't comment. They were both trying not to smile. But at least Caroline had come out of hiding to get a glimpse of their mother. Gemma was amused to see that she looked like the suburban housewife she was, all prim and proper and squeaky clean, with her blond hair in a ponytail. Kate was wearing her hair in the familiar braid down her back, so it didn't get in her way.

Kate turned the radio on to ease the tension. She chose a country music station, and Gemma flipped the dial to rap. Caroline groaned from the backseat.

"God, Gemma, you're as bad as my kids. They listen to that crap all the time. Peter yells at me about it, but I can't stop them. It's all kids listen to these days." Gemma mimicked it and knew the words to the song, and did such a good imitation of it that she had them laughing for the next several songs, as she got more and more outrageous, and then turned the music down. It had helped to relax all three of them. Gemma was a born clown.

When they got to Santa Barbara, they took the Montecito exit, which was the posh part of Santa Barbara where the expensive homes were, and some very famous people lived. Hollywood types who bought houses in Santa Barbara usually lived there.

"Shit, I hope she's rich," Gemma said to break the tension. "Maybe we can blackmail her or something. I wonder if she has a husband and other kids who don't know about us."

"We weren't illegitimate, for heaven's sake," Caroline said to her. "We're not like those people who show up on someone's doorstep and say 'Hi, I'm your daughter. You gave me away when you were fourteen. Remember me?' And then the mother drops dead from the shock, right after the husband says 'Who's that, honey?'" Her sisters grinned. All three of them were nervous, and had no idea what they were getting into, whether they'd even see her, or what kind of reception they'd get if they did. She might refuse to speak to them, throw them out, or call the police. "Maybe she has Alzheimer's and doesn't remember us," Caroline offered as an alternative. Kate slowed the truck. They were on a street of handsome homes, not the fanciest in Montecito, but pretty houses of human scale, the right size for a family, with neat landscaping and attractive gardens. Then she stopped.

"That's the house." Kate pointed. It was a medium sized, fairly elegant traditional house, with a flower garden in front and well-trimmed hedges. It was attractive and well kept. It looked like proper people of comfortable means lived there.

"Now what do we do?" Gemma whispered, as though their mother could hear them if they talked too loud.

"I don't know," Kate answered. "Do you want to sit here for a while and see if someone comes out?" She hadn't formulated a plan

for what to do when they got there. All her energies had been focused on finding the address, which had been easy.

"Yeah, let's wait for a while," Gemma said. Her heart was pounding and Caroline was staring at the house and not saying a word.
Kate found a parking place by backing up, just a few car lengths from
the house. They had a perfect view of the front door and the garage,
in case anyone entered or exited.

They'd been there for half an hour, and were just starting to relax,
when the front door opened, and a well-dressed older man came
out, opened the garage, got in a silver Mercedes sedan, and drove
away, and the garage door closed on its own a few minutes later.

"Are you sure you have the right address?" Gemma asked Kate.

"How many Scarlett Jane Carsons can there be in Santa Barbara,
or the whole country, with the right birth date?" she responded, and
Gemma nodded.

"Good point."

A few minutes after the man left, the front door opened again, and
a tall older woman walked out. She was wearing white jeans, a pink
silk blouse, and white running shoes. She dug in her bag for her
keys, locked the house, and used a remote to open the garage. She
looked right at them in the truck for an instant, as though she knew
they were there, and there was a collective gasp. It was the woman
they'd seen on the Internet. She looked exactly like Gemma with
white hair, and a little bit like Kate. She had their height and their
build, and her face was an older version of Gemma's. She was still
beautiful at her age. They knew that she was sixty-two years old.
And as though pulled out of the truck by a magnet, Kate got out of
the car, walked a few steps, and just stood there to get a better look

at her. She couldn't take her eyes off her, and as the garage door opened, Gemma got out of the truck too, and went to stand next to Kate. They didn't have the courage to approach, but just stood there, watching her. There was a white Mercedes station wagon in the garage, but instead of getting into it, the woman stopped and turned, and looked at them again. No one moved for an eternity, and then she slowly walked toward them, with a stunned expression. Both Kate and Gemma wanted to turn and run, but they couldn't. She stood a few feet from them in her driveway, and Kate spoke up in a choked voice.

"I'm sorry," she fumbled, "we were just admiring your house. . . . We're tourists . . . from L.A." But Kate looked more like Wyoming than L.A. in her plaid shirt and cowboy boots.

"I know who you are," the white-haired woman who was Gemma's lookalike said softly. "I gave up hope years ago that this would ever happen." Kate nodded, not knowing what to say, since they hadn't hoped for it. They didn't even know she was alive until their father died in May. There was a long, awkward pause, and they could see her hands shaking as she held the remote and her keys. She looked very pale. She was even prettier up close, and when she smiled, she looked even more like Gemma. It was like looking in the mirror. Gemma could see it too. "Would you like to come inside?" They hesitated and both nodded, and Kate felt obliged to say something.

"Yes, thank you. I'm Kate, and this is Gemma." The woman smiled broadly then.

"I know. I can tell. You haven't changed since you were two and three. Not much anyway. How did you find me?"

"We didn't know you were alive until our dad died last month. We found your divorce papers in his safe. We didn't know about that either. I did an internet search, and there you were. Have you always been here?"

"For about twenty-five years. I lived in L.A. before that. I came to California about a year before you did." She had been this close. As they were talking, Kate sensed some movement behind her, and turned to see Caroline standing behind her and Gemma.

"This is Caroline," Kate introduced her. Caroline looked paralyzed for a moment, like a deer in the headlights, and then nodded.

"You're all here. I'm sorry about Jimmy. I didn't know."

"It was very sudden," Kate said, and Scarlett nodded, with a pained look on her face. It was clearly not a happy memory for her, hearing his name.

"Let's go inside," she said gently. She led them into a front hall that was beige and white marble and led into a living room with a spectacular view, all the way to the ocean, with a terrace outside. There were comfortable seating areas and an outdoor fireplace for chilly nights. She led them outside, invited them to sit down, and offered them something to drink, which they refused. She excused herself for a minute, called someone on her cellphone, and canceled a lunch date. She said something important had come up and she was sorry, and then turned her full attention to her daughters.

"I'm sorry. I don't even know what to say, I'm so stunned to see you. I didn't think I'd ever get to see you again. I thought by now, you'd forgotten me," she said in a wistful voice. She seemed like a gentle person, but who knew what she had been like in her youth. She might have mellowed with age.

"We thought you were dead," Gemma said with her usual bluntness. Their mother nodded and wasn't surprised.

"I know he told you that when you were younger. I thought by now he'd have told you the truth."

"It would have made him a liar. I guess he didn't want to admit that," Kate said more diplomatically. "We found your divorce papers in the safe after he died. We never knew you were divorced. That's what made me look for you online. There was no death certificate with the other papers." It was obvious why not now. "And we found the relinquishment papers," she said more softly. "It was too late to ask Dad what really happened, so we wanted to see you. We would have wanted to meet you anyway," she added, "now that we know you're alive."

"I made a terrible mistake. The worst mistake of my life," she said, referring to the papers she had signed. She went to an outdoor bar then, and poured them each a glass of water, and one for herself, and sat down with them. "I suppose you want to know what happened." She was grateful for the chance to tell them herself, and was suddenly glad they hadn't heard it from their father, who might have told them a different version of the story. The gospel according to JT. She knew he had never forgiven her for what she'd done, and the punishment had been severe, a life sentence for her, which he thought appropriate in the circumstances, and most of it had nothing to do with their children.

"I was nineteen when I met Jimmy. He was twenty-one. He was an itinerant ranch hand, going from ranch to ranch and town to town. My father was a minister, and he didn't want me to be with him. He said he'd never amount to anything. He was wrong about that. I married him anyway, and had you ten months later," she smiled at Kate, "and Gemma a year after that. I worked at an all-night diner when your father came home from work, and he took care of you while I worked. Times were hard in Texas then, there had been a drought, crops were bad, money was tight, we could barely afford to feed you and ourselves. They used to give me leftover food at the diner. Most of the time, that was all we had to eat. We were dirt poor, with no future on the horizon. And your father . . . he wasn't an easy man. He had a vision and he expected me to follow him. He expected me to live by his rules, and do what he said. When you got sick, we couldn't take you to a doctor. My parents helped when they could. I never met Jimmy's family. They were from another part of Texas, and most of them were dead or in jail. His father had died in a bar fight. Jimmy was no different from most ranch hands, except that he was smarter and stronger and tougher, and he expected me to follow him blindly. I was madly in love with him. It was hard not to be. He was dazzling and he expected me to follow him off a cliff if he said so, without questioning him, and I got scared. I was terrified about what would happen if one of you got really sick, or he did. We should have been on welfare but he was too proud. He tried to save every penny he could, which meant we had even less to live on. I washed your clothes every night before I went to work so you'd have something to wear the next day." It was hard for them to imagine the kind of poverty she was describing, but she did it well. They could almost taste her desperation and the dust of Texas as they listened raptly to every word.

"I got pregnant with Caroline when Gemma was a year old, and Kate was two. We didn't have enough money to feed ourselves, let alone another child, but you were born and you were beautiful." She smiled at Caroline, who had tears in her eyes, listening, trying to imagine what it would be like if she were that poor and had to take care of her children, with little food, few clothes, and no medical care. "We lived in a one-room shack on one of the ranches he worked on. We couldn't have paid rent. We had one crib for all of you, which Jimmy built himself, and a mattress on the floor for us. He said things would get better one day, but I didn't believe him. I was twenty-three years old and exhausted, after four years of desperation. I felt like I couldn't hang on anymore. And I met someone one night at the diner. He was just a boy my age. He'd saved up a little money, and was heading to California. He used to come see me in the daytime when Jimmy was at work. He was no better than the man I had, or not much, but Jimmy never listened. He didn't want to hear what I was saying. It was just too hard. I couldn't do it anymore. I was too scared. I wasn't as strong as he was. I thought it would never get better, and we'd just starve to death or lose you to the state if they found out how we were living with three kids. My father threatened to tell them, so you'd have decent lives and have food and medical care with foster parents. Jimmy swore we'd make it through, and I'm not sure when but I stopped believing in him. I got sick of being told what to do, and to stop complaining and just do what he said. He could be a hard man, although he meant well. He worked as many jobs as he could get. Once I fell in love with someone else, it was all different. Bobby, the other man, wanted me to go to California with him, and said we'd come back for you later. I refused to go with him and leave you, but it made me see that I couldn't stay with Jimmy anymore. It's hard for love to thrive in that kind of atmosphere of deprivation. I felt like a slave, harnessed to a hard man I thought didn't love me. I don't know if he did or not by then, but he wouldn't divorce me. He said we were hitched forever." Traces of her old Texas accent came through as she talked about the distant past.

"I begged him to divorce me and he wouldn't. I wanted to take you with me, but I didn't have the money to do it. And I couldn't afford a divorce myself. Bobby pleaded with me to go with him to California, and swore we'd come back for you as soon as we could. I told Jimmy what I was going to do. He borrowed the money for a divorce from the rancher he worked for. He liked Jimmy. He divorced me, on condition that I give up all custody and rights to the three of you. He said he'd pay me three thousand dollars if I did. That was a fortune to me then, and I thought with that money, I could set up a life in California, come back for you, and a judge would cancel the relinquishment. It was the only way I could get enough money to leave, and set up a life for you, and I never believed any judge would uphold the paper I signed, if I said I didn't mean it and came back. I was young and stupid," she said humbly. "And I figured Jimmy would mellow eventually too. So I signed the papers and got the money and left. I figured I'd be back in six months.

"Things were harder in L.A. than I thought. I couldn't find a job at first. Bobby blew through some of the money. He got into drugs. I didn't. And a year after we got there, he was killed in a motorcycle accident, drunk. It didn't work out with us once he got into drugs. After he died, I had a small apartment and some of the money was left, and I went back to Texas to get you, but your father had left with you by then. There was no trace of him. No one knew where he went. It took me a year to find you in the Valley. I went from ranch to ranch until I found him. I'd been gone for two years by then. I had a job as a waitress. I took him to court to overturn the relinquishment. Your dad was making decent money on the ranch where he worked. The judge upheld the relinquishment. He said I couldn't have supported you, but your dad had told you I was dead, and the court-appointed psychologist said that it would be too confusing for a five- and four-year-old to be told that their mother was dead, and then she came back to life again. So I lost. I tried to appeal the decision, but I didn't have the money to take it too far. I was twenty-six years old by the time I lost the last hearing, and I had lost my kids, and in my mind, I had nothing to live for. Jimmy was relentless. He wouldn't let me see you, and the psychologist said you were all happy and he was a responsible father, which is true, he was. But I was your mother and wanted to be part of your life.

"After that, my life got ugly. I had been so sure the court would overturn the papers I signed giving you up. If I thought they wouldn't, I would never have signed them. But I did. And after that, nothing mattered. I got into drugs for the first time. It was a way to escape everything, my hopes, my dreams, my past, my life. My parents had died and I had nothing left in Texas anyway. I just stayed in L.A., wasted on drugs, and in the gutter for ten years. I was homeless a few times, dealt drugs for a while, wound up in jail three times for possession. I never got into prostitution, but I did everything else, mostly involved with drugs, until I ended up in jail for a year for possession with intent to sell. Some social worker got hold of me, pulled me out of jail, sent me to rehab, and I slowly crawled back into the human race.

"I drove around Santa Ynez once or twice, hoping to see you, and hung around the school. I saw you once when you were about sixteen, fifteen, and thirteen. I saw Jimmy pick you up in his truck. He didn't see me, or he would probably have called the police. I wrote to him and begged him again to let me see you. He said he wouldn't, that I had made my decision and had to stick with it, and that there was no way he could tell you I had returned from the dead. Seeing me would make a liar of him. He said you didn't need me. He didn't know I'd been in jail, but I did, and I figured maybe he was right.

"I gave up then. I got a job working in a hotel, and met a nice man, and my life changed after that. That was twenty-six years ago. My partner is an architect and he's Italian. He built this house and we moved here. We've been together for twenty-six years, and never married. We don't really need to. I never wanted to have more children. I do some decorating for his clients occasionally, and we have a good life. He's very good to me." She wiped away the tears which had been pouring down her cheeks when she told the story, and her daughters had cried as they listened. She smiled at Caroline. "I've read every one of your books. I saw them in a bookstore one day. They're wonderful." Caroline had written them using her maiden name. She turned to Gemma. "And I've watched your show every week for the last ten years," she said proudly. The one she had never seen was Kate, working hard in the Valley for her father. "I want you all to know that I bitterly regret my terrible mistake giving you up. It was the worst thing I ever did. Nothing could ever make up for it. I thought I could undo it later, but I never could. Your father would never let me, and the court supported him. I have regretted it and missed you and loved you every single day of my life since. You were never forgotten," she said, as she stood up and went to hug each one of them. Caroline sobbed as they embraced, and she had been the one who hadn't wanted to meet her.

Gemma wiped the tears from her cheeks. "How could he not back down and let you see us, and how could he not tell us when we grew up? Who cared if he looked like a liar? It was always about him, how he looked, what people thought of him. What if you had died before we met you?" Gemma said, horrified at the thought. "We thought we had no mother all our lives, but we did. We had a right to know that." But they all knew that was how their father functioned. He made the rules, and this was an extreme example of it.

All things considered, Scarlett was very fair about him, and willing to admit her own mistakes. He never had. He never did. And they had been cheated of a mother as a result, in order to punish her, and so he could be the only star in his daughters' lives. It was a devastating revelation for them all. None of them could imagine her ever going to jail, or being on drugs for ten years. They realized she was a strong person if she had survived all of it and turned her life around. She looked proper and respectable and wholesome, and seemed like an honest, open, very loving person, even if she'd been foolish in her youth. And how could anyone guess what they would do, faced with that kind of poverty and despair?

"It's ironic," she said quietly, "that he died first, and you found me as a result. I'm surprised he never destroyed the paperwork, so there was no evidence." It surprised her daughters too.

"He probably forgot," Kate said in response, "or meant to do it later. He died very suddenly of a heart attack, and he was quite young, at sixty-four. I'm sure he expected to live much longer and thought he had time to destroy the papers."

"Did he ever remarry? Did you have a woman in your life?" she asked gently.

"No, he didn't. He's been with the same woman for twenty-four years, almost as long as you've been with your Italian friend," Gemma answered. "She's very discreet, and treated us more as friends. Dad never wanted anyone too involved with us. They didn't move in together until Caroline left for college. He was pretty proper about things like that."

"Are you all married? Do you have children?" Scarlett wanted to know everything about them, and Kate laughed.

"I'm not. I run the ranch, and have worked for Dad for twenty years. Gemma's not married either. She's been too busy being a star." They all laughed. "Caroline is married and has two kids, a son, eleven, and a daughter, fifteen."

"My daughter looks a lot like you," Caroline said softly. Her sisters had noticed it too.

They were all shocked to realize they had spent two hours with her, while she told her story. It had been a heavy emotional experience for all of them. Her partner, Roberto Puccinelli, let himself in as they were chatting at the end. She introduced him to all of her daughters, and he looked deeply moved.

"Your mother speaks of you almost every day." He smiled at Gemma. He was a handsome, distinguished-looking man with lively blue eyes and white hair. "And we watch your show every week."

"You'll have to watch reruns now," she said sadly. "We just went off the air."

"Oh no!" he exclaimed, and Scarlett smiled at them.

"May I see you again?" she asked cautiously, afraid of what they'd say. Maybe they only wanted to satisfy their curiosity, but didn't want her in their lives now. Anything was possible. Jimmy had successfully gouged her out of their lives for nearly forty years.

"Of course," Caroline was the first to say, and Gemma and Kate were quick to respond positively.

"Will you come to the ranch to visit us?" Kate asked her. "We're all staying there right now, which is very unusual for us."

"Where do you all live normally?"

"I live in L.A.," Gemma volunteered, and Caroline said San Francisco. They had never been very far from her.

"I would love to come to the ranch," Scarlett said, and Kate extended the invitation to Roberto too.

They all had much to think about, and a little while later, the sisters left, after promising to all get together again soon. Roberto stood next to Scarlett with an arm around her and they waved as the girls drove away. Kate noticed that her lip was trembling. The poor woman was overcome with emotion to have seen her daughters and told them her story.

There was silence in the truck for the first few minutes after they drove away, and Caroline and Gemma dabbed at their eyes again.

"What an amazing woman," Gemma said. "I can see how it all happened. How could Dad do that to her, not let her see us?" But they all knew he had a vengeful side. If you crossed him, he didn't forgive you. Leaving him for another man must have been the ultimate betrayal, and he made her pay for his broken heart and his bruised ego, and had clearly never forgiven her. Her life sentence was to make her stick to her agreement to give up her daughters. They believed her that she thought she could get him and the courts to relent but she couldn't. She was trapped by her own agreements, and by a man who would never forgive her. By some miracle fate had intervened. They were all glad they had seen her. They each felt as though a piece of them that had been missing had been restored. The mother they knew virtually nothing about had reappeared. She hadn't been a disappointment, as they had feared. She had been a gift.

Chapter 8

Much to Scarlett's delight, Kate called her the next day to thank her for seeing them, and being so open with them. After so long, and so much pain, she could have refused to open her heart again, but she hadn't. Kate said that hearing her story and knowing the truth had helped each of them. They had all been enormously impressed by her, her grace, her simplicity, and her honesty.

Kate invited her and Roberto to the ranch for lunch on Sunday, and Scarlett was thrilled to come, and said Roberto would be too. She knew about Jimmy's enormously successful ranch, of course, but had never been there. She asked if their father's companion would be upset by their visit.

"I don't think so," Kate said. "She's a wonderful person. She's not a jealous woman. I'll tell her. She doesn't have to come to lunch if she doesn't want to. I'll give her fair warning, but she's probably curious to meet you." Oddly, although her father had been difficult, and even domineering, from what Kate knew, he had a penchant for exceptionally nice, gentle women. There wasn't a bitchy side to Juliette or

Scarlett, from what Kate could see. On the contrary, they were both quite docile in some ways, even meek, so were willing to play by his rules. Stronger women wouldn't have agreed to do that. A woman like Gemma would have killed him. But Kate had done what Juliette and her mother had. She had let him take the lead, and never challenged his power or right to tell her what to do. He had done the same to Scarlett, and to Juliette for twenty-four years, and to Kate for twenty years of working for him. Only now was she finally able to make important decisions on the ranch. She couldn't during his reign. He wouldn't tolerate it. And he had unilaterally decided to keep Scarlett away from her children, no matter how it impacted them, and all because she had left him for another man. In his mind, they didn't need a mother, so he had wiped the slate clean and forced her to live by the terms of the cruel paper she had signed in order to divorce him. And it suited him to rule, and to parent them, alone.

It took them all several days to digest what they'd heard. They were all haunted by it, and Morgan and Billy were curious about meeting their unknown grandmother on Sunday. Caroline had explained it as delicately as she could, that she'd thought her mother was dead but she wasn't, and she had just met her. She didn't explain the part their grandfather had played in it.

The day that they all spent with Scarlett and Roberto was exceptionally wonderful. Kate had gone out of her way to organize a picnic lunch from a barbecue chef they sometimes used for events at the ranch. His wife made the best pies in the Valley. It was a genuine celebration. Kate invited Thad to join them, without going into detail, and he looked startled when she introduced Scarlett as her mother.

He found a minute alone with her just before lunch, and looked confused.

"But I thought she was . . ." He was embarrassed to say it.

"So did we. We found some papers in Dad's office safe, which led us to her. She's been living in Santa Barbara for all these years. We just met her this week."

"Gemma looks just like her, and you too a bit, and Morgan. She seems very nice," he said quietly.

"She is," Kate agreed.

"And Jimmy told you she had died?"

Kate nodded. "He lied. For all of our lives." He was a man of many facets, and not always the hero he appeared, as they all knew. He used the truth when it was useful, but he was not above lying, if it served his purposes better. Thad knew it too.

Kate showed her mother and Roberto around the barns after they arrived, and the various aspects of the ranch. And Juliette joined them right before lunch. Kate had warned her of the visit, and explained the circumstances to her. She was shocked.

"I didn't know any of that. He never told me," Juliette said with a disapproving look. "I would have told you or made him tell you."

"He kept it a secret from all of us too," Kate said to her.

"That is so wrong," she said in her heavy accent. "I would have made him allow you to see your mother, if I'd known. Girls need their mothers, and boys too. And I could not be a mother to you, only your friend. I think he wanted you to himself." Kate thought so too. It was incredibly selfish of him, which wasn't a surprise either. Their hero had feet of clay.

There was no tension when the two women met. Scarlett greeted

Juliette warmly, and Juliette hugged her and told her that she was so glad she wasn't dead, which made everyone laugh. Scarlett sat surrounded by her daughters, and chatted with her grandchildren, while Roberto entertained everyone with stories about growing up at his family's vineyards in Tuscany, and the grandmother who ruled them all, and still did at a hundred and four. Roberto was the same age as their mother, and they both looked younger than they were.

They all went for a long walk after lunch, and Scarlett and Roberto reluctantly left at six o'clock, with promises to host lunch in Santa Barbara soon. She wanted to get to know each of her daughters. They couldn't recapture the past, but she wanted to take full advantage of the present. She had even spent some time talking to Morgan and Billy.

Kate made them promise to come back to the ranch. The whole family stood waving at them as they left, and Scarlett was beaming and crying again. It had been a truly remarkable day.

"Dad must be spinning in his grave," Gemma said to Kate with a grin as they drove away. "He lied to us for thirty-nine years, he's barely cold in his grave, and she's back and we're all in love with her. It serves him right. What a rotten thing to do to her and to us. He ruined her life."

"She seems all right. Roberto's a nice man," Kate said gently.

"Yes, but imagine not seeing your kids for nearly forty years, and our growing up with no mother. How do you live with impacting that many lives? Answer me that."

"He didn't ruin ours. We all turned out okay, in spite of it. And she made a bad choice. She says it herself. He forced her to live up to it, which was wrong of him. Maybe he thought he was doing the right thing." Kate always tried to be fair.

"I think it was his revenge because she left him for another man. You don't like to admit it, but he had a cruel streak, and he could be a son of a bitch when he wanted to be." Kate didn't deny it, but she forgave him more easily than her sisters. Caroline couldn't get over what he'd done either, and said it would have killed her to lose her children.

"But you wouldn't leave yours either," Kate reminded her.

"I don't think any of us know what that kind of poverty is like, total hopelessness and no money to feed your kids or go to a doctor. People steal in situations like that, and kill people. They're lucky they both got out. Most people don't," Gemma said with compassion. "It must have been frightening for both of them."

"But he had us. I think Dad was terrified of ever being poor again," Kate said, and they all knew that about him. It was why he was so proud of Gemma and her luxurious lifestyle. To him that was the pinnacle of achievement, but in fact a lot of it had been smoke and mirrors, and his was by far the greatest accomplishment to save his money, and own a ten-thousand-acre ranch to pass on to his children. Gemma was well aware of it and the hollow victories of her success, no matter how glamorous they appeared.

She was looking extremely stressed as she continued to get calls from her creditors, demanding that she pay her bills. Several were threatening to sue her. She was still waiting for her severance from the show, and they promised it would arrive any day. It hadn't yet. Her tenant was covering her mortgage payments, but there were countless other bills that were continuing to arrive, and her maid in L.A. was forwarding them to the ranch. She looked unhappy every time the mail came.

She told Kate that she wanted to get out from under the crushing weight of what she owed. She was going to sell the house at the end of the summer lease, even though she loved it. She wanted to pay off her debts and start fresh. And she had decided to cash out her share of the ranch and start investing money. She could stay there at her little cottage anyway, even if she was no longer a part owner.

"Do you think Thad is really serious about buying my third? Or is it just talk?" she asked Kate one night after dinner. "Or do you want to?"

"It's not a great time for me to come up with the money, and I know you need it right away." Some of the people she owed money to were threatening to sue her. "I'm sure Thad means it. He loves this place as much as Dad did. I haven't figured out what part I would sell him yet. I think the pastures at the north end. I've got to get an assessor out here to figure it out, and then we need to set a price on it. I'll start the wheels turning."

"Do you hate me for it?" Gemma asked her.

"No. I understand, you need to get on your feet, and have money in the bank. I just hope Caroline doesn't decide to cash out too, and that Peter doesn't talk her into it. I hate to start chopping up what Dad worked so hard to build." But with ten thousand acres, they knew that a third of it on the far side of the land wouldn't make too much difference, and Thad would be a good neighbor and an ally they could trust, which was important too if they were going to sell. They didn't want someone spoiling the area, or building a hotel, or some commercial venture. Thad would never do that, he wanted to set up a small ranch, and continue to run theirs, which was an ideal arrangement, and Kate needed his help.

They had a meeting with him two days later, where he confirmed his interest to Gemma, and Kate called in an assessor after that. They found a perfect piece of land, which wouldn't have an impact on their main areas of operation, and Thad liked the location that Kate had picked. The size was almost exactly a third of the land they owned, but in an area they wouldn't miss. Thad was going to have a narrow road built to connect it to the ranch, for only his use and theirs. Both the realtor and the assessor helped them come up with a fair price, which Gemma was pleased with, and Thad could afford, at fair market value.

Gemma was greatly relieved that that money was coming, and Thad made a good faith down payment, which gave her some relief from her debts. But she still wanted to sell her L.A. house. She had made the decision and stuck to it, and had notified her tenant, in case he was interested in buying it without a realtor's commission, before it went on the market. He was thinking about it. And Gemma started to look more relaxed.

They all enjoyed the rest of Caroline's stay, and she and the children were genuinely sad to leave. They had covered a lot of ground. Morgan and Billy had fun, the girls had met their mother, and they'd spent some good time together on the ranch among sisters.

Gemma and Kate saw them off the morning they left, and their nephew and niece hugged them and thanked them for a wonderful time. They were sorry now they were going to Aspen, and wanted to stay. But Caroline wanted to see Peter. She felt slightly guilty for having been gone for more than a week, but it had done her good. And she wanted to tell him all about Scarlett, and how meaningful it had been to her. She'd told him on the phone, but wanted to tell him the details in person. He had been very moved by the story.

Caroline had had a lovely time with her sisters. She enjoyed the ranch so much more now without her father looming. But she was anxious to see Peter before they left for Aspen. She was grateful that he had been so understanding about letting her spend the time with her sisters on the ranch. He had been very sweet about it, and sent her text messages every day, hoping she was having fun and relaxing.

Caroline and the children were home in Marin by lunchtime, and the house looked surprisingly orderly. He hadn't left a mess. The refrigerator was full. Their cleaning person had left everything tidy, and Peter was good about that too. He was organized and neat, and she never came home to a mess. Once she was home, she realized how much she had missed him. They had texted and talked on the phone while she was away, but it wasn't the same as face-to-face, or having his arms around her. He was planning to be home for dinner that night, and she bought steaks, which she knew he loved, artichokes, his favorite dessert, and put flowers on the dining table. Both children had plans to go out with friends, so Peter and she would have time alone, and maybe enough time for a little romance before they got home. She smiled at the thought. He was a thoughtful lover, and even after seventeen years of marriage, they had an active sex life that they both enjoyed. As reserved as he was, in their private moments, he could be very loving. And he had told her several times on the phone that he couldn't wait for her to get back.

She unpacked that afternoon after she dropped Morgan and Billy off at their friends', got almost everything put away, and opened the drawer of her night table to drop in a book she hadn't finished reading, and her reading glasses, which she had just gotten, and stared into the drawer with a look of surprise. She usually kept things to read in it, a pad and pen, and now her new glasses. Instead, she found herself staring at several packets of condoms, some flavored sex lubricant, and a blue Goyard datebook that wasn't hers. She felt as though she had been stabbed, or a bomb had gone off in her face when she opened the drawer. Her head was reeling and she felt sick. There was no way to explain the condoms and the lubricant except that he had used them with someone else. They didn't use condoms, because they didn't have other partners and she was on the pill, and had been for years. And she was allergic to lubricant, and they didn't need it.

She took the datebook out, feeling strangled, and wondering who it belonged to. She didn't have far to look. The girl's name was written on the front page, Veronica Ashton, with her address, phone number, and email address, in case the datebook was found. Not even feeling guilty, but suddenly ill, she flipped through it and rapidly found printed out photos of a woman in various highly suggestive positions, and three photos of them having sex, two of Peter naked, smiling at the camera, and two more of his erect penis, and she had drawn a heart around it in red marker. Caroline didn't know whether to cry, scream, or throw up. She suddenly realized why he had been so encouraging of her spending time with her sisters at the ranch.

She went through the drawer and didn't find anything else, but that was enough. There was no thong underwear under the bed, and feeling even sicker, she went around the bed, and checked the drawer in Peter's night table, where she found half a dozen gynecological photographs of the same girl, which left nothing to the imagination. He had obviously forgotten the photographs in the drawer, or didn't know they were there. She sat on her bed, feeling paralyzed, and burst into tears. She lay there for what seemed like hours, and then got up, washed her face, didn't bother to change as she had planned, put the photographs from his drawer in the stack with the others, and sat in a chair in the living room, waiting for him to come home. She had no idea what she was going to say to him, or where to go from here. Should she leave him, divorce him, move out, throw him out, demand an explanation, or call a lawyer? There was nothing he could say to undo what she'd found. It was obvious what had gone on in their bed while she was away. And how often had it happened before? Every time he said he had to work late on a deal, was he cheating on her? Had he done it before? Despite his natural reserve, and cool conservative demeanor, and his long working hours, she had always believed that their marriage was solid and he loved her. She had always thought he was completely trustworthy, and clearly he wasn't. She felt as though her heart had broken in a million pieces that afternoon. Was he in love with Veronica Ashton, or just having sex? Or did that even matter?

She heard his key in the door at seven-thirty. He walked into the living room and saw her there, came across the floor in rapid strides, picked her up and swung her around with obvious delight, and was about to kiss her, when she pushed him away and stood staring at him. He hadn't realized at first that she was limp in his arms and not responding.

"What's wrong?" he said with a puzzled look.

"Everything," she said in a small tight word, and stepped away from him.

"What does that mean?" He sounded hurt when he said it, and she turned to face him again.

"Why don't you tell me what it means, Peter?" Her voice sounded cold and jagged.

"I've missed you. I was excited to see you. Why are you upset?"

Without saying a word, she walked into their bedroom, opened the drawer in her bed table, gathered up the photos, the condoms, the lube, and the datebook and walked back into the living room and handed them to him. He stood juggling them for a minute as the blood drained from his face. Clearly, he recognized them.

"The pictures are great, by the way, terrific angles. You get a really good view. I didn't call her to return the datebook, although her numbers are in it. I thought I'd let you do that."

"Caro, I can explain," he started, with the oldest line of all cheaters, and she held up a hand to stop him.

"No, you can't. One picture is worth a thousand words, your penis, with a heart around it, her vagina, some interesting positions, condoms, lube, what part of that do you want to explain, how you took the pictures? Or that you had a stunt double screwing her? For chrissake, don't make a fool of both of us. One is enough, and I'm it."

"I was lonely. It was stupid. I was drunk and I called an escort service. It's never happened before," he said, sounding lame and unconvincing.

"Jesus, you must think I'm brain-dead. Escort service girls don't put their datebooks in someone else's night table, and you don't look drunk to me, and frankly I don't care if you were drunk or sober. You're as big a liar as my father," she raged at him. "You had that girl staying here, in my bed, using my night table, fucking my husband."

"Who told you that?" He looked panicked.

"You're pathetic. Get out of my house. I was happy I was going to see you too. For about five minutes, until I opened my night table."

"You're not serious about wanting me to leave?" She looked at his handsome blond aristocratic WASPy East Coast looks that had always made her melt, and thought of all the times he had said and implied that she was a redneck because she'd grown up on a ranch.

She almost hated him, and knew she could get there, and was well on her way. He had made her feel inferior for years because of her background and his family was so much fancier, but she had never cheated on him or been disloyal to him, and now he had.

"I'm dead serious. And you can cancel the house in Aspen, or take her and continue your photo project. I'm not going, and neither are my children. You're not taking them anywhere. I'm calling a lawyer tomorrow."

"Caroline, please . . . I made a mistake . . . be reasonable . . . I'm sorry . . . this is the first time I've ever done anything like this. I don't even know her."

"If I go through that datebook, how many times will I see your name, and how long have you been sleeping with her?" She made a grab for the datebook, and he pulled it away from her so she couldn't reach it. She was normally a quiet person, but she was not a fool. "I thought so. Get out. Now. You can come back for your things later. I don't want you anywhere near me."

"Caroline." He tried to reach for her, but didn't dare put down the offending evidence, so he was juggling it in one hand and trying to reach for her with the other. This was not the homecoming either of them had planned. "Please . . . can't we just put this behind us?" he begged her.

"It looks like you were doing that to her in one of those photos. You really should frame them. Get out! I don't want you here." He stood staring at her for a minute, and knew he had lost the battle. He walked through their bedroom to his closet, and started dumping things in an overnight bag, along with what she'd found, and five minutes later, he stood in their bedroom, looking beaten, and then decided that the best defense was a good offense.

"What do you expect, Caroline? You leave me alone here, you're always working on your books, you're busy with the kids all the time. . . ."

"And that justifies you having an affair, letting some girl sleep in my bed while I'm with my sisters and our kids, and you're taking porn pictures of her? How do you figure that computes? What if I did that and you found the pictures?" He would kill her and they both knew it. He had a jealous streak, and didn't like other men anywhere near her. It was one of the ways she knew he loved her.

"I told you. I made a mistake. She was a hooker, an escort."

"And you're a liar. Go." She pointed to the door, and he walked out of the bedroom and a minute later, she heard the front door slam as hard as he could slam it, which was his first sign of real anger, and at least more honest. He was livid at having gotten caught, and his little-boy innocent act had gone nowhere. Caroline was shaking from head to foot and sat down on their bed. And a minute later, she walked into their bathroom and threw up. She wondered if she should have kept the photographs as evidence to show a lawyer, but adultery was no longer grounds for divorce in California. It was just evidence for her. The courts wouldn't care about it.

She wondered if she would really divorce him for this. She wasn't sure. But she was incredibly hurt. And she could guess where he had gone with his photos and his lube and his condoms, straight to Veronica Ashton, who was assuredly not a hooker or an escort, but probably someone he worked with.

She washed her face in cold water, brushed her teeth, and went to her laptop, and looked up Peter's firm, the directory of employees. And there she was, top of the list, alphabetically. Veronica Ashton, junior trainee. She had graduated from Stanford a year before. She was twenty-three years old. It made Caroline furious all over again. She typed in Peter's email address.

"Check out your staff registry for the firm. Veronica Ashton, top of the alphabetical list, trainee, twenty-three years old. Good one, Peter. She works nights for an escort service? You're toast. I'm done."

He had been a total fool, and a liar. She wondered how long it had gone on. She put the ingredients for their dinner back in the fridge, unset the table, and didn't bother to eat. She couldn't have. She lay on her bed in the dark, until the kids came home. Billy came home first, dropped off by his friend's father.

"Where's Dad?" were his first words to his mother. He was anxious to see him, after being away.

"He had to work late," she said vaguely.

"He said he'd be home when I got in." Billy looked disappointed and she wanted to say "He lied," but she didn't. She was going to have to tell them something if she didn't let him stay there, but not tonight. She couldn't deal with more than she already had. Billy went to his room to play videogames, and Morgan came home an hour later. She'd been happy to see her friends.

"Is Dad home?" She looked hopeful, but tired.

"No," Caroline said, and Morgan didn't press the point. She went to her room to call a friend, and that was the end of it. Caroline turned off the living room lights, closed the door to her bedroom, and turned off the lights in her room, wondering how many nights Veronica had stayed there. Just thinking about her and what they'd done made her feel sick. She lay there for hours, with the room spinning, as her world fell apart and lay in splinters at her feet.

Caroline heard from Peter by email the next morning. All he said was "Were you serious about Aspen? You're not going?"

"Totally serious. No, I'm not, and neither are the kids," she responded. She was not going to live her life as a fraud for the summer, pretending nothing was wrong. She was not going.

"Fine," he responded. "They won't return our deposit." She didn't bother to answer, and three minutes later, he sent another email. "Caro, I told you, I'm so sorry. I was drunk out of my mind. She means nothing to me. She's a total stranger. It was a moment of insanity. I love you." Caroline didn't respond to that email either. Instead, she called a friend's husband, who was a lawyer. She trusted him, and she said she was calling as a client and it was confidential.

"Sounds serious," he said, trying to keep things light. "Client-attorney privilege. You're covered. What's up?" They had sons the same age in the same class at school, which was how she knew most people now, through her kids. She told him the whole sordid story and what she'd found.

"I'm sorry, Caroline. That's nasty, and it feels like shit when it happens." He had a gentle style, and a sympathetic voice, which made her want to cry again.

"Yes, it does," she agreed.

"What do you want to do?" he asked her.

"I don't know. I threw him out last night and told him he couldn't stay here."

"That's reasonable, in the circumstances. Now what? How can I help you?"

"I haven't figured that out yet. Do I divorce him? Make him move out? What do people do?"

"There's a whole range of possibilities here. It's entirely personal, depending on how you feel about him, and your marriage, until now, and going forward. Can you forgive him? Could you get past it?

Could you trust him again? Do you want to? Has he cheated on you before, that you know of?"

"I don't know if he has. Maybe. Probably. I think he's having an affair with her. Not just a fling. She's twenty-three, and a trainee in his office. She must have been staying at our house, if she had her datebook in the drawer of my night table."

"Sounds like a fair assumption. Do you want to suggest to Peter that you take a break until you decide? That's reasonable too. He can't expect you to just gloss over it and forget it."

"I think he did. He tried telling me he got her from an escort service and it was a one-off."

"Not with her things in your drawer."

"Exactly. What do I tell the kids?"

"That's up to you too. You hold the cards here. You need to decide if you want out of the marriage. What about telling the kids the same thing, that you're taking a break?"

"It'll be shocking for them. I don't think I should tell them why. Maybe that we need to figure some things out. I don't think he'll dare contradict me. He's going to be scared I'll tell them the truth. I can't do that to them."

"Some women would."

"They don't need to know that."

"Why don't you try what we said? Maybe give it a time limit. Till the end of summer, when school starts. That gives you two months to figure out what you want to do. And he can make other living arrangements for eight weeks."

"He'll probably move in with her," Caroline said, sounding depressed.

"Caroline, if that's what he wants, you can't stop him, and it's best to know. If he's in love or obsessed with this girl, you can't win. So he either fights like a dog to get you back, or he's made his bed with her, and that's it. You don't want to be looking for her underwear under the bed every time you leave the house to drive the kids to school. That's no way to live."

"You're right. I'll tell him we'll decide at the end of August. Can I take the kids away?"

"You can do whatever you want. You don't have a formal agreement. If he complains, or they do, you can negotiate it on a time-by-time basis. Where were you thinking of going?"

"My family ranch in the Santa Ynez Valley."

"Sounds terrific. It's not on the moon. He can drive down, or fly down if he wants to see them. Let him make some effort to redeem himself, that'll tell you something too."

"Thank you, Charlie. I'm sorry to tell you all this."

"I'm sorry it's happening to you. I'm going to charge you a dollar for this consultation by the way, to protect the attorney-client privilege."

"Thank you."

She felt better when they hung up. She had a plan. And a lawyer. She sent Peter an email, and told him they needed a break, or she did, until the end of August, and he needed to stay somewhere else in the meantime. She didn't mention the children or the ranch, and wouldn't until he did. She wanted to give them a few days to see their friends in Marin, which she had promised, and then she wanted to go back to the ranch until the end of the summer. She was happy she had it now. It was hers too. And this time, when she left, she wouldn't be running away, as she always had before. She would be going home. There was a difference. And she wasn't going to let Peter get away with this. He couldn't cheat on her and lie, and not be accountable. She wasn't going to be the silent, invisible wife anymore. Those days were over.

Chapter 9

Shortly after Caroline and the children left the ranch for San Francisco on Sunday afternoon, Gemma's agent called her. He had an audition for her in L.A. He wasn't overly enthused about it, and didn't want to get her hopes up, but she had said she would try out for anything, and he took her at her word.

Walking into the audition, Gemma had a shock. Most of the girls trying out were half her age. None of them had appeared in anything worthwhile, and it was a second-rate made-for-TV movie for a less than stellar cable network. They were auditioning her for the part of the star's mother. She had no idea what they were going to pay her if she got it, but whatever it was, it wasn't enough to humiliate herself to that degree. She was profoundly depressed when she left the audition, called Jerry on his cellphone, and got him in his car.

"Okay. Uncle. I give up. I said get me anything, maybe we should notch that up a little." Knowing that Thad was going to buy out her share of the ranch, and her summer tenant was promising to make an offer on her house and wanted to buy some of her art, she felt a little less desperate than when her show was canceled. "They wanted me to play some little hooker's mother, and I think it was a vampire movie. Either that, or the starlet I auditioned with needs to see her dentist immediately and get her eye teeth filed down." Jerry laughed at her description.

"I'm sorry, Gemma. I took you at your word. I've actually got something interesting cooking right now. They're not ready to cast it yet, but you'd be perfect. It's being put together by a brilliant British producer/director who's had nothing but hit shows. He does quality period dramas, and there's a fantastic role for an American in it. It spans both world wars, and you'd play an American doctor who left the country for some reason. They won't start shooting till the end of the year, and they're casting in September. It's high quality stuff for British TV, which will play in the States subsequently. There's only one hitch, two actually."

"I need to be twenty-two years old, and the part's for a guy. No problem. I'm not afraid of a little surgery." He laughed again.

"No. They shoot a lot on location, in some pretty exotic places. They're starting off with a safari in Africa, and not everyone is dying to spend Christmas with a bunch of snakes and lions and tigers, living in a tent. The Brits love that stuff, and they don't mind being miserable on location. You'd get double pay for it, which could be an incentive. And the other hitch is that the show is based in England. They're shooting thirteen episodes to start out, and with a show like that with major costumes and complicated hair, you can't commute from L.A. They want someone based in England. You'd have to move to London to do it. I didn't know how you'd feel about that." She thought about it as she listened to him, and she wasn't sure herself.

"It depends on how good the show is."

"The guy never misses." He reeled off some of his shows and Gemma knew them all, and had watched them and loved them. It was high quality work.

"Keep me in the running and I'll think about it. I don't really have anything to tie me down here, but that is a big change."

"I'll let you know if they're interested."

"What's the age range?"

"About right. Mid-to-late thirties. You can't be a kid if you're playing a doctor. They want someone with substance, experience, looks, talent, and a name."

"It sounds a lot better than the vampire movie, playing the mother of Dracula's daughter with the pointy teeth. She almost deafened me when she screamed in the audition."

"I'll keep you posted. How are you? Recovering from the shock of the show ending?"

"Trying to. I miss it already."

"We all will, for a long time. I think they made the right decision, but it always hurts to shut down a successful show while it's still working. You always wonder if you should have kept it going for a couple more seasons, but that's probably the right time to call it a day. Sad, though. It's a loss."

"Yes, it was." It had been a hard two months between her father dying and the show folding, and being broke. But she was enjoying her sisters and the ranch, and she had loved connecting with her mother again, although it cast a terrible shadow on her father, who had cheated them all of Scarlett for their whole lives. She had a feeling Caroline would never forgive him, particularly since their relationship hadn't been strong. But at least she had Peter and her kids. You couldn't have everything in life.

The part he had described to her sounded interesting but she also knew that the British were partial to their own, and more likely to hire a British actress who could do an American accent than a real American. She wasn't counting on it for now. And they weren't ready to cast anyway.

He promised to keep her informed and they hung up.

She had a meeting with her tenant that afternoon about the possible purchase of her house. Then she went to the hairdresser and got her hair colored. She was staying at a small hotel she knew that wasn't too expensive. She was planning to spend a week in L.A., and see some friends. She was enjoying the ranch, but it was nice to get out of the sticks, and come back to the city, where she belonged. She might have been born in Texas and raised in the Valley, but they were never going to make a country girl of her. She had L.A. in her blood. Caroline felt the same way about it. She loved San Francisco, and any big city. But as a temporary rest stop the ranch was fine, even fun at times. And she loved being with her sisters. They each brought something different to the table, irreverence, in Gemma's case, and glamour and style, which was good for Caroline and Kate.

It seemed too quiet on the ranch to Kate after Caroline and the children left, and Gemma went to L.A.

"Gemma will only be gone for a week," Kate told Thad. They had signed all the papers for his purchase of the land, and were just waiting for approval from the county, to split it off from the ranch, but they didn't expect any problems with it. They expected the approval to come through in July. He asked Kate to ride out there with him again at the end of a day's work. He wanted her to see where he was thinking of situating the house he was planning to build and he wanted her advice.

"You know, this is the first thing I've ever owned in my life," he said shyly, when they got there and looked around. They had picked some beautiful acreage on the border of the property, with a stream running through it, and some handsome tall trees that would provide shade. He was planning to build a house for himself, a bunkhouse, and a barn, which was all he needed for a start.

"My father felt that way too when he inherited his first piece of land out here." He had told her about it often and what it meant to him. She felt guilty selling some of that now, even to Thad, but it was Gemma's decision not hers. And she didn't want to buy her out, nor did Caroline.

"I've never owned a house, land, or even a horse. It feels like it's time. Your father was about my age when he started," he reminded her.

"He was a little older. I think he was forty, or a few years older, when he started buying. But he had three kids. That makes a difference. He had started early." Thad nodded, looking at her, remembering what she had looked like when he'd met her. She was twenty-three. She hadn't changed much, in his opinion, she had only improved with time, and didn't look very different at forty-two. He had been an eighteen-year-old kid when they met, just a boy.

"I want to build a house like his, with a porch around it, and enough bedrooms, if I need them one day, but not so big that I'll get lost in it. I'm used to living in a cabin barely bigger than a horse stall. It's going to take some getting used to, having more space. I'm really grateful that Gemma is willing to sell me her share."

"She's grateful to you too," Kate said. "She wasn't ready for it when they canceled the show. It really left her high and dry. So you're helping her out too."

"I couldn't do it without the money your dad left me," he said, and pointed to the spot where he wanted to build the house. It looked perfect to her, with the tall trees nearby. "I don't want anything too modern. I like old houses."

"So did my dad." She smiled at him. "I like old houses too."

"I always wanted to live in a house like that when I was a kid, shuffling around from place to place. I never thought I could do it, and now here I am." He looked so proud, standing in the tall grass on the land that was about to be his. He had a manly quality to him, and the sexy appeal of real cowboys. It reminded her of her father and the kind of men she had always liked and used to meet at the rodeo. You couldn't tell the cowboys from the ranchers sometimes, they all had that easy, sexy, masculine look.

"You can do anything you want to, if you try hard enough. That's what my dad always said. I believe that. No dream is too big if you keep plugging away at it. This ranch is proof of that. And now yours will be too." They sat down on a log together, looking out over the land into the Valley, their horses tied loosely to a tree, happily grazing.

"What about you, Kate? Do you think you'll keep the ranch forever?"

"I hope so. What else would I do? This is what I know, and there's nowhere else I want to be. This is it for me." She looked at peace. She had always known she belonged here, unlike her sisters. She had no yearning to be anywhere but where she was, doing what she did every day. All she wanted was to do it a little better, but it provided all the challenges she wanted, and she did it well. She was one of the most responsible ranch owners he had ever known, and she was more creative and open-minded than her father, which would take her far.

"How's your romance going?" she asked, and he laughed. She could never keep track of them.

"She had a fling with the bartender at the bar where she works. That did it for me. That's what you get with the young ones. Fickle, and no morals."

"And you're so moral?" she teased him. "Shit, you have a new girl every week. I can't keep up with you."

"I do them one at a time, though," he said, and she grinned. "Besides, I've had a problem for years." She was suddenly afraid that he was going to tell her something she didn't want to know. They were pals, but there was a limit to everything. Most of the ranch hands thought of her as one of the guys. "I've been in love with the same woman for years. But I didn't have anything to offer her. Nothing but a cabin and a horse I don't own. It's different now, with all this," he said, with a wave at the land he was buying from her sister. "I've got some substance to offer a woman now. A real woman, not a kid."

"And is she in love with you?" Kate asked him, relieved that he hadn't told her about some sexual dysfunction she didn't want to hear about. He had her worried for a minute.

"I've never asked her."

"She'd be lucky to have you, Thad," she said. "Any woman would. You're a fine man, a great foreman. You'll be a wonderful ranch owner one day." And now all his dreams were coming true. She was happy for him. He had earned it, and he deserved it. She turned to smile at him, and he was looking into her eyes seriously. He had never looked at her that way before, and her heart skipped a beat.

"You're the woman I've been in love with, Kate, since the first time I laid eyes on you at eighteen. There's never been anyone else I cared about, except you. I had nothing to offer you, and I still don't compare to what you have. But I'd like to make the ranch grow with you, and take it places your dad would never go to. We could do it together."

"We're doing that anyway. We're running it together," she reminded him.

"I want to be partners. I want to be married to you, Kate. I'm never going to love any woman like I love you." He said it so gently it was like a whisper in the wind. She didn't know what to say. She had never guessed that he cared about her or was in love with her, and she had never thought of him that way.

"I'm five years older than you are," she reminded him, and he laughed.

"Is that supposed to scare me? I don't give a damn how old you are. You're the most beautiful woman I've ever seen." And before she could come up with another objection, he put his arms around her, held her tight, and kissed her as she'd never been kissed before. It took her breath away and stunned her. She closed her eyes then and he kissed her again, and didn't stop until they had to come up for air. He was even sexier than she had ever imagined.

"Wow, I wasn't expecting that," she said softly.

"It's been a long time coming," he whispered, and kissed her again and she didn't resist him. She wondered what her father would say. If he'd have been outraged, or would have approved, and as she kissed Thad back, she suddenly didn't care what her father would have thought. She had never been as attracted to anyone in her life. She had almost forgotten what it was like being a woman, and Thad was reminding her. He smiled at her when they stopped. "You're even sexier than I thought you'd be. Good things are worth waiting for. You'd have slugged me if I'd kissed you when I was eighteen."

"Yeah, I would have." She grinned, but she had no inclination to slug him now. "Are you serious about this, or just bored between barmaids? I don't like being part of a crowd."

"Neither did I," he said. "I've never been more serious about anything in my life, except maybe this land. But you're part of that. We belong here, you and I. The Valley is part of us, the ranch, everything we do here. It wouldn't mean squat to me without you."

"I've always felt like I was married to the ranch, like a sacred vow. There's never been room for much else in my life. And I didn't think a man would understand it."

"I do." And she knew he did. "We can build something beautiful together, on the foundation your father left us. What do you think, Kate?"

"I think you're crazy." She grinned at him again. "You should be with some sexy young thing and have ten babies with her, not be with someone like me."

"We can have ten babies if that's what you want. We should start soon, though," he looked at his watch, "like tonight maybe."

"Oh, shut up. You know what I mean."

"No, I don't. I've never loved any woman like I love you, and I never will. I had to fight myself not to tell you before this. Now you know, and I'm not going to take no for an answer, and I don't give a damn about five years. You're better looking and sexier than any woman in this valley, any age. Gemma's a star, but I think you're way more beautiful than she is. You're real."

"Gemma's real too," she defended her sister, and then she laughed, "well, parts of her are."

"That's what I mean." He laughed too. "Fly with me, Kate. Let's show everyone what we can do. As husband and wife, not me working for you, or even as business partners. I want to go to bed with you every night, and make love to you." Now that he had said it, he couldn't contain himself anymore. He pulled her to her feet and pressed his long lanky body against hers, and she could feel the passion he felt for her. It was dizzying, and she didn't want him to stop or go away. She had run away from most of the men who had pursued her, but she wanted to run into Thad's arms, not away from them. Suddenly, he felt like the only place she wanted to be. She clung to him, as the sun began to set slowly, and she didn't want to let go. Without knowing why or if it was right, she looked into his eyes and nodded.

"Yes . . . I think we're crazy, but maybe you have to be a little crazy in life . . . yes . . . but let's take it slow. Let's get used to it ourselves first. I don't want everyone to know right away. This is going to surprise a lot of people," including her sisters, but she wasn't sure she cared about that either. All she cared about at that exact moment in time was him.

"We can go as slow as you want. As long as we get there in the end. I've waited nineteen years. I can wait a little longer. Not another nineteen years though, I hope."

"I'll be a hundred by then," she said with a grin.

"No, you won't. You'll probably still be sexy when you're a hundred. I'll be ninety-five then." He kissed her again and they walked through the grass to their horses in the place that was going to be his house one day, their house, if all went well. He gave her a boost into her saddle, and got up on his own horse with ease, and turned to look at her with the broadest grin she'd ever seen. "I love you, Kate, just remember that. I always will." She nodded. She believed him. He was an honest man, maybe the only one she'd ever known.

"I love you too." They rode back to her part of the ranch then, and got to the barn as the sun was setting. It was the beginning of a beautiful life together, they were sure of it. And the end of a perfect day.

They went out to dinner that night to celebrate, and he drove her back to her house afterward. She hesitated on the porch and didn't ask him to come in. She didn't want to rush things, and wanted to savor the beginning, and he didn't press her about it. He just kissed her, and then clattered down her stairs before he wouldn't be able to resist the temptation to sweep her up in his arms and carry her to her bedroom. They were both smiling as he drove away.

Chapter 10

Kate and Thad made every attempt to keep their growing attraction from showing around other people. He looked serious when he came to her office. She spoke to him as she always had in the breeding barn. He found a lot of downed fences and grazing fields to show her at the far edges of the property, and as soon as they were out of sight, they dismounted and lay in the grass together, hugging and kissing, and feeling each other's bodies. They made it through four days after he had declared his love for her, and she couldn't imagine how she had lived without him in her arms for the past nineteen years. They were cooking dinner together in her house one night, and he put down the fork he was using, grabbed her in his arms, and turned off the flame on the stove so they didn't burn the house down.

"I can't stand it anymore," he said in an agonized voice as he held her.

"Neither can I," she said, breathless, and they raced each other up the stairs to her bedroom, pulled each other's clothes off, and made love for the next four hours, as neither of them had made love before. It had all the hunger and passion and desire and hoping and dreaming of everything he had felt for her before, and everything that had been born in her since he first kissed her. And after making love to her until midnight, when he finally pulled himself away from her, all he wanted was to do it again.

He was starving after that, and they went downstairs and finally cooked dinner, and then went back upstairs and made love again. They hardly slept that night and for several days afterward. Kate was afraid someone would see him coming to her cottage early in the evening and never leaving, with his truck conspicuously parked outside, so he started driving home, and coming back on foot at midnight, and staying until she got up at four-thirty. It made for short nights but some epic lovemaking. By the time Gemma got back from L.A., Kate was starry-eyed and looked dazed.

"You look happy," Gemma commented when she first saw her. "Everything okay on the home front?"

"Fine. Nothing new. Thad is over the moon that you're selling him your share."

"Me too." Gemma looked pleased.

"He's going to build a house out there." She didn't have the guts to tell her sister that she was going to live there too and they wanted to get married. She was afraid that she'd be shocked that Kate wanted to marry the foreman. She needed time to figure out how to announce it to her, but for now, they had everything they wanted, nights together, and their plans and dreams for his property. She was going to tell her sisters soon. She just didn't know when.

"Have you talked to Caroline this week?" Gemma asked her.

"Actually, come to think of it, no, I haven't. I figured she was busy getting ready to go to Aspen. I think they're leaving this weekend."

"Apparently not," Gemma said, as they sat on Kate's porch drinking Cokes at the end of the day. "She sent me a text today. It fell through. She wants to come back with the kids till they go back to school. She didn't tell you?" Kate looked surprised.

"She's welcome of course, but that's a little weird. She hadn't been here in three years and now she can't tear herself away. Is Peter coming too?"

"She didn't say."

"I doubt it. He hates it here. He thinks we're all rednecks, except you of course. You're Hollywood Elite." Gemma laughed. "Did you get work this week, by the way?"

"Not a bit, unless I want to play mother to Miss Frankenstein in a vampire movie. Jerry says he might have something for me in a new British series, but they don't start casting till September, and it's a lot of location work. My tenant says he's going to make an offer on my house any minute. If he buys it, I'll have to put everything in storage, until I buy something else, smaller, like a condo. I'm in no hurry. It'll be nice having money for a change. It feels good to be back." She smiled at her sister. "I missed you this week. This place is addictive. I never realized that before, now that the Big Bad Wolf is gone," she teased. She loved her father but she didn't like what she had learned about him since his death and what he had done to their mother. It was hard matching that up with all the moralistic preaching he'd done in his lifetime.

Kate got a text from Caroline that night too. She said she'd be back in the next day or two, and would love to stay for July and August if it was okay. Kate texted back that it was, and didn't ask about Peter. She had the odd feeling that something was off but didn't want to ask. That was a major change of plans if she wanted to stay for two months. She wondered how the kids felt about it, and Peter.

Kate drove to Santa Barbara the next day to see their mother. It was the second time she'd gone to see her on her own. She was enjoying spending time with her. She was a good woman, and loved getting to know her daughters. They talked for hours, and when Kate got back, Gemma said she wanted to go with Kate next time. Scarlett entering their lives took away some of the grief of losing their father.

Even when Gemma was back, Thad continued his nightly visits, staying until ten o'clock after dinner, driving to his cabin, then coming back on foot at midnight and staying until Kate got up in the morning. It made for short interrupted nights, but they agreed that it was worth it. Their affair had taken off like a rocket, and was continuing at a frantic pace with the white heat of their passion for each other. Kate had never had anything like it, and Thad said he hadn't either. They hadn't figured out when to tell people, but it still seemed too soon to Kate. He wanted to shout it from the rooftops.

Caroline packed everything she thought she and the children would need for a two-month stay at the ranch, mostly shorts and jeans and bathing suits, some T-shirts and blouses, sweatshirts if it got cool at night. They didn't need anything fancy, and what they didn't have, they could buy in town. They didn't need a wardrobe at the ranch, and neither did she, unlike Gemma, who had to go to L.A. for auditions occasionally, and had to look the part. She had an image to maintain, now more than ever, since she was trying to find work.

The children were shocked when their mother told them that the house in Aspen had fallen through. She said the owners were planning to use it themselves. But they were even more surprised when they realized very quickly that their father wasn't coming home at night. That was harder to explain.

"Where *is* he, Mom?" Morgan asked her pointedly over breakfast on the third night of his banishment. Caroline hadn't talked to him, they had emailed and texted, and he said he wanted to see the children. She told him to take them to dinner if he wanted, but he hadn't called them yet to set it up. Caroline guessed that he was embarrassed, and probably terrified about what she had told them. So far, she had said nothing, and didn't intend to about what had really happened. They weren't old enough to know, and shouldn't.

Caroline took a deep breath when Morgan pressed her again. Billy was at the table too, so it was a good time, but he wasn't paying attention. He was watching something on his iPad.

"Dad and I have decided to take a little break, till the end of the summer. We need to think about some things, and work out some problems." It was the official line she had decided on.

"What kind of problems?" Morgan looked panicked.

"Grown-up stuff, husband and wife stuff. We haven't been getting along so well lately. We haven't said anything, because we didn't want to upset you." Billy stopped what he was doing and looked up.

"Are you getting a divorce?" he asked her.

"No, just a break, for now. A time-out." He nodded and went back to his iPad. The details didn't interest him at eleven, just the end result.

"Is that why we're not going to Aspen?" Morgan asked her and her mother nodded. She didn't want to lie to her more than she had to.

"We didn't think it would be a good idea, and the summer seemed like a good time to do this."

"So what are we supposed to do all summer? Everyone's going away. All my friends are going east or to Europe," she said plaintively.

"I thought we'd stay at the ranch for a while," Caroline said cautiously, wondering what they'd think of the plan. Morgan thought about it for a minute and nodded. She didn't seem to object and Billy didn't comment.

"Will we see Dad?"

"He can come down to see you, or you can fly up here to see him. I don't know what his plans are." Or Miss Ashton's, she thought. She wondered if he was going to use the house in Aspen with her. It wouldn't surprise her. She was still furious at him, and he had done nothing to repair it. She suspected he was having a major affair and had lost his mind in some kind of midlife crisis. He was twenty-one years older than Veronica Ashton.

"When are we going to the ranch?" Caroline was relieved that they seemed to have no serious objections to spending the summer at the ranch. They were more concerned about their parents taking a break and what it meant.

"This weekend," Caroline said with a sigh about when they were leaving Marin.

"Do you think Kate would pay us for the chores we do?" Morgan asked her.

"I don't know. She might. You should talk to her about it."

"Do you think you and Dad will get back together?" Morgan asked with frightened eyes, and Caroline looked at her seriously.

"I don't know. I hope so." Morgan nodded. A lot of her friends' parents were divorced. It wasn't unfamiliar to her, and Billy's too, but it worried them anyway. He chimed in then.

"Arnie Rivers's parents took a break. His father had a girlfriend. They got divorced and then he married the girlfriend," he supplied, and Caroline's stomach turned over when he said it.

"Thanks, Billy, that's really helpful," his mother said sternly.

"Dad doesn't have a girlfriend, stupid. He and Mom are just having problems," Morgan said to him in a fury, and then looked at her mother.

"Does he?"

"I hope not" was all she was willing to say on the subject. Less was more in the circumstances. But the fact was he did, and maybe he would marry her, if she didn't mind marrying a man twenty-one years older than she was. It still made Caroline feel sick when she thought about it, and the photographs, especially the one of his penis with the heart drawn around it. That used to be hers. Now it belonged to Veronica Ashton, with the fancy Goyard datebook. Maybe he had bought it for her. She thought of them constantly, which only made things worse.

On Saturday morning, Caroline and the children flew to Santa Ynez, and Thad picked them up with the truck, and drove them to the house they had recently furnished. It looked homey and cozy when they walked in and Gemma and Kate arrived a few minutes later to welcome them.

Gemma could see immediately that something was wrong. Caroline was pale, had deep circles under her eyes and looked like she'd lost ten pounds.

They helped them settle in, and the kids took off with Thad half an hour later. He and Kate exchanged a look, which no one saw, and his hand gently swept hers as he walked by, which made her whole body thrill at his touch.

As soon as the kids had left, Caroline sat down on the couch and looked at her sisters.

"Peter's having an affair with a twenty-three-year-old trainee at his office." She told them what she'd found when she went home. Kate looked shocked, and Gemma disgusted.

"Oh, for chrissake, what a jerk. That's so juvenile, dick pics yet," Gemma said, familiar with the concept.

"He tried to claim that he got her from an escort service, which is bullshit. She works for him. I haven't seen him since the night I got home and told him to leave."

"What are you going to do?" Kate asked her.

"I don't know yet. I don't know if I can forgive him, and he lied to me on top of it. I don't know how long it's gone on or if it still is." Since she'd thrown him out, she was sure he was still with Veronica.

"That kind of thing usually burns itself out pretty quickly. She'll get tired of him. Let's face it, he's not a very exciting guy," Gemma said, and Caroline nodded. He wasn't exciting but she loved him, and their marriage. Her sisters had always thought him too uptight and conservative, and a snob in some ways, but he suited Caroline and he was her husband. She didn't want to lose him, but it felt like she already had.

"I love him. I thought we had a good marriage. And the whole time I was here, he was screwing her. I don't think I could trust him again." She looked miserable, and her sisters felt sorry for her.

"What have you told the kids?" Kate asked her quietly, deeply sympathetic to her.

"That we're taking a break for the summer."

"Is he going to see them?" Gemma asked.

"He hasn't asked yet. Maybe he's too busy with her. I think he's embarrassed and doesn't know what to say. Neither do I." Caroline looked devastated and exhausted, but it was good to be back with her sisters, and the kids would be busy on the ranch. It was the best she could hope for right now. She knew he wouldn't stay away from the kids for long. But she wondered if their marriage was over. It seemed like a distinct possibility. She wasn't sure what she wanted. She was still too shocked and upset to make up her mind. She kept going back and forth between wanting a divorce and wanting him to fix it. But how could he? Her heart felt broken forever.

"You two need to talk at some point," Gemma said sensibly, "and have an honest conversation about it. He needs to level with you about her, and what she really means to him."

"I don't know if he will. He hasn't tried. Maybe he'll marry her," Caroline said with tears in her eyes. His silence seemed like a bad sign to her.

"If he does marry her, then you lost him a long time ago. This isn't just about what you want. He needs to figure out what he wants now. A twenty-three-year-old, or his wife. He's being an idiot." And they all knew that only time would help make the decision. For Caroline, it was going to be a long summer. And she wasn't sure she could ever forgive him.

* * *

With both sisters settled in their cottages at the ranch, Thad and Kate were discreetly managing to spend nights together. He didn't come to dinner every night, but tried to make it more sporadic, when Kate didn't have plans with her sisters. But he did show up every night around midnight to spend the night with her. He said he couldn't live without her anymore.

"I'm addicted to you," he said happily, as he slid into bed with her, and she laughed. Their romance had taken off so suddenly, and with such force that neither could imagine being without the other now. They spent much of their days together, and now nights as well. She liked talking to him over dinner, but sometimes that was harder to manage. Either Gemma or Caroline dropped by in the evening sometimes, especially Caroline to talk about the situation with Peter. She was hearing very little from him. A few emails, mostly about the children, but not much more. After his initial denial, she had hardly heard from him again. And he hadn't tried to fight the separation for the summer, or the children going to the ranch with her. He hadn't asked to see them yet, which Caroline found very suspicious, and so did her sisters. Kate had talked to Thad about it, for a male opinion, and he was shocked at the way Peter was behaving. He felt sorry for Caroline and her kids. It didn't sound to him like the situation could be fixed. He was obviously besotted with the young girl, which Caroline thought too. He had lost his mind over her.

Caroline had just left Kate and headed back to her cottage minutes before Thad arrived to spend the night.

"Wow, you just missed my sister," she said when he got there and let himself in. She never locked her doors at the ranch. They'd never had a problem. He looked at Kate seriously.

"Is that going to be a big deal if they find out?" He was worried.

"I don't think so." Kate smiled at him. "But they'll be surprised. I don't usually tell my sisters about my personal life," she said demurely, and then laughed at herself, "but then again, I haven't had one in a long time." She had given up on men for several years. After her one serious boyfriend in college died in a car accident, and several left her and cheated on her, she focused mostly on the ranch, and time had just sped by. Her father kept her too busy and monopolized her time, and dumped everything in her lap, and she never turned him down. He knew she was free at night, so he took full advantage of it, and expected her to take projects home. She was trying to do less of it now, especially since Thad had started spending the night.

"They won't think I'm good enough for you, will they?" He looked worried and upset when he said it. "I never finished high school and never went to college." She knew he had gotten his GED certificate and had taken college classes online for a few years, even if he didn't have a degree. And he was intelligent and read a great deal about anything that related to their work on the ranch. He was essentially self-educated, which Kate admired, but he was sure her sisters wouldn't, particularly Caroline and Peter, who were highly educated, with graduate degrees.

"Gemma didn't go to college either. And I was a lousy student. The only brain in the family is Caroline, and my father thought her going to college was a waste of time." She smiled as she said it. "She writes juvenile books, she's not a nuclear physicist."

"I'm just a ranch hand, though," he said, in a funk about her sisters, and Kate knelt in front of him where he sat on the couch and looked him in the eye.

"You're an extraordinary person, Thad. You run this ranch like a well-oiled machine. The employees, the livestock, our breeding operation. My father respected you more than anyone else, and relied on you, and so do I. You're up to date on all the modern technology. I'm lucky to have you in my life, and luckier still that you love me. You're more than 'good enough' for me, and my sisters will think so too. I just don't want to get them all wound up about us yet. I like having time to get used to each other before the whole world knows and has an opinion, even if it's a good opinion. Right now our future belongs to us. This happened very fast, like lightning. I want to get comfortable with it before we share it. I've never been this serious about anyone before. It's all new to me."

"You look pretty comfortable to me, Ms. Tucker," he teased her, slid a hand into her blouse and a moment later, took it off, and her bra, and pulled her up the stairs with him to her bedroom, where he took off all her clothes and his own. She forgot about her sisters for the rest of the night, until she had dinner in town with them the following night.

"Was that Thad I saw walking toward your house last night around midnight?" Caroline asked with a blank expression, after they ordered pizza with the kids.

"I don't think so. If it was, maybe he was just out walking, or checking on something. I think he checks things at night." Caroline smiled as Kate said it, and then glanced at Gemma, who raised an eyebrow.

"Are we dallying with our foreman?" Gemma teased her, and Kate paid no attention to her.

"Of course not."

"Why not? He's a mighty handsome hunk of man. I've thought of it a few times myself." That was an interesting tidbit Kate didn't react to either. "I just figured Dad would have a fit, so I didn't mess with it. But Dad's not here now," she reminded them. "Are we hot on the trail of something here?" She pressed her and Kate didn't take the bait. She wanted to protect her relationship with Thad for as long as she could, for both their sakes. It was no one's business.

"Don't be ridiculous," Kate said, and chatted with Morgan to avoid them, but the following night, Gemma visited Kate and there were a pair of Thad's cowboy boots in the front hall. Gemma took one look at them, broke into a grin and looked at her sister.

"When are you going to level with us?"

"About what?" Kate feigned innocence and Gemma pointed to the boots.

"Either your feet have grown dramatically, or your foreman left here barefoot. For chrissake, Kate, we're your sisters. We've all known him since we were kids. He's a great guy and we love him, and if you're in love with him, I think it would be the best thing that could happen to you and he loves this place as much as you do." Kate looked like a kid caught with her hand in the cookie jar.

"It's just embarrassing to have you guys know everything I do, and we weren't sure how you'd react," she finally admitted. They couldn't hide it anymore.

"We're happy for you. So is that it? Is that who you've been turning your bedroom lights on for every night at midnight, and then turning them off about five minutes later? I can see your house from my bedroom, you know." Kate laughed then. They had tried to be so discreet, and it was obviously pointless. Her sisters were too smart and they were too close, now that they were all at the ranch.

"Yes, that's what's going on. So you're okay with it?"

"I'm not Dad, Kate," Gemma reminded her. "You don't answer to me or to anyone. You're a grown-up, and you do a fantastic job running this ranch, with his help, and if you two think you can work it out, more power to you. You deserve to have a good man to love you. And he is a good man," she confirmed.

"He was afraid you and Caro wouldn't approve, and wouldn't think he's fancy enough, or educated enough."

"He's a cowboy. So was our father. That works for me. And he's a way more decent guy than that asshole who's married to our sister and cheating on her with his secretary or whatever she is."

"Trainee, I think."

"Caroline should divorce him. He's a lying shit." Kate didn't disagree with her and was worried about how it would turn out. Caroline hadn't heard from him since she arrived, and he certainly wasn't remorseful, from what she said. Caroline wanted to try to work it out, or at least talk about it, but she felt he should take the first steps if he wanted to save their marriage. They all suspected that he was continuing the affair, and taking full advantage that his wife was away for the summer, and maybe thought he could fix it later. It was foolish of him. The longer he waited, the more hurt and the angrier she got. "In any case, you can tell Thad that he can stop tiptoeing around for us. You have our full approval, if you need it, mine and Caro's. We've been waiting for you to tell us. I just couldn't stand the suspense anymore."

"He'll be relieved." Kate smiled at her, and half an hour later, he showed up, to get his boots. Gemma winked at him, patted his arm, and left, and he looked at Kate.

"What was that about?"

"They figured it out, they're happy for us." She smiled at him and his face broke into a smile and he pulled Kate into his arms and kissed her.

"Well, hallelujah. That's a load off my mind." They went upstairs and celebrated shortly after, and they agreed that from then on, he could come for dinner and spend the night. He didn't have to show up after dinner, or pretend he was just walking by. It was going to make their lives a lot easier, and more relaxed.

"Just like real people," he said, pulling her close to him, and kissed her again. It meant a lot to him that her sisters were happy for them. Her family meant everything to him and was like his own. They were the only family he'd ever had.

The next time Kate went to see their mother, Gemma and Caroline went with her. They had a lot of catching up to do. And Gemma had gone to see her once on her own. Caroline was too upset about Peter, and didn't want to see anyone. She had taken Peter's affair very hard, and felt it as a personal failure that her marriage was falling apart. But she joined her sisters for the drive to Santa Barbara. They took Scarlett to lunch at the Biltmore.

Scarlett was a quiet, sensible woman. She had seen a lot of hardships in life, a failed marriage, losing her children, drugs, jail, the death of the man she left her husband for, and finally a successful relationship with Roberto for twenty-six years. She was above all real, and wise, and humble. They had discovered that she was very religious, which she said was how she had survived, but she didn't force her religion on anyone.

She was enjoying getting to know her daughters and appreciated how different they were. All of them were discovering that they could say anything to her, without her being shocked or judging them. Motherhood was new to her, but all three girls agreed that she was good at it, and had a light touch, unlike their father, who had imposed his will and opinions on all of them with a heavy hand.

Kate ended up telling her about her new relationship with Thad that day, and it was obvious how happy she was. Scarlett thought it sounded perfect for her. Gemma confessed that she was terrified her career was in the tank and might never recover, although Scarlett thought that was unlikely and Gemma's sisters agreed with her. She was a major star, and they all thought it was just a lull, a bad patch that she'd get through. At the end of lunch, Caroline blurted out that she and Peter were taking a break for the summer because she'd discovered his affair. Scarlett turned to her and told her not to come to any rapid conclusions, not to listen to other people's advice, and follow her heart. They had seventeen years invested in their marriage, and two children, no one knew their marriage as they did. The twenty-three-year-old was lightweight compared to that, and probably wouldn't last.

"But how would I ever trust him again?" Caroline asked with tears in her eyes.

"You won't at first, and maybe not even for a long time. Love will get you through it, if you genuinely love each other. We're all human, and sometimes we make terrible mistakes. What's important is that you learn from them. I don't know your husband, whether he's a good man or not. If he isn't, you'll have to have the courage to get away from him before he takes you down. If he is, it might be worth staying with him and giving him another chance. You'll know what you need to do. Some time to yourself now will do you good." Caroline felt peaceful. It struck a chord with her. She thought Peter was a good man and a good husband and father, even if he was cold and pompous sometimes, but underneath it all, they loved each other, or they had. What she needed to know now was if he still loved her, and if she could forgive him. She didn't know the answer to that yet.

She was quiet on the drive back to the ranch and turned to her sisters with a serene look on her face.

"I like having a mother. She's nice. I really missed that growing up. Dad was always telling us what to do. He never listened. She doesn't do that. I wish we'd found her a long time ago. He really cheated us of that." She didn't look angry, just sad.

"I wish we had too," Gemma said with a smile. "She reminds me of Kate a lot. She doesn't go off half-cocked like me and react, or hide like you. She's strong and quiet and sensible, like Kate." They all smiled and Kate was touched by the compliment.

It had been a nice visit. It had been every time. She brought something new and important to their lives. They would never get back the years they had lost, but she had come back at just the right time, for all three of them. They needed her now, maybe more than they ever had.

Juliette left on her trip to France the day before their annual summer picnic. She was sorry to miss it, but she was meeting her brother, and she admitted to Kate that the picnic would be too hard for her this year without Jimmy. She had been very brave about continuing her life there without him, and Kate dropped in on her frequently, but she seemed lonely and sad. He hadn't been gone long, so she hadn't had time to adjust, but her life on the ranch was empty without him.

She had done the books diligently until she left, and all three girls came to say goodbye and hugged her.

"We're going to miss you," Kate said gently. "See you at the end of August." Juliette shed a few tears when she left and Thad drove her to the airport. She was flying to L.A. to make her connection to Paris, where she was going to stay with her brother for a few days, and then they were driving to Bordeaux and visiting friends there. And after that, they'd go to the house in the Camargue. It was going to be a nice trip for her.

After Juliette left, they had their huge annual picnic for all the ranch hands and employees, their families and neighboring ranchers. Two hundred people came for great food, delicious barbecue, and a spread that people always talked about afterward for weeks. There was line dancing, and Gemma had gotten a country singer she knew from L.A. The party was one of the best they'd had. Thad and Kate made their debut as a couple that night. She'd forgotten what a good dancer he was. They square-danced and line-danced and slow danced to country music, and they made a handsome couple. Everyone noticed the love in their eyes when they looked at each other. There was no mistaking what had happened between them. Thad said he had never been so proud and happy in his life. And Kate was radiant in a white lace dress Gemma lent her for the night.

She sat with her sisters for a few minutes to catch her breath between dances, and he went to get them all some beers.

"You look happy, Kate," Caroline said quietly. She looked as troubled as she had since she arrived and they all knew why. Peter had gone silent on her, and she was beginning to think it was just as well. She was determined to wait to hear from him, and not chase him, which was agony for her, but seemed like the strong thing to do. If it was over, she needed to face it and couldn't run away from it. It wasn't what she wanted, but it was the hand she'd been dealt. She wasn't going to run away from what he'd done, turn a blind eye, let him get away with it, or pretend it wasn't happening. It was, and she was willing to face it head-on, if he reached out to her. And if he didn't, she would move on, and find the strength to do it. "I'm happy for you and Thad," she said, and Kate could tell that she meant it.

"We both are," Gemma seconded it. "Somebody has to be happy around here and it's definitely your turn." Kate had played hand-maiden to their father for twenty years, which was more than enough. And he had left her the legacy of Thad, almost like his blessing of their union, if she needed that.

He came back with the beers then, and sat down with the three of them. "If I eat any more ribs, I'm going to pop."

"Me too," Gemma said with a groan. "I may have to get my fancy trainer up here if I keep eating like this. I'm starting a biking program with Morgan tomorrow. But I might have another piece of the apple pie first, with vanilla ice cream."

"I always forget how good the food is at our barbecue," Kate said with a smile and leaned over and kissed Thad. He looked like the happiest man on earth. They were signing the papers for his new land in two weeks. A contractor in town was working on plans for the house, modeling it on JT's, only slightly larger, with more bedrooms, and he was in love with the love of his life.

They went back to the dance floor after that, and led the next round of line dancing. Scarlett and Roberto joined them for a last dance before they left, and said they'd had a great time. She asked Caro quietly if she'd heard from Peter yet and she shook her head.

"You will," she said confidently, and hugged her. And Caroline felt safe in her mother's arms.

The party lasted until two A.M., and all three sisters stayed until the bitter end. As the party finally wound down, Thad held Kate in his arms and looked into her eyes.

"Thank you for making me so happy." He didn't ask her when they were going to get married. He didn't want to rush her, but it was all he could think about now.

When the party was over, they walked up the road to her house hand in hand, for everyone to see, and up the front steps into her house. It was where he belonged now. The owner and the foreman, proud to be together. Gemma watched their bedroom lights go out a little while later and smiled. And wherever their father was, she hoped he was smiling too.

Chapter 11

After the big summer barbecue, the days just seemed to roll by with bright blue skies and hot weather. Thad and Kate together everywhere on the ranch became a familiar sight, more than ever. She gave him her old office, next to her father's, which she was using now, and they were always consulting each other about something, or working on a project together. Their breeding barn was busier than it had been in a long time. And their livestock and Thorough-bred auction almost doubled in size because of Thad's bulletins about it ahead of time on the internet. He was good about using social media to increase their business. They worked hard all month, while Caroline went on outings with Morgan and Billy, and Gemma went to L.A. for auditions several times, but nothing had borne fruit so far. She felt lazy on the ranch and spent hours reading in a hammock Thad had set up for her. And whenever they got the chance, one or all of them visited their mother in Santa Barbara.

It was in many ways a perfect summer, although different. It was their first without their father. Juliette was away, and sent postcards from all over France. And Scarlett and Roberto came to lunch several times on Sundays when Kate and Thad weren't working. Caroline had heard from Peter a few times, and he met Morgan and Billy in Santa Barbara for a weekend. Caroline had Thad drive them there to meet him. She didn't want to see Peter.

Roberto and Scarlett had been to the ranch for the day in early August, it was Saturday, and Kate and Thad were lying in bed that night at her house, talking about them, and Kate said how nice it was to suddenly have a mother at her age. She had just said that to Thad when he sat bolt upright in bed, sniffing the air and listening. And before he could say a word to her, he had leapt out of bed, jumped into his jeans, grabbed his boots and pulled them on, put on a T-shirt inside out, and grabbed his denim jacket as she watched him intently.

"What's wrong?"

"Fire . . . I'm sure I smell something." She got out of bed just as quickly, and pulled her clothes on. She was heading for the stairs when he was already at the front door, and as soon as he opened the door, she could smell it. They ran outside, and the night sky was lit up in the distance. It was bright orange. It wasn't close yet, but that could change in an instant. There was a light breeze, and he left her at a dead run to sound the alarm. Kate called both her sisters on her cellphone, while she ran to the old fire bell they still used as backup. The sirens came on less than a minute later when Thad turned on the alarm, and within minutes men came running from everywhere, the bunkhouse and the barn. They grabbed hoses and started hosing down the roof of the barn and the other structures. Thad had called 911, and was waiting for them, ready to head to the fire with them in his truck.

The fire department was there in less than ten minutes, the regular force and the volunteers on their heels, and Thad took off with them. Her sisters and Morgan and Billy came to find Kate at the barn, and she gave Billy the job of continuing to ring the old fire bell, while Morgan, Caroline, and Gemma helped the men spraying the roof of the barn with hoses. Ranch hands were getting as many horses as they could into trailers. The horses were looking wild-eyed, but they wanted to have them ready to move at a moment's notice if the fire turned in their direction. From the distance, Kate couldn't tell which way it was going. A few minutes later, a helicopter swooped by overhead to check the fire from the air. They would call in the fire planes if they needed them later, but it hadn't reached those proportions yet. Gemma flashed by on her way to help the men getting the horses into the trailers. Fire was their worst fear on the ranch, and they had at least one bad one a year in the area, sometimes more, once the grass was dry, and the temperatures rose. It had been a dry year, so this could be severe.

By four that morning, the planes to spray the fire were hard at work. Kate was dying to get in her truck to follow the fire trucks to the fire. She hadn't seen Thad since he drove off and left her. Most of the horses were in trailers by then, frightened and whinnying, but ready to move if they had to. There were hundreds of men spread out across the ranch, doing their jobs, and at seven o'clock they could see men and trucks starting to return, and the planes flew back in the direction they came from. Kate could tell from all the signs that the fire had been contained and the worst of the danger was over. At this time of year, a small fire could become a blaze and wipe out thousands of acres, homes, and livestock. She had seen it before and sometimes it took days to contain the fire.

By ten o'clock that morning, Thad came back filthy, his face blackened with soot and ash, and red from the heat, but everyone had done their job. Two of the fire trucks followed his truck back to the ranch, and the drivers stopped to talk to Kate and the men. They weren't going to put the horses back in the barn yet, waiting to make sure that the fire was as contained as they believed it was.

Kate was standing with Caroline when the men got off the trucks, and ranch hands handed out bottles of water, when she saw Caroline give a start and look at one of the men.

"Tom McAvoy?" she said, as he gratefully took a bottle of water and drained it. They'd been in the thick of it for eight hours, and they were wet from the hoses, and hot from the flames in their heavy suits with their masks and helmets slung over their arms. He grinned as soon as he saw her. His red hair was plastered to his head and face, and he had streaks of soot all over his cheeks, but she had recognized him in an instant. He had been her boyfriend senior year in high school, and he had gone into the fire department when she'd left for college. And a year later when she came back, he was married and had a baby.

"Caro?" he said, as his face broke into a broad grin. "What are you doing here?"

"I'm here for the summer. Gemma's here too." She was talking to some of the firemen she had recognized from school, and they looked shy with her, knowing she was a big star now. But there was nothing shy about Tom McAvoy and never had been. "How are your kids?" she asked him.

"My oldest is applying to veterinary school at UC Davis. The twins are at UCSB, and my baby just graduated from high school. She's getting married in September." They started young in the Valley, and it was impressive that he had three in college. She had lost track of the fact that he had four kids. "What about yours?" She pointed to Morgan and Billy handing out bottles of water to firefighters. Thad had just given the order to get the horses back into the barn. The danger was over. They'd been lucky. August was usually the worst month for fires all up and down the California coast, and especially in the valleys.

"How's Ellen?" Caroline asked him politely about his wife, a girl she'd gone to school with and never liked.

"Happy, married to someone else, with two more kids. We got divorced about ten years ago. I don't think you've been here for a while."

"No, I haven't," she admitted.

"What about you? Still married?" It was an interesting question at the moment, for which she didn't have an easy answer. She hesitated just long enough for it to catch his attention.

"Yes, I guess I am," she finally responded. "Peter stayed in Marin for the summer. I'm here with my sisters." Without spelling it out to him, he got the distinct impression that something was wrong, and he nodded.

"We got lucky with the wind tonight," he told her. "It could have been a bad one, if the wind had turned on us. It didn't. We had a couple of real bad ones last year, wiped out acres of homes, and the Canyon Ranch." She had heard about it from Kate and forgotten. It was a worry for them every year too, and there was little you could do to protect yourself from it, except keep the brush cleared away, and react quickly when it happened. As he chatted with her, one of his men came up and addressed him as "Captain."

"You're a captain now?" Caro smiled at him.

"Hell, I should be. I just turned forty. I've been in the department since I was eighteen." Like a lot of the kids they had gone to school with, and even Gemma, he hadn't gone to college. "I'm planning to retire from the department in ten years and run my own business. I've got a small business started now. With three kids in college, I'll be working for the next hundred years to help them pay off their student loans. By the way, I'm sorry about your dad. Our guys came out right away, but there was nothing they could do." She nodded and thanked him, as more of his men came up to talk to him. They had left a detail where the fire was, and they wanted to get the trucks back to the firehouse, so the men could rest and take over the shifts later that afternoon, to stay near the fire until it was fully out. "Duty calls." He smiled at her. "I'll call you if you'll be here for a while."

"Till the end of the month." He patted her arm, and followed his men, got in the cab of the biggest fire truck and they took off a minute later. He waved as they drove by.

"Was that Tom McAvoy?" Kate asked her and she nodded, still looking surprised. "He hasn't changed since high school."

"He's divorced, and he's got three kids in college, one who just graduated from high school and is about to get married. Shit, that makes me feel old."

"They get a head start in the Valley," Kate said, echoing her sister's thoughts. "He came out with Dickie Jackson for Dad," she said, which Caroline vaguely remembered Kate telling her. "It's funny how a lot of the people we knew are still here. Like me," she said, and laughed, but she had gone away to college. Thad came and joined them then, and a little while later, a hearty breakfast was served by the staff for everyone in the barn, as they all stood around and talked about the fire. Everyone was on deck, all thirty-five ranch hands, and all the office employees had showed up and pitched in. Billy was enjoying the excitement and talking to the men, and Morgan was helping serve breakfast. Gemma came and stood with her sisters, and had seen three or four men she had gone to school with too. "Did everyone we went to school with end up in the fire department?" she commented.

"Or working on ranches," Kate answered.

"They all said their wives watch my show."

"We should have set up a table to have you sign autographs," Kate teased her, and a little while later they all went back to their houses. It was almost eleven by then, and they could still see smoke in the distance.

Kate went upstairs to take a shower, and a little while later, Thad came in and joined her, and they wound up making love. It was Sunday and no one was going to work. They'd spend the day cleaning up and trying to calm the horses, who had had a rough night. The men were still on an adrenaline rush, and Kate and Thad went out to the barn, to make sure none of the horses had gotten hurt while unloading them from the trailers. Everything went smoothly as they got the horses back in their stalls.

It was a long day and everyone was tired when they went home at six o'clock. Thad came back to Kate's place, and stretched out his legs, sitting on the couch, while she organized something for them to eat.

"It's a good thing you smelled the fire last night. I didn't smell anything till we got outside," she said, sitting down next to him, and handing him a plate. All she'd been able to rustle up for him was a turkey, cheese, and tomato sandwich, but it was all they wanted.

*   *   *

By the next day, the ranch was back to normal, and the fire department still had a detail of men watching the embers and hosing them down in the back pasture, and Caroline was surprised when Tom McAvoy called her. He left a message for her at the main office of the ranch, and she called him back that night.

"It was nice seeing you last night, Caro," he said easily. "You haven't changed a bit."

"I wish that were true." She smiled, thinking about him when they were in high school. He hadn't changed much except he had less hair, but he was still attractive. He was a big, burly guy.

"Do you want to have dinner tomorrow night?" he asked her.

"Sure, I'd love that."

"Great. I'll pick you up at seven."

She told Gemma about it the next day, and she teased her about it.

"Going back to old boyfriends, are we?"

"I'm married and he has a million kids," Caroline said with a quelling look at her sister. The truth was that she had no idea how married she was at the moment. She and Peter had spoken on the phone now, but their conversations had been awkward and didn't touch on the significant issues. But at least he'd called, and it seemed wiser not to broach the big issues until she got back to the city and saw him. She'd know more when she could see his face, and read what she saw in his eyes. She realized that there was a strong possibility that they were headed for divorce. She wasn't sure if she had done the right thing kicking him out of the house. She had the feeling that she had thrown him right into Veronica Ashton's arms. But letting him stay with her wouldn't have changed that, if that was the case.

When Tom showed up that night at seven, he was driving his captain's car. He said he had just come from work, but she had the feeling he was trying to impress her. It was fun getting in with him, and he showed her how the siren worked. He let her put on the flashing lights on the way to dinner. And they went to the same diner they used to go to as kids. It was still there, and so were two of the old waitresses, who recognized her. It was like a time warp. And Tom said he still ate there regularly.

"So what have you been up to for the past twenty years?" he asked her. She'd run into him once but hadn't really talked to him. He'd been carrying the twins, his wife had a toddler by the hand and she was pregnant. Caroline had felt sorry for her. It was exactly the life she had wanted to escape when she left for San Francisco.

"Not much, being married, two kids." She answered his question, and she told him about her young adult books, which he said sounded interesting. He asked what her husband did and she said he was in venture capital.

"A big guy, huh?"

"Not really. To be honest, I think we're separated at the moment." She tried to sound nonchalant about it.

"But you're not sure?" He looked puzzled. "When my wife told me she wanted a divorce, believe me, I was sure. She threw a frying pan at me." He laughed at the memory.

"Did you cheat on her?" Caroline asked, curious.

"No, I used to take three-day shifts at the firehouse to get away from the kids, and play poker with the guys. I lost a lot of money and she was pissed. I'm a good boy now. I can't afford to play poker anymore. The kids need the money. She married my captain. He retired and runs a security alarm business, and does pretty well." It was a small life with people struggling for money. Just hearing about those lives used to make her feel trapped, terrified that she'd become one of them. They didn't scare her anymore, but they sounded sad to her. None of them had had a chance to live and get out of the Valley. Tom had been a bright boy. He had wanted to get a football scholarship to college, but got his girlfriend pregnant and got married instead.

"This must all seem very small town to you now," he said, as though reading her mind. "I remember how desperately you wanted to get out of here. Are you glad you did?"

"I was until a month ago, now I'm not so sure. Things work out in either place, or don't work out. I like living in San Francisco, but my marriage is a mess. We're probably going to get divorced," she said with a sigh.

"You'll survive it, Caro. You're a winner. You always were. If he's not the right one, you'll find a better guy than the one you have. If he's making you unhappy, it's not worth it. Ellen and I were never right for each other. She wanted a lot of kids, and she got them, two more after me. But as soon as we had them, she lost interest in me. She's ambitious in a funny way, but she wants to do it here. She's very grand now, married to the guy who owns the alarm company, a retired captain. I mean, let's face it, in the real world how la-de-da is that? And look at your husband. It's great that he's in venture capital, but if you're unhappy, who cares?" He had a down-to-earth way of looking at things that she had always liked, and he hadn't changed. And he was good-looking and in great shape at forty. He still looked like a football player. But she couldn't imagine herself with someone like him. It just never fit, even then, no matter how cute he was. She had wanted someone very different from the hometown boys, like Peter.

"He cheated on me," she explained about her husband.

"He's an idiot, married to someone like you. I used to think about you when I was married to Ellen. She bitched all the time about the money I wasn't making. And I'm pretty sure she slept with my captain before she left me. Who needs that? There are plenty of good people out there. You just have to find one." She nodded, agreeing with him, not sure if Peter still qualified or not.

"It's not going to be easy, starting over, dating again. I thought I was set for life."

"We all think that. It's chutes and ladders. You're up at the top, and then you slide down to the beginning again. But it can be fun. I've actually enjoyed dating for the last ten years and not being married. I got it ass backward. I should have played till I was thirty or thirty-five and then gotten married. Instead I got married at eighteen and divorced at thirty, and now I'm having fun." She laughed at his description of it, and he was right. "You'll be happy again, Caro, if you wind up getting divorced. Just give it time. It's a mess at first, especially with kids. But then you start to meet nice people, and you feel good about yourself again." He was actually being helpful, and she was grateful for his advice. He made the future sound bearable, and not like a tragedy that had befallen her. "You should try dating online. It's a little like gambling. You never know what card you're going to get. Luck of the draw." She laughed, and couldn't see herself computer dating, although a lot of people she knew did. She'd thought she had it all worked out with Peter. Tom was right, now she was back to the beginning again. And she wasn't sure how she felt or what she wanted. She was confused. She loved Peter, and she missed him, but every time she thought of him now, she thought of the photos in her nightstand. She was still in shock, angry, and sad. He had broken the sacred trust between them, and her heart. She had no idea where to go from here or whether to get a divorce.

They talked for a long time over dinner, and then he drove her home.

"I'd like to see you again sometime, Caro, if that's okay with you. I can be your summer fling while you're here." He put it on the line and she laughed.

"I don't think that's what I need right now, but thank you, Tom. I don't want to complicate my life more than it is. I have to figure out my marriage, and what I want to do, before I start dating or having flings. I don't want to screw your life up either, or cheat on Peter if we're going to get back together. But I'm up for an evening like this, dinner and good friends."

"Fair enough. You were always straight up, Caro. I admire that about you. I should have stuck with you." She had never cheated on him, Peter, or any man she'd gone out with.

"No, you shouldn't," she told him. "You did the right thing. I'm sure you have great kids." She knew more than ever that she couldn't live there. It just wasn't enough for her, and never had been. But he was a nice person, and a warm memory. She couldn't imagine him ever being more than that for her.

"I'll call you," he promised, but she wasn't sure he would. She suspected that he wanted to sleep with her. And a fling was more what he had in mind, if he was big into computer dating. He was looking to make up for twelve years of a boring marriage, and he wasn't through playing yet. She had never been a player, even in college. Gemma had been, but she never was. She was the serious one, and so was Kate.

She kissed his cheek, thanked him for dinner again, got out of the car, and walked into her house. Billy and Morgan were watching TV and looked up when she walked in.

"Who was that?" They heard him drive away.

"An old friend from high school." It didn't sound interesting to them so they didn't question her further. But it had been nice, re-examining the patchwork of her life. It made her glad all over again that she had left. Life in the Valley just wasn't for her, no matter how handsome and sexy Tom McAvoy was. She had outgrown him in high school, and that hadn't changed. Now she had a decision to make about Peter, about whether she had outgrown him too. She hadn't thought of it that way before, but that's what it came down to. Could she start over with Peter and trust him again, or was it over for her and time to move on? And did she still love him, or did he kill that? She wasn't sure. She was hoping she would know when she saw him again. Until then, she felt like she was floating in space.

Chapter 12

The end of August was a turning point for all of them. There had been big changes in the past four months, starting with their father's death. Thad and Kate had a future to plan, new paths to discover together, and new ideas they wanted to implement on the ranch. He had signed the papers and paid Gemma for her share. It was a big change for both of them. He and Kate grew closer every day, and were excited about their future.

Gemma's tenant in L.A. had to leave her house on Labor Day weekend, and hadn't made an offer yet. He said he was in love with it, but it was a big financial commitment. She had paid off most of her debts with Thad's money, there were still a few lingering ones that trickled in. She knew she had to confront her lifestyle now, and make major changes. For the first time in her life, she couldn't, and didn't want to, live from paycheck to paycheck. She didn't have one, and she wanted a cushion, so the bottom couldn't fall out of her life so easily again. She didn't want to live that way. Selling her house in the Hollywood Hills and downsizing would give her something to fall back on.

Almost three months after the show had folded, she was still out of work. Jerry, her agent, was still promising that the new British series was a strong possibility for her, but it hadn't come through yet, and she didn't know if it would. She couldn't count on it as a sure thing, or even a strong possibility. It might turn out to be a train that would pass her by. It happened a lot in TV series and feature films, someone told you that you were perfect for it after an audition, or that they were going to call you, and they never did. Hopes got dashed in Hollywood every day, and hers had in June.

She went back to L.A. the day after Labor Day, and she was surprised by how sad she was to leave the ranch. More than she had been when she left at eighteen after she'd graduated from high school. It had provided her a safe haven all summer, an opportunity to reconnect with her sisters, and find herself in the peace and silence of the Valley. She realized now that she'd been running away for years, living on distraction and overriding her inner voices with background noise, running away from age, her responsibilities, the need to put something aside for the future. She hadn't wanted to hear any of it. Her father had tried to warn her, but he liked the idea of her being a star, and the reflected glory it gave him. In some ways, she had been an accessory to him, to make him more important and look good. His daughter was a star. And stars didn't have to be responsible or even grown-ups most of the time. They had to show up at work, look great on camera, and know their lines. She had done all of that, to perfection, but she had been coasting for ten years, while the producers spoiled her, the public adored her, her father bragged about her, and she signed autographs. She had bought into all of it. It would have been hard not to. She would have had to face herself more often than she had. She doubted that she had faced reality at all. She had formed no deep relationships or friendships in the past ten years. Everything in her life was superficial, a façade.

She walked around her house when she got it back, and loved being there again. It was big and beautiful, elegant and showy, the furniture was perfectly placed, the art was attractive and expensive, and it gave her a feeling of well-being just being there, wandering around, and looking at the view. But she didn't need it, no one cared that she lived there. She had no one to share it with. It was ten thousand square feet of drain on her finances with no income now to support it. And even if she got another big show, did she really want to carry all that and work to pay the mortgage? She was sorry now she hadn't bought something smaller and easier to carry. With no show, the house was a rock around her neck, and a heavy burden.

She missed her sisters when she got back to L.A., seeing Kate and Caroline every day, and going on walks and daily bike rides with them. Seeing her niece and nephew and learning about them. She had made her sisters go to the nail salon with her to add "glamour" to their lives, as she put it. Kate had had the first professional manicure of her life.

Gemma missed their serious discussions too, about what the future looked like for each of them. They were all suddenly at a turning point, a fork in the road. Caroline hadn't figured out what to do about her marriage, and was worried about her kids. They asked her several times if she and Peter were getting divorced, and she told them she didn't know. They were handling it better than she'd expected, but the whole family couldn't hang in limbo forever.

Kate had big plans for the ranch, and with Thad, and it was different without their father, a huge change for each of them.

Their father was the ghost of Christmas past for Caro, the bugaboo she had feared and run from. He was Gemma's hero, and in the past she always knew she had him to fall back on if things got tough, but not this time. She had to bail herself out, she wasn't Daddy's Girl anymore. And Kate was thriving. He had repressed her and tacitly put her down for years, substituting her fresh new modern ideas with his, implying that everything he did was better and she couldn't make it on her own. She had to now, with Thad next to her, as a partner, not overpowering her as their father had. Her father's message to her had been strong, that she didn't have what it took because she wasn't a man, and without him she would fail. She wondered how one man could be so many different things to each of them. He had taken over their lives, tried to make their decisions for them, hidden their mother from them, and lied to them.

He had all but ruined Scarlett's life, with her full cooperation and innocence at twenty-three, and run their lives or tried to ever since. She and Caroline had had to run away from him in order to breathe, and Kate hadn't taken a deep breath in years without his standing over her, intimidating her, second-guessing her decisions. Now they were all breathing, in some ways for the first time, without him. He was the specter in the background, the savior when he chose to be, the judge of everything they did, the voice in their heads no matter where they went or how far they ran. There had been no escaping him, and now suddenly he was gone, and there was only the sound of their own voices, not his. It was finally beginning to sink in, for all of them. Their daddy wasn't there anymore. They had grown up and were adults now, and it was scary as hell. And it almost seemed meant to try them, that Gemma had run aground, lost the show, and was out of money, Caroline's marriage was on the rocks, and Kate finally had a man in her life, a real one, one who loved her, for the first time in a dozen years. It was about goddamn time for all of them. In the months since his death, they had all grown up.

Gemma called Jerry the morning she got back, to see if he had any work for her, but he didn't.

"Still nothing? How is that possible? The show wrapped nearly three months ago and all you've had are auditions for a vampire movie, the voiceover for a witch in a cartoon, and six commercials that didn't want me." And they both knew why. She couldn't play ingénues anymore, or even thirty-year-olds credibly. She had entered a new phase in her career, while she wasn't looking, the middle-aged actress. How the hell did that happen? She had aged with the show, and now the show was gone, and she was standing on the shore watching the ships pass her by. "There has to be something," she said in a plaintive tone. She had been harassing him all summer, even when he went to the South of France, and stayed at the Hotel du Cap, where she used to go, and could no longer afford. All the fancy trimmings and perks seemed fraudulent now, and irrelevant. She needed work, something she could sink her teeth into, and pay the bills with. Where was stardom now? Her star was in the tank, or that's what it felt like to her.

"There will be something," he said with certainty. "It just hasn't happened yet. You're a big name, they're going to want you for a decent part, but whatever that project is, it hasn't come together yet. It will have your name on it when it does."

"I wish I was as optimistic as you are."

"Do something," he told her. "Go to the gym, get a hobby, buy a dog, sleep with someone. Keep busy."

"I'm thinking of selling my house," she said, sounding morbid about it.

"Good. Buy a new one. Decorate. Buy things. Go shopping."

"That's what got me into this mess in the first place. If I change clothes six times a day for the next twenty years, I can't wear it all. My cleaning lady had more money in the bank than I did when the show closed." The story was familiar to him. Most actors lived that way. They started to believe the roles they played and the hype. They went around living like royalty or the dictators of small countries, with nothing to back it up. Gemma was not unusual in that. Fancy cars, houses, art, and jewelry changed hands frequently to bail them out. And then they did it all over again when they got another big part, and forgot that it would end again one day. Few of them had a grasp on reality, and knew how to cope with real life.

Their relationships evaporated as fast as their films. Very few of them had their feet on the ground. Gemma was no different, no better or worse than most of his clients, though she was one of the rare few who had talent. Most of them just had great looks, which they frittered away too, with too much plastic surgery when they had time and money on their hands. He had a famous client who had died that summer from an infection after her fourth liposuction in six months. The doctor was under investigation. And another one who wanted a million dollars a year in her spousal support to pay for plastic surgery. They were all a little crazy, but he loved them. He tried to be gentle with Gemma. He knew she was panicking, but she had to be patient.

"Just don't get work done on your face while you're waiting. Every time I sign someone for a big part after a slump, they show up with a new face and the producers don't recognize who they hired, and neither does the public." They both knew it was true and saw it often, actors and actresses who surfaced looking like strangers. "You're perfect just the way you are right now. Keep it that way." Most of the time he felt like a babysitter or a shrink or a combination thereof. "Have an affair," he advised her, "it's great publicity. Go break up a marriage." He was kidding, but his clients did that regularly too. "What about a younger guy? Women love reading about that. It gives them hope."

"I just want work, Jerry, not a face lift or a boyfriend."

"Then you're in the wrong business. Don't go getting all deep on me, or find religion." One of his biggest stars had become a nun, he had lost a shitload of money when she bagged on her contract in a big series. The producers had sued her, and him, for not honoring the contract, and won.

She was still hoping for an audition for the British TV series he had mentioned, but they weren't holding auditions yet, and he didn't know when they would.

Gemma went to a spinning class after they hung up. At least she could keep her body in shape while she waited. She'd been bicycling all over the Valley with her niece all summer, and was happy to say she could keep up with a fifteen-year-old, and occasionally even beat her. She could go back to the Valley too, but she thought she should spend September in L.A., and get her face out there, so people didn't forget her when they started casting series for the following year. But she actually missed the Valley now. It was a first for her.

Caroline and the kids had gone back to Marin County a few days before Labor Day weekend. She had to get them ready for school, which was starting on Tuesday. Billy had outgrown everything he owned except his shorts and flip-flops and his oversized T-shirts. Morgan said she had nothing to wear to school, and they needed all the usual supplies, pens and notebooks, a new backpack for Billy with the latest superhero on it. It was bittersweet going home and knowing Peter wouldn't be there. Neither of them had been in the house since the end of June, or so he claimed. It hit all of them when they walked through the door. Caroline knew she couldn't avoid reality any longer.

"So when's Dad coming back?" Billy asked her their first night home, when she took a frozen pizza out of the oven, and had burned it. His words hit her like an ice cold shower.

"She doesn't know," Morgan growled at him in an angry stage whisper. "Don't ask her!" They didn't want bad news either.

"Your sister's right," their mother said in a tired voice. They'd been home for six hours and she was already exhausted, and every time she walked into her bedroom, she thought of her discoveries there two months before. The room felt toxic. Their life hadn't been the same since, and probably never would be again. It had seemed easier to be brave and a little cavalier on the ranch, trying on different decisions, to see which one fit. So far, none did. Leaping into divorce seemed too extreme, moving back in together was impossible. They couldn't pretend it hadn't happened, she was incapable of forgetting it, and she couldn't sweep it under the rug anymore. A year or two ago, or ten years, she might have. Now she wanted to face it, and make the right decision for all of them. She knew that sooner or later it would take a toll on the kids. They had been good sports so far.

Peter called her that night and invited her to lunch the day the kids started school, since he knew she'd be free then. He knew what the week before school looked like, a frenzy of activity, planning, driving from store to store, and setting up carpool schedules with other mothers. There were additional carpools for their afterschool activities. Morgan wanted to start ballet again, and Gemma had gotten her hooked on yoga and Pilates. Billy had to go back to the orthodontist.

"How are you?" Peter asked her as though she were a friend he hadn't seen in years. Time had put distance between them. Her life seemed to be full of faces from the past now. She had run into them in Santa Ynez constantly. Now he was one of them, except that they were still married, or said they were, and she thought she still loved him, or who he had been before. She wasn't sure who he was now, and if she could love that man. The children had spent Saturday night and Sunday with him, but she was out when he picked them up, so she missed him. He'd only seen the children one weekend in two months. He said he was working the rest of the time. Thad had driven them to Santa Barbara to meet their father and a driver brought them back, so Caroline hadn't seen him since the end of June. She had to face the music now. They both did. They couldn't hang in space forever. She hadn't called the lawyer back. She had nothing to tell him. She wanted to talk to Peter first and see him and how she felt before deciding to divorce.

"I'm fine. How are you?" she asked politely when he called.

"Okay, it's been weird not being with you and the kids," he said in a sad voice, but so was finding pictures of his penis and his girl-friend's vagina in her night table. She thought of it every time she thought of him now, and hated their bedroom, knowing what had gone on there. It still felt like days ago. Two months later, the memory hadn't dimmed. Just hearing him brought it all back. She knew he had rented an apartment in the city, in a building that was famous for housing divorcing men, and couples having affairs. She wasn't sure which he was. She didn't know if the affair was over or not, which made a difference.

They agreed to have lunch at a restaurant near his office. It was noisier than she would have liked, if they were going to have a seri-ous conversation about their future. But someplace quiet would have scared her. She didn't feel ready for an intense exchange, didn't want an angry confrontation, and didn't want to cry in public. Noisy was better. Maybe she wouldn't hear him say it when he told her he wanted a divorce and was marrying Veronica Ashton. She was afraid of what he'd say, but she wanted to know.

She dropped both kids off at their respective schools on the first day, and went home to dress for lunch with her husband. She didn't know what to wear. Sexy, no, ridiculous and pathetic. Formal. She took out a suit she hadn't worn in two years, and would look like she was going to court or a funeral, which was why she had bought it, when a friend's mother died. Casual looked too sloppy, jeans like she wasn't even trying. She looked in Morgan's closet since they traded clothes sometimes, but she'd look like she was trying to compete with his twelve-year-old girlfriend. She finally settled on a black skirt and white sweater, and a pair of heels she pulled out of the back of her closet, and brushed her blond hair back in a ponytail. She wore mascara and lipstick, and had a deep tan. She didn't want to look like she was trying to seduce him, she wasn't, but she wanted to look good enough that he'd have some regrets about destroying their marriage when she asked him for a divorce, if that seemed like the right answer over a salad.

She had indigestion thinking about it, and arrived ten minutes late because the nearest garage was full, and she had to walk five blocks to the restaurant from where she parked.

"I'm sorry I'm late" was the first thing she said to him after not seeing him for two months. He was wearing a suit and a pale blue tie, and she assumed he had meetings that morning, although he rarely wore a tie to them, except with clients who flew out from New York. She knew all his routines, just as he knew hers, and she realized that this was different than the people she ran into in Santa Ynez who wanted to know what she'd been doing for the last twenty years. Peter had become a stranger in the last two months, but everything about him was still familiar.

He was waiting for her at the table, and was drinking a Bloody Mary. He normally didn't drink at lunch. He looked nervous, and so was she. This wasn't like a first date. It felt like their last one, and they both wanted to get it right.

They made small talk about the kids until after they ordered. She told him how well they rode now. He ordered a steak, and she a chicken salad and didn't think she could eat it, but she could push it around on her plate. He commented on how much Billy had grown over the summer, and asked if she had set up the math tutor for Morgan. She had. She was back at her job as perfect mother, having failed as perfect wife. If she hadn't, he wouldn't have been sleeping with twenty-three-year-olds in their bedroom.

He finally touched on the subject halfway through lunch. She had been dreading it since she got there, but it was why they were having lunch in a busy downtown restaurant, and he wouldn't be coming home to her that night.

"So where are we headed, Caro? I've got the apartment for three more weeks, and I need to know what I'm doing." That was it? The apartment? What about their life? Her heart? Their kids? Their future? Was it time to divide up the books, the furniture, and their sports equipment? And decide who got the couch?

"I don't know. I'm not sure. Where do you think we should be going? What's happening with you?" She wanted to sound stronger, but her heart was pounding so hard she could almost hear it and was sure he could too.

He sighed when he looked at her, and almost visibly deflated, like a balloon with a hole in it. He wasn't the man she remembered, confident, cocky, strong, hers. She noticed that he'd lost weight over the summer, and he noticed the same about her. She looked fit, and her tan was golden brown. He hadn't dared tell her she looked great when he saw her.

"I think I went a little crazy two months ago. Some kind of midlife crisis or something. Maybe I was afraid of getting old. I can't make excuses for what I did. And I don't know if you can forgive me. It might have just screwed us forever. I hope it hasn't, but I wouldn't blame you." She had never heard him sound so humble and contrite.

"Interesting choice of words," she said tartly, and he looked embarrassed, as he should have.

"Whatever. You know what I mean. Do you want a divorce?"

"Want one? No. Need one? Maybe. I'm just not sure I can get past it. I want to, but I can't get it out of my head. I can hardly walk into our bedroom without feeling sick. You broke my heart," she said as tears filled her eyes, and she struggled to hold them back.

"I'm so sorry, Caro. I don't know what happened. I went nuts. That's all I can say. I feel terrible. I didn't want to hurt you. I wish I could erase it for both of us."

"And now?"

"It's over. I ended it. She quit. She went back to New York a few weeks ago. She's young, she'll get over it. I spent a lot of time this summer trying to figure out why it happened. It was like a drug."

"And the next one, just like her, if you go nuts again?"

"There won't be a next one. I love you." He had finally said it. She wondered if he would. She didn't say it back, because she was no longer sure if she still loved him. That was the problem. Her feelings for him had been frozen since June, and nothing she thought or said or tried to remember seemed to defrost them. After the initial agony, she had been numb and confused ever since. "I love our life, our kids. I don't want to do this to them or to you."

"You should have thought of that two months ago."

"I should have, but I didn't. I was a massive fool. It's like I thought I was single for a minute, in a way I never had been. I never did things like that before we got married. It's all different now. It's cell-phones and selfies and texting and fast sex from dating sites. Instead of ordering pizzas, they order people. It's a giant supermarket of bodies, fast lays like fast food and no feelings. I don't know how they cope with it. It made me crazy, and it scares me to death for Morgan, out there in a few years. I don't know how any of them handle it.

OkCupid, and Tinder, and Twitter. I'll lose my mind if that's what I have to do now. I don't want a divorce. I want to come home, if you'll have me."

She didn't answer him for a long time, as she looked at him and thought about it, and tried to figure out what she wanted. She wanted to turn the clock back to before June, and she knew that couldn't happen. She didn't want what they were left with either. Anger and bitterness, and a broken heart over what he'd done to their marriage, and indirectly their kids if they were going to be the children of divorce now. She would have never cheated on him, or done what he did, or lost her mind over a twenty-three-year-old. Why did he get to do that, act like a maniac and then come home to her like nothing happened? It had happened, right in their own bedroom. And she couldn't forget anything about it.

"I'm not ready for you to come home," she said sadly, knowing that leaving him out there meant that he might find another Veronica and do the same things with her, while Caroline sat in her ivory tower and mulled it over. But the idea of sleeping in the same bed with him again made her feel slightly sick, and if he touched her, she would have killed him. Not after the pictures she'd seen, that were engraved on her memory forever. Maybe that was her answer. The word "forever." She didn't think she could get past it. "I wish I felt differently. I just can't get any of it out of my mind." She didn't go down the list. He knew what she was upset about.

"I'd probably feel the same way you do," he said. "But I don't want to lose you. I don't know what it would take for you to forgive me, but I'll do whatever you want." She nodded. It was better than his asking for a divorce, but it didn't change what had happened. Nothing would.

"I just want to forget what happened, but that's all I think about every time I think about you." He looked as though she had slapped him. She had always been so gentle and forgiving, but this time she wasn't. She couldn't run away from this the way she had from his comments about her being a redneck because of where she grew up, and her father being a cowboy, or the dismissive comments he made about her books in the early years of their marriage. He had gotten past that. This was different. He had stabbed her in the heart of her marriage, everything she held dear and respected about him and their marriage and loved about him. Now all that was gone, or dead, or seemed to be. Where did one go from there? "I need to think about it. I've been thinking about it all summer, and all I know is I'm not ready for you to come home. I don't know if I ever will be, but I'm definitely not there yet." He nodded, there was nothing he could say to her honesty and to erase what he'd done. He couldn't rewind the film and edit it to make it different. High tech did not apply to real life. You were stuck with what was on the film forever. She wasn't sure if memories like that ever faded. So far they hadn't for her, even if Veronica was gone now. There would always be another girl like her around the next corner. She didn't think she could ever trust him again.

"I understand," he said, trying not to cry, and she almost felt sorry for him, but not really. He had done it to himself, and to her. "I'll extend the apartment till the end of the year."

"I think that's a good idea," although she wanted to make a decision before that. She didn't want to be in limbo forever either. She wondered if they should sell their house, whatever they decided to do. It was tainted forever now. Veronica would always be in the room with them, and in their bed. And as she realized it, she had an idea, but didn't say anything to him. It wasn't up to him. At least not for now. He didn't live there anymore.

"What are you going to tell the kids? You've been terrific with them," he said gratefully.

"That we need more time, and we haven't worked things out yet. It's the truth." He nodded, and he could tell from seeing them on the weekend that she hadn't told them anything about what he'd done. It meant the world to him. Other women would have, but Caroline was too decent to, no matter what he'd done or how badly he had hurt her, she hadn't told their kids. "They've seen their friends go through it, although most of the time, as Billy says, after a break like this, their friends' parents get divorced. But at least if we do, we'll be sure." She wondered if one was ever sure. There were always the things you loved about a person, and the things you hated and couldn't live with, and in this case, couldn't forgive. That was the crux of it. Could she forgive him or not? She didn't know. She didn't think so, but she wasn't sure.

"Could we go out to dinner sometime, or have lunch?" he asked her hopefully. She didn't answer, but her eyes said no. He realized as he looked at her now how far away from him she'd gone. He wished that he'd called her more often over the summer instead of only a few times. He had wanted to but thought she needed space. Maybe she didn't. And ending it with Veronica had been messy. He'd had a rotten summer, and missed Caroline and the kids fiercely.

He asked for the check then, and while they waited for it, he asked her about the ranch. "What are you doing about that? Are you asking Kate to buy out your share? You never go and you hate it there. It doesn't make much sense. And there are better investments to make than a ten-thousand-acre ranch in the Santa Ynez Valley, although the land is valuable." She didn't tell him that Thad had just bought Gemma's share. It was none of his business.

"It's better without my father. That was always the problem for me. It was nice being with my sisters this summer, and it was good for the kids. They loved it, and so did I." They had told him as much when he saw them. And he was surprised to hear she'd loved it too. He hadn't gone to see his parents in Maine at the end of August, as they always did. He didn't want them to know they were having trouble.

He paid the check then, and they left the restaurant together. "Thank you for lunch," she said politely, but she looked less nervous than she had when she arrived. In spite of everything, it was nice to see him.

"Thank you for talking to me," he said with a small wintry smile. He wasn't sure if it was the beginning or the end, and neither was she. He leaned toward her and kissed her cheek, and she smiled. "I'll email you a schedule that works for me to see the kids, let me know how it works for you. I'd like to try to keep this informal for now." She nodded. She agreed. Her car was in the opposite direction from his office, so they left each other outside the restaurant.

He had his head down as he walked away. It hadn't gone as well as he'd hoped, and hadn't been as bad as she'd feared. She had wanted to be more decisive and ask for a divorce, but she realized at lunch that she wasn't ready to do it. Once she was across the table from him and she looked him in the eyes, he wasn't as easy to walk away from as she thought he would be. The good memories were still in her mind too with the bad ones. They had a lot invested in their marriage, and it was hard to throw the good away with the bad. As she hurried toward her car, she remembered the idea that she'd had at lunch, and was determined to start on it as soon as she got home.

She drove to Marin as fast as she could within the speed limit and with the traffic. She didn't want to be late for Billy's carpool, and he had soccer practice in San Rafael that afternoon. She was left with what she'd had in their marriage, all the chores and errands and responsibilities. The only difference now was that he wouldn't come home at night. She didn't have to cook dinner for him, talk to him, or care about his problems. She didn't have to have sex with him, and clearly she must have bored him, if he wanted the kind of stuff she had seen in the photographs of Veronica. She was thirty-nine, almost forty, not twenty-three, and her ass was never going to look like Veronica's again no matter how many Pilates classes she went to or even if she had an ass and boob lift like the people Gemma knew in Hollywood.

She had a new book to work on now that she had started at the ranch that summer. She had her kids to take care of, and a life to live alone, to try it on for size. It wasn't entirely a bad thing, it was different, and some things would still be the same. But it would be a life without Peter. She needed to clear out some of the past. After she got back to the house after dropping Billy off at soccer, she made the first call. Another mother would be driving him home. She called a secondhand furniture store and arranged to have them pick up all the furniture in their bedroom. They had spent a fortune on it, but she didn't care. It was part of the ugliness he had left her with, and she didn't want it anymore. She was getting rid of all of it. She was going to fill the room with beautiful new things. It was her bedroom now, not theirs. Maybe after she did, she would feel new too.

*   *   *

When Juliette got home on Labor Day weekend, she looked alive and well, and her eyes were bright again. She'd cut her hair just a bit shorter and it didn't look quite so wild. She was smoking French cigarettes again, and Kate noticed that her English had suffered a little, but she looked peaceful, had gained a few pounds, and said she had seen a lot of old friends all over France. She had mostly spent time in Provence, and visited the Camargue, where she grew up.

She looked both sad and nervous when she told Kate about the decision she'd made, but she knew she had to tell her. Kate looked shocked when she did. Juliette had decided to move back to France. She realized that she belonged there. It was her culture, her language, her home. It was too hard for her to be at the ranch without Jimmy. He was really her only reason to be there, and now he was gone, and she felt it was time for her to leave too. She said it had been a hard decision, but she thought it was the right one. She would come back to visit, but now she wanted to live in France again. She had come to California for a summer and stayed for twenty-four years, because of him.

"You and Thad should move into my house, your father's house," she corrected herself, "when I go." Kate had told her about them as soon as she got back, so she heard it from her first, and Juliette approved.

"Your father thought about that sometimes too. He said he was the only right man for you, but it would never work because he was the foreman, and a man needs to be the boss."

"We both will be, we work well together." Kate smiled at her, surprised by her father's comment. "He's going to build a house on the land he bought from Gemma. They're starting to lay the foundation in a few weeks."

"Your house is too small for the two of you, and it will take time to build his house." Kate liked the idea of moving into Juliette's, but she didn't want to rush her, and was sad that she was going back to France. She wanted to settle in Provence, and could afford to buy a nice house with the money Kate's father had left her. And he had left her enough so she wouldn't have to work.

"When are you thinking of leaving?" Kate asked sadly.

"Not too quickly. I will need time to say goodbye to the Valley." She looked at Kate with her big green eyes. She was such a good woman. Kate was going to miss her. "I'm thinking by the end of the year. Maybe in December. I'm going skiing with my brother for Christmas. I'll go before that." Kate nodded and hugged her and told Thad about it that night.

"I'm not surprised," he said softly. She told him about Juliette's suggestion that they move into her father's house, and he liked the idea. Juliette was right, Kate's house was a tight fit for the two of them. And now that everyone knew about them, they had nothing to hide.

There was no question about it. Four months after her father's death, change was everywhere and had touched them all. It was comforting for Kate to know that her father would have approved of her relationship with Thad. It was like a final tender goodbye from wherever he was now.

Chapter 13

In the third week of September, Jerry called Gemma as she was leaving the gym. She had had a good workout, her body had never looked better, and she was settling into her L.A. routine. It had taken a while after coming back from the ranch, and she had promised Kate she'd come up for a weekend soon. She'd gone to a premiere and several parties, just to keep her face out there. She had gone alone.

"What is it this time?" she asked him as she got into her car. "Another teenage horror movie, or an infomercial, selling mattresses at two A.M.?" She was kidding, but not entirely. Nothing had turned up so far.

"Don't be such a bitch. I told you the Brits would come through. I just met with the producer/director. They're ready to cast. They start shooting in December, on location in Zimbabwe. They'll be there for two months, and then go back to London. The show will be based there. And they're looking for an American actress for the part I told you about. I gave them your name first. We just watched you in two episodes of your old show. And you know, I hate to admit it, but damn, you're good." He was laughing and she laughed too.

"Is that a compliment or an insult?"

"Both. They want to meet you. The casting director is here with him, a woman, and the executive producer. It's a big budget show. A period piece. You're good at those. What are you doing at four o'clock?"

"Today? Oh God, I look like shit. My hair is a mess."

"They don't care. For that historical stuff, they use wigs. And you'll be working in a field hospital in World War I. You're supposed to look a mess. Whatever you're doing, cancel it. This is the best project I've seen in years and you're perfect for it."

"Don't I get to see a script first?"

"No. You're broke, remember? You haven't worked in months. I've got nothing here. And it's this or the infomercials you were just so rude about, or vampire pictures." He was in great spirits. The meeting had gone well, and he liked giving her good news for a change. She was a fine actress who deserved to work.

"I would have to live in London?"

"Yes, during the season, when they're not on location. You can come back during the hiatus. It's the best shot I've got for you for now," he reminded her. "It's going to be a great show and a huge hit."

"Okay, okay. I'll be there. Remind me of the director's name, I'll google him."

"Rufus Blake-Harte. He's one of the best directors in England. Everything he touches turns to gold, and if you turn this down, I'm personally going to kill you, and you lose your whining rights for at least six months. Don't be a diva, Gemma. You need the work and they need you."

"I get it," she said grudgingly. She googled the director on her phone and recognized everything he'd done. It was all top material and hit shows, and he'd written some of it himself.

She went home and spent two hours trying to figure out what to wear. She knew it didn't matter, her work history did, but she still wanted to look her best. She finally decided on black jeans, a black Chanel jacket, six-inch heels, a black alligator bag, and diamond stud earrings. Rich but not too rich, successful but not showy, youthful but not too young. She wore her shining dark hair down, and was satisfied with how she looked when she left her house. It was a half-hour drive to Jerry's office, and she arrived on time, and was ushered into his inner sanctum immediately. He was sitting with a group of people who were laughing and looked relaxed. The men were wearing tweed jackets and jeans, and brown suede boots or shoes. They had a polished look to them that American producers didn't. Stylish and sophisticated without trying, longish hair, some beards, and one in particular seemed to be studying her carefully from the moment she walked in. They all stood up when she entered the room, and the woman with them, the casting director, was young and beautiful and looked like an actress herself. They were a handsome group.

Jerry introduced her to Rufus Blake-Harte, who had been studying her so intensely. He smiled at her as they shook hands. "I apologize for staring. You're even more beautiful than I expected, even more than you are on screen. Thank you for coming in on such short notice. We're only here for two days." They all sat down again, and he looked to be about fifty. He had a well-trimmed beard and was very tall and lean with dark hair like hers, and intense blue eyes. He had a pronounced British accent, and what she'd read on Google said he had gone to Oxford and had been a Shakespearean actor himself at the beginning of his career, but became a film director very quickly, and had worked in TV series for the past fifteen years.

He admired her tan and casually asked where she'd spent the summer. She could sense that he was trying to get her measure and who she was in real life. She explained that her family had a ranch in the Santa Ynez Valley, and he looked pleased.

"You ride?"

"I do. I grew up on horses."

"Wonderful. It's so much easier than needing a stunt double for every shot, with actresses who are terrified of horses." They talked about the show she'd been on and how much she'd loved it, the writing, and her fellow actors, and how sad she was that it had ended. It had been like home to her for ten years.

"Well, we'd like to find you a new home for the next ten," he said warmly, and everyone in the room laughed. He seemed like a very intelligent, sensible, easygoing person, with none of the posturing of Hollywood, and he asked her how she felt about being based in England while they'd be shooting.

"That's fine with me," she said simply. "I'm not married, I don't have kids, no boyfriend, no dog. I'm unencumbered." He looked ecstatic. Another actress they were considering had four young children and wanted it in her contract that she'd be flown home every weekend, or her children, husband, and nanny would be flown to England. It was a nightmare of logistics they knew would never work. And she wanted special accommodations if she got pregnant again. They'd been asking around about Gemma and liked what they'd heard. Good actress, reliable, shows up and does her job, a consummate professional in every way, easy to get along with, well liked by director, crew, and cast. That was worth its weight in gold to them, not to have to deal with histrionics on the set, or actresses who didn't know their lines, and there were plenty of them, male and female in the business, who required twenty or thirty takes before they got it right. Time was money, and although the director said he was a perfectionist and people hated that, no one wanted to retake a scene ad nauseam because the actor hadn't learned his or her lines. Everything he had heard about Gemma so far had convinced him she was right for the part.

"We'd like to give you a script, and see how you feel about it. We'll be shooting in Africa for the first two months. Christmas, I'm afraid. You'd get to spend it with me and the cast, although we'll have a break in there somewhere." She looked unfazed by any of it. She hadn't gone home for Christmas in years, and usually tried to go away with friends. And Africa would be interesting. She'd never been there.

"I'll admit I'm not crazy about snakes, but I don't mind being on location over Christmas."

"I will personally protect you from them. We'll be in a very civilized, sophisticated, high-end safari camp. Most of it is for several episodes later in the season, and some for the first show, but we thought we'd get it out of the way right off the bat, and stay in England after that, with a few scenes in Paris during the war. Your character has an affair with a French army officer in the First World War, and she goes to meet his family at their chateau. He gets killed shortly after so that takes care of that." He smiled at her, and Gemma liked him. He seemed warm, personable, unpretentious, and human, and she liked the idea of working with him, and loved the concept of the show. "Your part is the second lead role. Your co-star is a very hot young British actress right now. She's twenty-eight, brand new, and a joy to work with. And from everything I understand, so are you. We need a British actress in the lead role to keep the folks at home happy on British TV, but as it will be seen worldwide, we want an American, a real one, in the second lead. You'd be the only American in the cast. The rest are all British. And we intend to do a maximum of publicity for the show. We want it to be the number one show in England a year from now. And with you on board, I feel sure we can do it." He smiled at her, and one of the other men handed her a script. "If you have time to take a look at it tonight, I'm sorry to press you, but I'd love to hear from you by tomorrow. There's no point chasing a flock of others if we can have you. You really are our top choice," he said, and Gemma glowed.

The meeting lasted for two hours and she was floating on air when she left. She went straight home, took off her shoes and jacket, and sat down to read the script. She called Jerry at nine o'clock that night. He was on the freeway on the way to a party and put her on speaker.

"Sign me up. I want it. I don't care if I have to sleep with the snakes in Africa, it's the best show I've ever read and the part is perfect for me."

"They think so too. The director is obsessed with you." He was smiling. "I'll give them a call right now. They'll be thrilled. You're okay about being stuck in England?"

"I'd be willing to be stuck at the North Pole to play that part."

"And you don't mind having a co-star this time?"

"I can live with it. It looks like a beefy part for me."

"They say it is. They want both characters to be equally strong. I'll call them. Talk to you tomorrow, and, Gemma, congratulations! I'm happy to see you back on top again." In reality, it hadn't taken long, only three months, but it had felt like centuries, thinking that her career was going to tank. But it hadn't. It was on the upswing again.

Three dozen roses and a magnum of champagne appeared at her house the next morning, and Jerry had the contract in his hands at noon. He was having it checked by his legal department, and she'd have to have it seen by her lawyer too, and add any special conditions she wanted. But Jerry knew that Gemma was usually reasonable, and didn't ask for the absurd stipulations and perks that some actresses did. He had told the producers that too.

Rufus called her himself that afternoon. "I can't begin to tell you how happy you made us, and me personally. I've loved watching you on your old show for years. I think this is going to be a very exciting shift in your career, more dramatic, historically based, we want to give it real substance, and keep it on the air for as long as we can. I don't quit when we're on top," he reassured her.

"I'm really excited," she said, and sounded like it. "When do we start shooting?"

"We're going to need you in Zimbabwe around December fifteenth, or thereabouts. Right in time for Christmas. But I meant what I said, we're going to make it as pleasant as possible for the cast, and make it a very special experience."

"I can't think of anything better," she said. She was floating.

"See you in Africa then."

She looked over the contract that afternoon, after Jerry cleared it. She added a few minor things, and sent it to her lawyer. They emailed it to Rufus two days later with her signature. He countersigned it, and by the end of the week, the deal was signed, sealed, and delivered. She called Kate as soon as it was.

"I have a job!" she screamed into the phone and told her all about it. "The show is based in England, so I'll be in London eight or nine months a year, but I can come home for three months in the summer, and you can come and visit me." Kate was thrilled for her, though sorry to hear she would be so far away, but three months in the summer would be wonderful. And Kate promised to try to come over, although she hadn't been away in years.

As soon as Gemma hung up, her phone rang again. It was her tenant from the summer. He had decided to make an offer on her house. It was raining blessings on her. She had already decided on a price, based on comparables in her neighborhood, and had communicated it to him. He knocked ten thousand dollars off the price on principle, and she accepted the offer. He said he'd have the written offer to her by the next day, and he did. He wanted a sixty-day closing and expected her to balk at it, but it was perfect for her since she was leaving for Africa in mid-December and could empty the house before. She told him she was planning to put all her furniture and art in storage. He called her back two hours later. For another two hundred thousand dollars, he wanted most of her furniture, which was a fair price for it and close to what she'd paid. She'd only have to store what he didn't take, her art and some personal effects. She was planning to sell some of her clothes, the ones she knew she'd never wear again. She was trimming down her life in every way.

She texted Kate about the house, and called Caroline, who was standing in the totally bare room that had previously been their bedroom. She had gotten rid of everything and was starting fresh. She was planning to go to the Galleria in the city, and redecorate her bedroom exactly as she wanted it, without a hint of Peter in it, or Veronica Ashton. She couldn't wait to start, and planned to sleep in the guest room in the meantime, and then replace that bed too.

"That's not a good sign," Morgan whispered to her brother when they saw it. "She's getting rid of everything that reminds her of Dad." She had already told them that they had decided to extend their time-out until the end of the year. But at least they hadn't filed for divorce yet. There was still hope they might get back together, but they were worried about the empty bedroom. Morgan was feeling stressed about it, and Billy didn't like it either. Now that they were home from the ranch, their parents' separation seemed all too real to them. Their mother tried to reassure them without lying to them. She didn't want to make promises she couldn't keep, and the future of their parents' marriage was uncertain.

Later that night, Caroline told Gemma about her new bedroom, she thought it was a great idea, and Gemma told her all about the new show she was going to be on. She made Caroline promise to come over and visit and bring the kids during a school vacation.

"We'll come in February, for ski week," she promised. So they both had something to look forward to, and Gemma was very happy with the money they were going to pay her for her co-star role. The money from the house sale was better than she'd hoped for, without a realtor's commission to pay. She was on top again, and even better than before. Losing the show had been a powerful wake-up call to her, and had taught her a lesson. She was never again going to let her finances slide out of control, with nothing tucked away. She was just lucky that she'd had part of the ranch to sell, and a house. And her salary on the new show was higher than the old one. She was on top of the world.

They both got an email from Kate a week later. With Gemma leaving the country in December, she wanted to be sure that they would all come home for Thanksgiving on the ranch. It was going to be their first one without their father. But ironically, now they would have their mother with them for the first time, which was not lost on any of them. He had exited, and she had entered. It was a constantly shifting scene. Juliette was going back to France in December, and Kate wanted her with them on Thanksgiving too.

"Your family seems to be on the move these days," Thad said when she told him about it. He was working on the plans for his house, their house, and Kate was going to freshen up her father's house and redo some things before they moved in. Everyone had a project and was busy as life continued to happen, and people came and went.

"It's kind of like a TV series," he commented, and Kate laughed.

"Yes, it is. Especially with my family." Caroline didn't know if she wanted to get divorced, Gemma was leaving for Africa and moving to London after that, and Juliette was going home to France.

"I'm glad you're not going anywhere," Thad said, as he wrapped his powerful arms around her in bed that night. At least the ranch was a constant they could all count on, even now that their father was no longer there. But his legacy lived on in each of them.

Chapter 14

Thanksgiving at the ranch was a joyous affair, far more than any of them had expected. It was the first time their father wasn't there, which they knew would be hard. But it was also the first time that all the girls had been together for the holiday in a long time. Gemma and Caroline had assiduously avoided holidays at the ranch for years, and this year, they were all there, and Caroline had brought her children. Peter was going to have them for a week over Christmas, so he had let her have them for all of Thanksgiving. He was going home to his parents' in New York.

Scarlett and Roberto were there, which was the most dramatic change of all. Not in their wildest imagination could they have thought a year before that on this Thanksgiving their father would no longer be there and the mother he had claimed was dead for nearly all of his daughters' lives would be with them instead. She added a happy presence and was thrilled to share the holiday with her daughters and grandchildren. Scarlett had brought all of the desserts, and kept looking at her daughters in wonder, as though unable to believe she was really there. Roberto was a welcome addition to the group, and male company for Thad in a heavily female-dominated environment. It was Juliette's final gathering with the family before she left for France on Sunday. Her bags were packed, and she was sad to leave, but excited about going back to France.

Kate made a toast to their father at the beginning of the meal, that without him they wouldn't be there and none of this would be happening. They were enjoying the home he had provided them, and the family, and she warmly welcomed Scarlett, who had turned out to be the best gift of the year. She acknowledged Juliette and how much they would miss her as the woman who had stayed for the longest summer in history, and they all laughed. She wished Gemma well on her exciting new journey and adventures and reminded her to Skype and FaceTime whenever she could. They were going to miss her so much too. They drank to all of it, and the champagne poured liberally through lunch. And everyone said that the pies Scarlett had brought were delicious. They were everyone's favorites, pumpkin, apple, pecan, and mince. That way there were no hard decisions to make. Everyone had a slice of each with whipped cream or homemade vanilla ice cream, provided by the cook Kate had hired to make their Thanksgiving meal.

"This is the best Thanksgiving I've ever had," Thad whispered to Kate, sitting next to her. He took on the role of host graciously, and Gemma smiled as she watched them. They made a handsome couple and looked happy. They were planning some improvements to the ranch that their father wouldn't have liked or approved of, but that Thad and Kate thought were necessary. The next generation was in control now, and Juliette agreed that it could never have happened while he was alive. He never would have let anyone run it or make changes, except himself.

Caroline was planning a trip with Morgan and Billy, to visit Gemma in London, and they promised Juliette they would come to France on their next trip. But she was coming back to the Valley in May anyway, for the unveiling of a memorial monument to Jimmy for all to see at the center of the ranch. They were putting it up on the anniversary of his death, and Juliette had promised to be there. She said she'd be starving for some good barbecue by then, and everyone laughed, but she seemed happy to be going home. She was ready, and the ranch no longer seemed like her home without him. His absence was as powerful as his presence had been, and Kate felt it too.

"I used to hate holidays as a kid," Thad admitted to Kate. "They were so bad in some of the foster homes I was in. People just took in foster kids to work them like slaves. A few of them were nice but not many. They took us for the money the state paid them. I never had a real Thanksgiving or Christmas or a birthday." But that had changed now, and he finally had the family he had dreamed of all his life, with Kate, not as the foreman, but as her partner in life. They had so many good things in store for them. Gemma was trying to convince them to come to London too, but they said they were too busy on the ranch to go that far and stay away for long. Gemma wasn't going to give up easily, and intended to harass them until they did. She was going to be back in time for their father's monument installation too. They agreed to delay it a few weeks until the end of May, so she could be there during her summer break.

* * *

Everyone was so full they could hardly leave the table at the end of the meal, and the weekend went by too quickly. It had seemed sad to Morgan and Billy at first not to have their father there. But Thad and their aunts kept them so busy that by the day after Thanksgiving they were in good spirits and having fun. Peter had called from New York, and had finally admitted to his parents that he and Caroline were separated. He told them that he was entirely to blame and didn't go into detail. He called Caroline and the children on Thanksgiving, and they talked to their grandparents.

They left on Sunday morning to go back to San Francisco. Gemma left shortly after, to go back to L.A. and finish packing. The movers were coming that week to remove the furniture she was keeping and put it in storage with her art, and she was leaving for Zimbabwe in two weeks to start work.

That afternoon, Juliette left to catch her flight to L.A. and then Paris. It was a deeply emotional moment when she left the ranch, as she and Kate clung to each other with tears running down their faces.

"Take care of yourself," Kate said through her tears, "and come back if you're not happy there. We love you. You always have a home here."

"And you too. Come to visit me." She patted Kate's face as the two women cried. "Be happy, Kate. Your father didn't understand many things and he was a stubborn man, but he loved you, and he wanted all of you to be happy. I don't think he ever knew what he did to you, telling you that your mother was dead." Kate nodded. She thought that too, and wasn't as angry as her sisters about it. "Be happy with Thad. There is nothing more wonderful than the love of a good man." She smiled through her own tears then. "I have no regrets with Jimmy. It was everything we wanted and needed. He was my world," she said softly, "and my sun and moon. I wish that for you and Thad." In a way she had been Kate's role model for how to love a man, with gentleness and loyalty and pride, and forgiveness for his failings. They had been good for each other, and she hoped that she and Thad would be too.

Kate stood and waved as the car drove away with Juliette, with Thad standing next to her with an arm around her shoulders. Kate hoped that she would be happy now, even without Jimmy, and that his love would carry her into the future, with the years they had shared.

"I'm going to miss her so much," Kate said, still crying when the car was gone. Her quiet presence had been a blessing to all of them, not only to her father. He had been a lucky man to have her.

"I'm here for you, Kate," Thad said gently. And they walked slowly back to Kate's house. They were moving into her father's house in a few weeks, after they gave it a fresh coat of paint. They would be officially living together then, until they moved into his house in a year, when it was ready. They had much to look forward to. And Juliette's warmth and daily presence on the ranch would be long remembered.

Gemma's arrival at Harare international airport in Zimbabwe, after a thirty-six hour trip from L.A., with stops in London and Johannesburg and a switch of airlines, was more rigorous than expected. It took them an additional hour to find one of her bags, which had mysteriously gone in with the freight. The customs officials were astounded by how many suitcases she had brought and she had to explain that she was not selling clothes, she was planning to wear them. Finally, in frustration, she told them she was a movie star, and luckily they believed her. They were fascinated by her. She had an armload of bangle bracelets on, and they wanted to know also if she was a jeweler. She knew that someone from the crew was coming to meet her, to take her to another flight which would bring her closer to their high-end camp where they would be shooting among elephants and other animals in a national park.

She came through customs feeling a little deflated and disoriented. The trip had been endless, and she suddenly realized that she was on the other side of the globe in a totally unfamiliar world. There were people in elaborate costumes, riotous colors, exotic sights and smells, friendly looking locals, and African dialects being spoken around her. She was fascinated by all of it and felt a little lost too. She looked around to find someone holding a sign with her name, not sure whether to laugh or cry or scream when a man holding a monkey smiled at her, and the monkey leaned out and patted her face.

"He friendly, ma'am," the owner said, and she whispered to herself with a grin, "Toto, I have a feeling we're not in Kansas anymore." Far from it, as three porters struggled with the eleven suitcases she'd brought. She wasn't sure what the dress code would be at night or when they weren't working, so she brought everything she could think of, including an entire suitcase full of PowerBars, bug-bite medicine, and insect repellent. She glanced around and saw Rufus, the director, leaning against a post, smiling at her, looking relaxed, as though meeting her at the airport with her mountain of bags was the most normal thing in the world.

"You came to meet me?" She was deeply touched. No director had

ever met her at an airport before, but she'd never filmed on location
in Africa before either.

"It was on my way to the supermarket to pick up a loaf of bread,
so I thought I'd swing by." He grinned at her. He was even taller than
she remembered, and his beard was neatly trimmed. He was wearing
a safari jacket, khaki pants, and heavy work boots, and had a jaunty
look about him, totally at ease in the exotic setting. "How was your
trip? Other than ridiculously long? It took me forty-two hours to get
here when I came, with delayed flights."

"I made it in thirty-six." She smiled at him. "Thank you for meeting me." She looked at him gratefully. It was nice to see a familiar
face, even if she didn't know him well.

"Be careful of the monkeys, by the way. Some of them bite, or they
grab your wallet and run up a tree. The perils of Africa."

"Better than snakes," she muttered, as he looked at her bags and
explained to the porters that there was a truck outside to take them
to a chartered plane waiting at another part of the airport. He must
have tipped them well because they all bowed and thanked him and
gave him a thumbs-up, and headed outside to load her bags into an
old truck waiting for them with a driver. Gemma had followed Rufus
out of the airport.

"I'm afraid you've got another short flight ahead of you. This one
will be easier, to Victoria Falls. From there, it's about an hour's drive
to the main camp. It's very comfortable and quite civilized. It was a
Swiss colony at one time, so there are even chalets. But we've put
everyone in the main building. We'll drive out from there to film with
the animals. But we wanted everyone in the most agreeable accommodations we could get." He helped her into the truck, and they
headed toward a remote part of the airport, and drove onto the tar-

mac, where an old cargo plane refitted for charter was waiting, and the pilot waved and smiled in greeting when he saw them. "This won't take long," Rufus assured her. The pilot loaded her bags and she saw sandwiches and biscuits set out for them and cold mineral water once they stepped into the plane. The seats were large, they had chartered the plane for the duration of their shoot to ferry the crew and equipment back and forth to Harare.

Rufus took a seat next to her, and a few minutes later they took off, and were in the air very quickly, cleared by the tower. The pilot said it would take them just under an hour. It was her fourth flight of the trip, and Rufus chatted with her as they flew toward the northwest corner of Zimbabwe, their ultimate goal being Hwange National Park. Rufus explained to her that there was an "Intensive Protection Zone" in Sinamatella, about seventy miles from their camp, where they would be shooting too. And the park had one of the largest elephant populations in the world.

"This is definitely premium service, the director picking me up at the airport, and flying to the camp with me," Gemma said with a grateful smile. She was tired, but excited to be there, and she had slept on the last flight.

"I told you we were desperate to have you."

"I get the feeling you've been to Africa before," she said, from his descriptions of the area.

"I've shot a few films here. And I spent some years in Africa as a boy. My father was a career diplomat. We got some of the worst posts imaginable until they finally took mercy on him and sent him to Rome and Barcelona, and I had a ball. But I enjoyed the time in Africa too, more than my mother did. I think she bribed the Foreign Office to send us back to Europe." He smiled and she laughed. "It's useful knowing some of the customs and the history, though. I think you'll enjoy shooting here. We try to make it as easy as possible," he said, "and Victoria Falls is spectacular, the largest natural falls in the world." He was already making it easy for her, meeting her, and accompanying her on the last leg of the trip in the comfortable chartered plane.

"I don't know how I got so lucky. My agent was sending me out for teenage vampire movies when my show closed." He laughed, and she ate one of the cookies and offered him some.

She was curious what the camp would be like, and the rest of the cast. She had recognized some of the names as well-known British actors, particularly one woman and two men. It was an all-star cast. Their young star was new, but the others were well seasoned and had been in many successful shows and movies. It was the hallmark of his work. He used big name actors in his series, including her.

They flew for a while without speaking, and then he asked her where she grew up.

"In the Santa Ynez Valley, on the ranch I mentioned. My father was a cowboy from Texas. He built it from nothing. I hated it growing up. I thought I'd been switched at birth, and was meant to be a princess somewhere. One of my sisters thought that too. She was sure that intellectual parents had lost her at the hospital, and she wound up in a hick town with no culture, and a bunch of rednecks. You have to have a strong identity and ambition not to get stuck there."

"I used to feel that way about England. Now I'm happy to be back. But it took a while to readjust. I thought I was Tarzan's son, meant to swing on trees, or the son of a rajah in India. I was certain that boring British parents and freezing winters were not in my genes. But apparently they are. The older I get, the more I enjoy my roots. There's something comforting about it." She smiled at him.

"I just discovered that. I spent the summer on our ranch for the first time in years, and Thanksgiving there with my sisters. I loved it. My father just died in May, and it's brought us closer together. I thought it would have the opposite effect, but it hasn't. I think he'd be pleased. He had to die to get us back there."

"It often works that way. I've inherited my grandparents' crumbling manor house in Sussex. My parents are gone now. I detested going there as a child. Now I kill to spend weekends there, and go shooting like my father, which I swore I'd never do. It's all so predictable and so British. Nothing ever changes there. I love that now. My children hate the same traditions and swear they'll sell the house the hour I die."

"How old are they?" She watched him carefully. He was fascinating to talk to.

"They're grown up, twenty-five and twenty-eight. I married when I was in diapers myself. Lovely girl, we grew up together. It seemed like a fine idea. It took us three years to come to hate each other. We divorced, she's been happily married to someone else for twenty years, with masses more children, married to another boy we grew up with. I never remarried, and have been happy ever since. I'm a bit of a renegade. I can manage the crumbling manor house, but not the lady of the manor that goes with it. So I run around the world, making movies and flying and chauffeuring glamorous actresses around. I can hardly wait to see what glorious costumes come out of those suitcases."

"Mostly blue jeans and insect repellent," she said, and he laughed.

"No toilet paper?" he asked, and she looked embarrassed. He had guessed.

"Just a few rolls. The customs man wanted to know if I was opening a store here."

"He probably wanted you to give him some."

"I thought so, but I didn't know if I'd need it. I'll give it to him on the way back." They chatted easily with each other, he seemed very relaxed and comfortable with her.

"Where do you live now?" he asked, curious about her.

"That's an interesting question. I'm homeless at the moment. I just sold my house in L.A., it's closing this week. And since we're based in London, I haven't bought anything to replace it yet. I can stay at a hotel or the ranch when I go back, though it's a long drive from L.A. I'll probably buy an apartment in Hollywood or Beverly Hills. The house was a big commitment. I loved it, but I think selling was the right thing."

"You can buy a flat in London, or rent one." She nodded. She hadn't figured that out yet, and was going to look around when they got to London in February. They had rented an apartment for her until they finished shooting for the first season in May, so she had time to decide what she wanted to do. "I have a flat in Notting Hill. It's a bit chaotic, like the Left Bank in Paris. I like that. I'm not so fond of stuffy neighborhoods. L.A. always looks a bit too grand to me when I get invited to people's homes. They look so perfect. I always want to mess them up a bit so they look lived in." She laughed. He was fun to talk to. "I think you'll enjoy the cast, by the way. They're a good mix of British types, a bit slutty, a bit naughty, some of the older actors take themselves quite seriously. We have a resident curmudgeon. And Natalie Jones, our star, is a really sweet girl, who loves everyone. She reminds me of my daughter, innocence itself. She works for a fashion magazine. My son is very serious. He's a biologist. I have no idea what he does. He's explained it to me a thousand times. It's all Chinese to me. He's an assistant professor at Cambridge. I can't imagine how I wound up with a boy that smart. Must be in his mother's genes, though she can't figure out what he does either. Half the time, she says he's a pharmacist, which drives him insane to have two such ignorant parents. He thinks I'm a terrible Bohemian. He's engaged to the daughter of an earl, and hides me whenever possible. His mother is a countess now, so she's considered respectable." He said it all with good humor, and had Gemma laughing for most of the short trip.

"You seem very respectable to me," Gemma said, smiling, as they each ate one of the sandwiches.

"I'm not at all respectable. That's only because you grew up on a ranch in America. By British standards, I'm a total outlaw. What about your mother? What was she like?"

"I was born in Texas, and she left when I was two, so we moved to California a year later. I never met her until this summer after my father died. He told us that she was dead, and we found out after he died that she wasn't. So we looked her up on the internet and found her. She's lovely actually. She lives with an Italian architect. So I didn't have a mother until I was forty-one."

"That must have been awkward, when you met her." He frowned sympathetically, thinking about it, and glanced at her.

"It wasn't really. Emotional, but not awkward. She's a very sweet woman. She ran off with another man and my father never forgave her, so he told us she was dead, and we were young enough to believe him. My younger sister was a baby, and my older sister and I were two and three when she left. And when I was three, we moved away. We were all babies really."

"Your father just took you and moved to California? Brave man."

"Yes, and complicated."

"Of course, who isn't?" He had a point. "That's what's so interesting about what you and I do. I direct actors to express emotion and pull it out of their souls, and imagine it. You try to connect with the material at an emotional level, and apply something you've experienced to what you're doing and channel it for the viewer. It's magic really." It was an intriguing way to describe it. "What you do is a pantomime of emotion really for people who want to feel and don't know how to, or don't know what they should be feeling, so you show them, and I tell you how to show them. It all fits together rather nicely. Like Kabuki.

"I lived in Japan for a year too. Fascinating people, gorgeous place. A little too foreign for me, though. And very repressed. It's important there *not* to show emotion. That doesn't work for me. Of course the British would like to be like that too. They're very proud of how cold they are, but they aren't really. I have them crying like babies with our shows," he said, looking pleased. She could hardly wait to work with him and see what it was like. "My son is very British. My daughter is more like me. She's an artist, when she's not working at the magazine. I thought she'd want to become an actress, but she didn't."

"My father loved that I'm an actress."

"Of course, you can express everything he couldn't." She had never thought of it that way and wondered if it was true.

As they approached Victoria Falls, which he pointed out to her from the air, he told her some things about the scenes they would be shooting, and the place where they were staying, and by the time they had exchanged histories, and eaten the sandwiches, they landed at a small airport, where a Land Rover was waiting for them, and a truck for her bags and the supplies he had picked up in Harare that morning. They were on their way to the camp twenty minutes later, once everything was loaded. Rufus drove her himself in the Land Rover, at first on tar roads, and then on gravel as they bumped along.

It took them just under an hour to reach the camp, where natives in starched white uniforms waited to serve the guests, sitting on wide porches with tables and chairs, drinking and eating. There were several buildings where the rooms were, and a cluster of tents. It looked more like a luxury hotel than a camp, which Gemma was relieved to see, and there was a fleet of vehicles they used to drive out among the animals. It was safari at its cleanest, safest, and most pristine. Many tourists preferred more rugged conditions in remoter areas, Rufus commented, but he knew his cast wouldn't.

"Not too bad, eh?" He smiled at her as he turned off the engine and half a dozen men in white uniforms ran toward them to assist them from the car. Her bags were already disappearing into the main building on the heads of porters.

"Thank you so much for driving me," she said warmly, "and coming to Harare."

"I wanted to get to know you a bit better before we start working together. You're a very interesting woman," he said appreciatively. And she thought he was fascinating with his boyhood and his background, his parents and his children, and the places he had lived, and all that he understood about their trade, and the artistry behind it. "Dinner with the cast at eight tonight. Jeans, long-sleeve shirt, boots, and insect repellent. No toilet paper needed," he instructed her and she laughed.

"I'll leave it in my room."

He gave directions to the head man of the fleet of porters and runners, and then with a wave he disappeared into the hotel. The manager of the camp appeared to walk her to her room, up a flight of stairs. When they walked in, she saw an enormous room, with a huge fan overhead circling lazily. Two women in bare feet and uniforms were already starting to unpack her bags. She peeked into the bathroom and it had a toilet, a sink, and a tub, and she was relieved. She suspected that their accommodations cost a fortune, but she was glad they weren't primitive. If she was going to shoot on location in Africa, this was the way to do it. It was not a real safari, but Rufus had promised that the animals they'd see would be extraordinary.

The two women unpacked her bags, put everything away neatly, and ran a tub for her. They brought her a cup of tea, watercress and cucumber sandwiches, and English biscuits on a silver tray. She wasn't hungry but ate one of the delicious sandwiches anyway, and lay down on the bed to relax for a while, after the long trip. She fell asleep, and a discreet knocking at her door woke her in time to bathe and dress for dinner.

When she came downstairs, she wore exactly what Rufus had suggested. There were about twenty-five or thirty people milling around, a combination of cast and crew. Rufus stepped forward to introduce her to everyone and there were some very famous British actors in the group, whom she recognized immediately. Her co-star was exactly what he had said, a really sweet, warm, naïve girl, who looked awestruck when she saw Gemma and said she had watched her show with her mother every week.

Rufus's production company had taken over the whole hotel. Gemma was seated at a table with the cast, next to Rufus. There were about a dozen of them. The other fifteen or so were crew and sat together. These initial days were a kind of orientation for all of them, to meet and get to know each other. Scripts were handed out at the end of dinner to begin studying. Gemma couldn't wait to get to her room and read it. And at the end of dinner, the entire cast bid each other a very formal good night and disappeared. They weren't a family yet, as they had been on her other show. But with Rufus in charge, pulling their emotions straight out of their souls, she was sure they would be soon. In the meantime, she had had a very good day, getting to know him. She could hardly wait for their African adventure to start. Being there was the most exotic experience of her life. And meeting Rufus and working with him was a privilege. He felt the same way about her.

Chapter 15

Caroline planned to spend Christmas with her children, as she always did. The difference this year was that Peter wouldn't be with them. They had tried to work out an equitable arrangement, and Caroline had been generous with him. Their school vacation had started on the nineteenth, they were spending the first week with her, and Christmas Eve, and Peter was picking them up on the morning of Christmas Day, taking them skiing after he celebrated Christmas with them. He was to return them to their mother on New Year's Eve.

Caroline had thought about taking them somewhere before Christmas, but they wanted to stay home and see their friends, and they were going skiing in Squaw Valley with Peter, so it seemed superfluous to make them go away with her. The ranch was bleak and depressing that time of year, so she didn't press them to go there either. And so far, they were weathering the new arrangements surprisingly well. She and Peter alternated weekends, when it worked for the kids. And during the week, he could take them out to dinner or they could spend the night with him whenever they wanted to. They both tried to make it as easy as possible for the kids. They were worried, but not panicked yet. And their grades hadn't slipped. Billy asked his mother frequently how things were going with Dad. Nothing much had changed since September.

Caroline had decided to stay home herself from Christmas Day until they returned to her six days later. She didn't mind being at home at Christmas, and she could catch up on projects in the house, and do some writing. She had a manuscript for one of her young adult books that she wanted to finish. She had started it that summer, at the ranch, and hadn't turned it in yet. It was about a thirteen-year-old orphan and the family who adopts her, and how she changes them.

Peter had been reliable about seeing the children every other weekend, but Billy's sports and extra classes and Morgan's plans with friends made it complicated, so Caroline had been generous about the holidays, to make up for any time he'd missed. She didn't want to use their children to penalize him, which he appreciated.

She and Peter hadn't had lunch or dinner together again. She didn't want to, and he could sense that, so she didn't encourage it, and he didn't push. He was pleasant when they spoke and so was she, but she still felt cautious about spending time with him. He didn't want to intrude on her so he waited for the kids in the car when he picked them up. He had literally not set foot in their house since June. Caroline felt like it was her home now, after he had violated it, so she didn't invite him in. And she saw their friends on her own. Word had gotten out after the summer that they were separated. It worried her that with separate social lives, they seemed to be drifting further apart, rather than back together. Caroline had

promised herself that she was going to broach the subject with him
again after New Year's. By December, she had made her decision
about a divorce, but didn't want to tell him before Christmas and
ruin the holidays for him or the children. It had been six months
since she'd discovered his affair. She wasn't angry anymore, or devastated, but she didn't feel any closer to him either. She was convinced now that the damage was irreparable.

Caroline made their traditional turkey dinner on Christmas Eve
and she, Morgan, and Billy ate in the dining room, on their best
china, with good crystal and silver, with a tablecloth and a center-
piece of poinsettias. She used the same decorations they always did.
They put up a tree together a week before Christmas, and made an
outing of buying it. She put Christmas carols on their stereo system
while they put the ornaments on the tree. Everything was the same,
except it was all different. Without Peter, there was a hollow feeling
to it, like a bell with no ringer.

He had told her that he wasn't decorating for Christmas, or getting a tree. His apartment was too small, and they were leaving for
Tahoe on the afternoon of Christmas, so there was no point buying a
miniature tree, since they were celebrating it with their mother on
Christmas Eve. And the kids said they were fine with it.

They exchanged presents under the tree after dinner, and Billy
screamed when he saw the new version of PlayStation from his
mother, and the games to go with it. He had wanted a video camera
desperately, which she had gotten him, and an iPad because his had
been stolen at soccer practice. She'd bought him a new ski jacket to
wear when he went away with his father. He had outgrown everything from the year before. And Peter had promised him new skis
and boots and a "cool" helmet. Morgan was always easier because

she wanted clothes. She had just turned sixteen and had given her mother a list of purses, shoes, skirts, sweaters, and a million other small things, and makeup, and she needed a new laptop, and Caroline got her the latest one. Peter was getting her the new cellphone she wanted, and new ski equipment too. So they had Christmas covered. Caroline had decided not to buy Peter a gift, and then two days before Christmas she felt guilty when she saw a sweater she knew he'd love. It was a black cashmere turtleneck he could wear skiing or on weekends. She bought it for him and wrapped it, and put it under the tree. Morgan noticed it immediately.

"You bought Dad a present?" She looked pleased and took it as a good sign.

"Yeah, I did." She felt stupid doing it, and didn't want to mislead him into thinking she felt differently. She didn't. But Christmas was a special time, and she felt mean not including him in the goodwill of Christmas.

"That was nice of you, Mom." Caroline didn't expect a present from him, and didn't want one.

After they opened their gifts, they went to midnight mass at the same church they always went to. They sang Christmas carols, and then went home. She made a fire the way Peter used to, and was surprised by how many things she was able to do without him. She was managing nicely on her own.

Eventually she sent the kids to bed since they were getting up early. They were half asleep when she went to kiss them good night, and they thanked her for a nice Christmas. She kissed them, and left the room, and went to sit in front of the fire, thinking of the past year.

It had been a year of difficult changes, losing her father, discovering that their mother was alive and he had lied to them, all hell breaking loose with Peter and their marriage falling apart. At first, she had felt like only half a person, but she was starting to feel whole again. She was lonely at times, and sometimes she missed him and the good times they'd had, but she had discovered she could function without him. She felt ready to face a divorce if she had to, and a new life on her own. After six months, it seemed like time to do something about a divorce. She had talked to Kate about it, and their mother. She just couldn't seem to forgive him, and had begun to believe she never would. He had broken what they had, that ephemeral bubble of love and trust that one could destroy so easily, and he had. She couldn't put Humpty Dumpty back together, and more important, she still didn't want to. She was comfortable the way things were now.

She sat thinking about it in the living room until the fire went out, and then she turned off the tree lights, and went to bed in her new yellow bedroom that was all floral chintzes, with a beautiful headboard on her new bed, and a canopy. The furniture was white, and it looked like a sunny summer day every time she walked through it, and it made her happy looking at it. It had been worth every penny she'd spent on it. She had bought it with royalties from her books. She had put in pale yellow carpeting, moved the bed to a different place, and put built-in drawers in the closet. She bought a beautiful antique desk to work on, and a big, comfortable chair covered in the floral fabric, and a fabulous new TV. It was fancier than any other room in the house, and the next best thing to an exorcism.

She woke the children at eight, wished them a Merry Christmas and kissed them, and went to make them breakfast while they dressed. Peter was due to pick them up at nine, and take them back to the city. He said they would leave for Squaw around lunchtime. He had it all organized.

She made them pancakes, which was their favorite breakfast, and they grumbled about having to get up so early. Billy was playing games on his new iPad when Peter rang the bell after waiting outside for ten minutes. She went to the door and he looked handsome in his ski clothes. He was dressed for their trip.

"Hi. Merry Christmas," she said, smiling at him. "They're ready, they're just slow eating breakfast. They're all packed." They had become experts at handing them off to each other, and were always punctual and respected each other's schedules, unlike many divorced parents who showed up early or late just to annoy each other, and wound up stressing the children even more than themselves. They were careful not to do that.

There was an awkward moment as he stood there, and then she remembered his present and invited him in. He hesitated for an instant and then followed her to the kitchen. She stopped in the living room, stooped down, picked up his gift from under the tree, and handed it to him. He looked surprised and touched and embarrassed as he took it from her. It felt strange to him being back in the house again.

"I don't have anything for you," he said guiltily.

"I didn't expect anything. It just looked like something you'd use." He opened it in front of her, and smiled broadly. He loved it, and he kissed her cheek to thank her, which embarrassed her. As he did, he looked over her shoulder and saw her bedroom through the open door. It looked like a summer garden, and he was startled.

"You changed our bedroom?" He said it like a child who discovered his parents had sold the house and didn't tell him.

"Yes, I did. It was looking tired," she said by way of excuse but didn't need one. He knew why she had done it. They both did. It cut through him like a knife, and reminded him of how deeply he had hurt her. She couldn't even live with their furniture after what he'd done.

"It looks very fancy." He could see into the room and that there was a canopied bed, pretty fabrics, and entirely different furniture. "Very girly," he commented, and she laughed. "What did you do with the old stuff? I liked it."

"I got rid of it. It's nice having a fresh look. I have a desk in my room now, so I can work and the kids don't have to be quiet in the living room. And I had built-ins put in the closet." She was proud of what she'd done. She'd used a closet expert, and consulted a mother from school who was a decorator. She had helped her get the fabrics at a discount. She'd done the rest herself.

"It's nice," he said, not knowing what else to say. It had dragged his transgression right up into their faces on Christmas morning. He wondered if she had just sent all their old furniture to the city dump. She had wanted to, and him along with it.

They went to find the children then, they had finished breakfast and were talking quietly, wondering what their parents were saying, and careful not to interrupt them.

"Mom got you a present," Billy announced when they walked in.

"I know, it's a gorgeous sweater. I can wear it in Tahoe." He smiled at her and she looked relaxed. It was easier having Peter in the house than she'd expected. It felt almost normal.

"That was nice of her," Billy added.

"Yes, it was," Peter agreed, and both children stood up. "We'd better be going." They went to get their backpacks, and he got their suitcases and carried them to the car. He noticed that their bedrooms hadn't changed, only their mother's.

They put on their jackets and she hugged them, and then Peter and Caroline looked at each other, and didn't know what to say.

"Merry Christmas," she said again, sounding cheerful.

"Thank you for the sweater," he said, and kissed her cheek again, and then they walked out to his car, got in and she waved as they drove away. Caroline stood in the doorway with a lump in her throat, smiling and trying not to cry. She closed the door behind her, and felt as if someone had sucked the air out of the house. The life went out of it the minute they left. It was going to be a lonely Christmas Day without the children, but this was what they had agreed to. She went out to the kitchen and rinsed their dishes, and then she went to her desk in her new bedroom, pulled out her manuscript, and sat down to work, trying to see the words through her tears. It wasn't a very merry Christmas. Suddenly all she could think of were the happy times she and Peter had shared for so many years, and for the first time in six months, she really missed him.

On Christmas Day, the cast and crew had been in Africa for ten days. They'd started shooting a week earlier, and agreed to take two days off for Christmas. They'd had a nice dinner the night before, and sang Christmas carols, and some of them had lovely voices. They admitted the next day that they'd had way too much to drink. Gemma tried to call Caroline and Kate on Skype, but couldn't get through. The connection was terrible where they were. There had been years when she hadn't bothered to call them on Christmas, but this year was different. There had been losses, and gains, and changes in their lives, and she felt a need to reach out to them and hear their voices. And she wanted to tell them about the wonders she'd seen since she'd been there. The animals were as amazing as Rufus had promised.

They all spent a lazy day, somewhat hung over, and that night, they all agreed to dress for dinner. They put on the best things they had brought, which in Gemma's case was a slinky black knit dress that molded her spectacular figure, and Jimmy Choo black suede high-heeled sandals, and chandelier earrings.

"Okay, you win," Rufus teased her, but he looked impressed. Her co-star had worn a silver dress that was just as sexy, but she looked a little like a Christmas angel on top of the Christmas tree. Gemma looked like a femme fatale. "How on earth have you escaped marriage?" he asked her, as they sat by the fireplace before dinner drinking the Cristal his crew had brought for the cast.

"I date unsuitable people," she said proudly, smiling at him. "Married, confused, relationship-phobic, addicted to substances or bad habits, or my favorite, in love with someone else."

"Do you do that on purpose?" he asked, and she laughed.

"Apparently. I've never placed a high value on marriage. And I never wanted kids unless it was a two-parent affair, and my partners have been even less suitable for that. I didn't enjoy growing up without a mother, and only a father. I didn't want to risk doing that to someone else. It doesn't work so well. There's no balance. I was lucky. I was my father's favorite, but that's not a pleasant role either, and it was hard on my sisters."

"How do you know you were his favorite?" He was fascinated by her. She had given him some incredible performances that week and memorable moments on camera, she could pull nearly any emotion out of her gut and tear your heart out. She had even had him in tears twice, which almost never happened. And the cast was new to her. He couldn't imagine what she would be capable of six months down the line. It couldn't all be manufactured emotion. She was an actress, not a magician. There was someone very interesting in there, and he wanted to get to know her better.

"He told us," she said about being her father's favorite. "He never made a secret of it. He told all three of us that I was his girl, his favorite."

"Did your sisters hate you for it?"

She shook her head. "No, we loved each other anyway. My younger sister hated him . . . or not hated, but didn't like him, and resented him. I thought he was domineering. I battled with him constantly. My older sister just did whatever he wanted, to please him and win his praise, and never got it."

"It's amazing what we do to our children. I always worry about the influence I've had on mine, and the mistakes I made."

"Being a parent seems very complicated to me. Being a human being is hard enough. My sister actually seems to be doing a good job with hers, though. It's a full-time job. I like my job better," she said, and he laughed. "It comes with better clothes. She's looked like a housewife since the day she had them, and she's a pretty woman. She just doesn't care how she looks anymore. She's about to get divorced."

"How she looks is her husband's fault. Women who feel loved are a lot more attractive than neglected wives. They stop caring about how they look. It always makes me sad for them." Gemma nodded. She agreed.

They had dinner with the others, and they all played cards and parlor games and charades after dinner, which got hilariously funny. They were a clever crowd, and knew how to amuse each other. Gemma started a poker game and several of the men joined them, Rufus among them. She won fifty pounds from him, with glee.

"Where did you learn to play poker like that?"

"The ranch hands on my father's ranch. Cowboys love to play poker. They taught me when I was about ten."

"You're a dangerous woman, Gemma Tucker." And an irresistible one. He was reminding himself to be careful, and hoped it wasn't too late. But one way and another, they managed to share a memorable Christmas, and Gemma didn't mind being in Africa at all. She loved it.

Kate and Thad had followed all of their usual traditions on the ranch, but it was different this year without her father, and Juliette. She hadn't had Christmas with her sisters in years. She thought Gemma would call on Skype, but she didn't. She called Scarlett and they had a brief but loving conversation. Roberto was cooking pheasant for their Christmas dinner.

And she managed to talk to Caroline on Christmas Day. She sounded lonely and sad without the kids, but she was a good sport about it and didn't complain. She said she had seen Peter when he came to pick them up. There was something odd in her voice. Something gentle, that hadn't been there for months. Kate didn't ask her about it. She didn't want to upset her and make her feel worse.

They had a long talk about forgiveness, and she tried to explain why she couldn't forgive Peter, and Kate understood. She'd had her own problems trying to forgive her father for hiding their mother for thirty-nine years.

She and Thad had dinner alone on Christmas Eve, and went to church, and then went back to her father's house, where they lived now. They had just moved in. It didn't feel like theirs yet, but there was more space. And it was familiar to her, since it was the house she had grown up in. She couldn't believe how small her bedroom had been, and she had shared it with Gemma. Caroline had an even smaller one down the hall. It felt like a major luxury to have the house to themselves. Thad was building a much bigger house on his new land.

They went to look at the progress on the house on Christmas Day, and spent the rest of the time tucked into their home, talking and making love. At the end of the day, he looked at Kate, naked in his arms, and told her how much he loved her.

"This was the best Christmas of my life," he said to her.

"Mine too." She smiled at him. He had given her something no one else had before. When she looked into his eyes, she knew she was loved.

Chapter 16

When Peter and the kids woke up in Tahoe on the morning of New Year's Eve, they looked out the window and saw that a blizzard had started. They could hear the dynamite being set off on the mountain to prevent avalanches. They were planning to go home that day, and Peter wondered if the roads were passable. And if so, he knew they wouldn't be for much longer. He had promised to have them home to their mother by dinnertime.

"We'd better go," he said, looking worried.

"Should we stay?" Morgan asked him. "Is it safe to go?"

"I think if we go now, we'll get through. I don't want to upset your mom and bring you home tomorrow. Get packed. I'll go pay the bill." He was back twenty minutes later and they were ready. The snow was swirling in the heavy winds outside. It was eight in the morning, and normally it would only take them four hours to get back to Marin.

They were about to get in their car when Morgan looked at him.

"We should get something for Mom at the gift shop." He was about to object to the delay, when Billy looked at him mournfully.

"You didn't buy her a Christmas present, Dad, and you've been wearing the sweater from her a lot."

"Okay, okay." They rushed to the gift shop, and looked around. There was nothing she'd want, and everything had the hotel logo on it. Suddenly Morgan picked up a yellow teddy bear, and handed it to her father. It had a name tag that said Buttercup. "She won't want that," he objected.

"It'll look nice in her bedroom," Morgan insisted. They paid for it and rushed back to the car. Their skis were on the rack on top of the car, their bags in the trunk. The kids had bought candy and snacks in the gift shop, and they were on the road ten minutes later, heading toward the highway. The snowplows were ahead of them, and the roads were still relatively clear. It took them an hour and a half in spite of that to get over the mountain, and the snow was still falling steadily. His GPS told him the roads were passable, so they kept going and didn't turn back. By noon, they had made little progress. Peter said nothing to them, and kept driving and focusing on the road, while Morgan manned the radio, and Billy watched a movie on his iPad with earphones. They were perfectly happy. At one o'clock they stopped for lunch. They were starving. They had been on the road for four and a half hours and were halfway there. He figured they'd make it by five if they were lucky.

They bought sandwiches at a truck stop, and took them back to the car and kept driving. The trip seemed to go on for hours. They finally got to Sacramento at five o'clock and hit heavy fog, and had to slow down to a snail's pace.

"Call your mom and tell her we'll be a little late, so she doesn't worry," he told Morgan. She took out her phone and it was dead.

"I forgot my charger in Tahoe," she said, and so had Billy, and his phone was dead too. Peter took his out of his pocket and handed it to Morgan, and she laughed. "Yours is dead too, Dad."

"Okay, we'll get there when we get there." It was nearly seven by the time the fog cleared, and they kept going and finally picked up speed.

Caroline was at the house in Marin, watching the Weather Channel. She could see that there was a blizzard in Tahoe. There had been a record snowfall, the roads were closed by then, and there had been an avalanche in Tahoe that morning. She'd been trying to call her children all day, and their phones were off, and so was Peter's. She could imagine them under an avalanche, or buried in a snowdrift somewhere, or freezing in a car that had run out of gas or crashed into something. Only the worst possible scenarios crossed her mind, all of them involving death from hypothermia, carbon monoxide, or suffocation.

At seven o'clock, she was panicked. It was New Year's Eve and Peter was never late. If he was going to be ten minutes late, he called her. She called the hotel and they had checked out at eight A.M. She wondered if a drunk had hit them and killed them all instantly, or they were in comas in a hospital somewhere and didn't have her number on them. She was watching the news with tears running down her cheeks when the doorbell rang at eight o'clock. She ran to the door, and there they were, tired, rumpled, hungry. Peter could hardly see from driving in snow all day. They stumbled into the house and she hugged them.

"Twelve hours! *Twelve* hours from Tahoe. We left at eight-thirty this morning," he said, exhausted. He was wearing the sweater from her. He loved it.

"That's only eleven and a half hours, Dad," Billy corrected him. It was eight P.M.

"I thought you were all dead," Caroline said, wiping the tears off her cheeks, and hugged Peter. "Thank you for bringing them home."

"We left early because I didn't want to disappoint you. I know you wanted them home tonight, and I didn't want you to be alone." He hugged her back, and Morgan handed her the bag from the gift shop, and she pulled out the yellow bear.

"I love it!" she said. "It'll look great in my bedroom."

"Told you, Dad," Morgan said smugly, and he rolled his eyes.

"The alternate was a pack of golf tees with the hotel logo on them."

"Are you starving?" They all nodded and left their parkas on the floor and went to their rooms to leave their backpacks. Peter left his parka in the front hall.

"I should be going," he said politely.

"You must be wiped out." And then she realized he probably had a date. "Do you have plans?"

"Yes, wiped out. No plans. I don't want to horn in on your dinner with the kids."

"Stay," she said and meant it. The blizzard in Tahoe had transformed into sheets of rain in Marin. They had been through every kind of bad weather in the last twelve hours, and he had brought them home to her so she wouldn't be alone. "Stay for dinner."

"You're sure you don't mind?"

"Not at all. It's New Year's Eve," she said, and poured him a glass of wine. He had earned it, and it would wear off by the time he left after dinner.

She added another place to the table she had set in the kitchen, and had dinner ready in half an hour. She had steaks, salad, baked potatoes, and she had a spare, she always did. They ate ravenously, and then the kids disappeared to their rooms to call their friends. Their suitcases were still in the front hall, and he carried them in for her, and came back to the living room. The rain had gotten worse. It looked dangerous.

"Why don't you stay till it lets up?"

"I don't think it's going to." He looked exhausted, and then she startled him by what she said next. It was almost ten o'clock.

"Why don't you spend the night?"

He looked confused for a minute as he thought about it. "Would that be too weird?"

"What difference does it make? We're still married, and you just drove twelve hours to bring my children home safely. You're so tired you'll fall asleep on the bridge."

"You don't mind?" He was stunned by the invitation. "I'll sleep in the guest room."

"Actually, you can't." She laughed. "I decided to redo that too, or at least get a new bed. They took the old one, and the new one isn't here yet. We can sleep in the same bed, it won't kill us."

"What will the kids think?"

"I don't know. You're tired, it's late, the weather's awful, you've been driving all day. Do we need their permission?" He smiled at her answer.

"No. Only yours," he said gently.

"You have it. I don't mind letting you sleep here. It's a big bed. I got the next size up." He agreed to stay then, and poured them each another glass of wine, since he didn't have to drive.

"Happy New Year, Caro. I can think of more glamorous ways to spend it, but I'd rather be here than anywhere else."

"Me too," she said simply.

He built a fire as he always did, and they sat in front of it talking quietly. The children were in their rooms, and when she checked, they were both asleep on their beds at eleven. She went back to the living room and they sat watching the fire and talking.

They waited until midnight and he wished her a happy new year and kissed her on the cheek. And then they turned out the lights and went to her bedroom. She opened the bed on both sides, and let him use the bathroom first, and he came out in boxers and T-shirt. Then she went in, and came out in an old warm nightgown, and climbed into her side of the bed, keeping her distance. He lay on his side looking stiff and awkward.

"It feels strange being back here," he admitted.

"Yeah," she agreed, turned off the light, and they lay there stiffly in silence, remembering better days.

He didn't know how it happened and she wasn't sure either, but he reached out silently to her in the dark, and pulled her into his arms, and kissed her, properly on the mouth, the way he had wanted to all night, and for months, instead of little pecks on the cheek. All his longing for her came at him in a rush, and engulfed them both. She thought she was over him, but she wasn't. He had unlocked something in her again and she wanted him desperately. They were ravenous for each other and found each other easily. He was inside her where he wanted to be in seconds and she couldn't get enough of him. They couldn't stop and didn't want to, and their lovemaking was so intense and so good it was almost painful. They couldn't stop or slow down until it was over, and when they stopped, she knew that she had forgiven him. There was no room for Veronica Ashton in their life anymore. She had lived with them long enough. She was gone.

"Are you sorry?" he whispered afterward, terrified she'd be furious and make him leave.

"No, I just love you," she said, and he pulled her tighter again, and lay glued to her, holding her.

"What'll we tell the kids?" he asked, worried.

"Just that. That we love each other." She was calm and happy and felt as though she had come home when he did.

"Do you want me to leave before they wake up?" He wanted to respect her boundaries, whatever they were. He didn't want to lose her again. It had been the worst six months of his life.

"No, I want to make love to you again," she whispered back, and he laughed in the dark.

"Thank God I drove home from Tahoe," he said, and she knew how true that was. She'd been planning to call the lawyer and file for divorce on Monday, and now she was falling in love with him all over again. If he hadn't driven home, she wouldn't have slept with him, and this would never have happened. There was no telling about timing, or destiny. No predicting the heartbreaks, or if hearts could be mended. All she knew was that she still loved him. She had her answer. It had taken her six months to figure it out. And now she had.

Chapter 17

Peter moved back in the weekend after New Year's. The children were ecstatic. Their parents explained it as simply as they could, that they hoped they had worked out their problems and wanted to stay married.

Peter knew that Caroline was giving him another chance, and he was determined not to blow it. His punishment and eternal reminder was that he hated the color of her new bedroom, but he didn't say a word about it. She loved it. It had been her first act of independence from him. And he found with time that she had changed. She wasn't as trusting or as quiet. She spoke her mind now, was more confident, and had her own ideas. She no longer apologized for their differences. She was proud of them.

She had called Kate to tell her as soon as he moved back in, and she was happy for her, if it was what she wanted.

"It is. But he's on probation, probably for the next forty years. I may give him a break for the last ten."

Kate laughed.

Caroline told Peter that she was taking the children to London to see Gemma in February during ski week, and if he cheated on her, she would divorce him immediately. He swore he would never cheat on her again. And she sent an email to Gemma that he was back.

Gemma was loving Africa and what they were shooting on location. She had emailed both of her sisters that the cast was fantastic, the smartest, most interesting, best actors she had ever worked with, and the director was amazing. They were going back to London the first week in February, and she was going to L.A. in March for a few days, and wanted to introduce the director to them. She wanted to invite him to the ranch for the weekend.

Caroline called Kate immediately. They had both gotten the same email.

"Do you think she's sleeping with him?" Kate asked her.

"I hope not. She always moves too fast, and if she screws it up, they'll throw her off the show."

"She's too smart for that," Kate reassured her.

They were both right. She wasn't going to jeopardize her career for a romance, or a night of great sex. She hadn't slept with Rufus, but four weeks after they had arrived in Africa, after working together intensely, he had told her he was in love with her. She was too. And she was refusing to sleep with him. She told him she wanted to move slowly and not do anything stupid that she'd regret. They were inseparable, and had had some remarkable experiences, following the animals, filming episodes for the show, going out at dawn together to revel in the magic of Africa. It had been unforgettable.

He had to go to L.A. in March for some business meetings, and wanted her to go with him, and she wanted him to meet her family.

She had never done that before either. Her lovers came and went without introductions, and her sisters read about them in the tabloids, not in emails from Gemma.

They picked the weekend that worked for Rufus, and Caroline promised to go to Santa Ynez with Peter and the children. Before that, Caroline was going to London for ski week in late February, when they were back from Zimbabwe.

"What if they hate me?" Rufus said to Gemma one night, while they sat on the porch of the hotel, long after everyone else had gone to bed. They had to be up in a few hours, and could hear the elephants trumpeting in the distance. It was the music of Africa which they had both come to love, and was the background sound to their late night conversations, where they talked about everything they cared about and hoped. He couldn't believe that she wouldn't sleep with him, and neither could she. She had never done that before, but she wanted it to be different with him, because she was different now.

"They're not going to hate you, they're going to love you," she said about her family. She wanted him to see the ranch because it was part of her history. And meet her sisters, and her mother.

He wanted her to move in with him in London, but she wanted to take her time about that too. She didn't want to spoil anything by moving too fast.

By the time they left Africa at the beginning of February, they were almost soldered to each other, and knew everything about each other. He could almost sense her instinctually, and he was the most sensitive director she'd ever worked with, and a huge talent, and he thought the same of her.

The cast didn't even seem to object to their close relationship, because they were so enjoyable to be around, and Rufus remained attentive to the entire cast. Their love for each other spread good feelings wherever they were.

When they got to London, she stayed at the apartment the production company had provided for her, and he stayed at his London pied-à-terre, and took her to see his "crumbling drafty" manor, as he called it, and she loved it, although she could see why his kids objected to it. It was in need of some serious attention, a lot of paint, and more heat. It was damp and cold and dreary.

They had dinners at Harry's Bar and danced at Annabel's when they weren't working, and on Valentine's Day he sent her three dozen red roses. He was totally besotted with her.

When Caroline came to London with Morgan and Billy, Gemma took them everywhere. She asked Rufus for two days off and he shot around her. She took them to the Tower of London, and the queen's stables, and Madame Tussauds, and all the corny tourist attractions they were dying to see and she wanted to see with them. And he let them come on the set to watch her filming when she came back to work. Caroline was struck again by how talented her sister was. She was a brilliant actress, and she thought Rufus was wonderful, and a great director. They were an extraordinary team.

When Caroline left, they had a Sunday off, and spent it together, walking in the park, they had tea at Claridge's, and went back to her apartment when it started to snow. They were going to L.A. in two weeks, and they were going to see Caroline again with Peter and the children, and Kate and Thad, and Scarlett and Roberto. Having met Caroline, and seeing how sweet and easygoing she was, Rufus was no longer nervous about the others.

"I'm the family bitch," Gemma said. "You don't need to worry about them." But she wasn't a bitch with him. Far from it, and she had never been happier in her life. She loved the show, and she loved him. She just wanted to be sure it wasn't an on-set romance that would be over in five minutes. She wanted this to be real and it appeared to be. When Caroline left London, they had known each other for more than two months and so far it seemed solid.

They talked about it that night with the snow falling. There were so many things they wanted to do together when they had time. He was forty-nine years old, and she was forty-two now. Even their ages seemed perfect.

Rufus looked at her then, and knew what he wanted was right. He smiled and said in a soft voice, "I'm not leaving. I want you so badly I can't stand it. I love you, make love with me," he said so enticingly that she smiled a Mata Hari smile and led him to her bed. He peeled her clothes away instantly, and she took off his, and they fell into bed like starving people, but for the first time in her life, she had waited, she was sure, and she knew that they loved each other. It wasn't a wild, crazy fling or a one-night stand with a guy who meant nothing to her. She had had too many of those. And afterward, they were both glad they'd waited, and did it again, and again, and lay in each other's arms until morning, savoring every minute of their first night together.

"Gemma, you have turned my whole life upside down," he said in an awestruck voice, unable to believe what had happened. He had wondered if it would all stop in Africa, or when they got back. But it hadn't. Their love for each other and attraction had just gotten stronger when they got home.

* * *

Rufus and Gemma flew from London to L.A. together in March. He went to his meetings, and Gemma went to see Jerry and thanked him again for getting her the part. Her house was gone so they stayed at the Peninsula for two nights, and then drove to the ranch in the car Rufus had rented. It was a big American SUV, which he loved.

Caroline and Peter were meeting them at the ranch with the children, and Kate was excited to see them. The sisters hadn't all been together since Thanksgiving, it had been four months. And they were all getting together again in May, for the memorial for their father on the one-year anniversary. It seemed like an enormous number of things had happened in the ten months their father had been gone. But the ranch was running smoothly, and Thad's new ideas were working out well. He was handling the whole breeding operation now, and they were both involved in the auctions.

When Rufus saw the ranch, he fell in love with it. He spent hours riding with Thad to get a feel for the size of the property. And Gemma rode with him for part of it. He got on well with Peter too, so the sisters left him to look at the livestock with the men, and the breeding operation.

The girls had a glass of wine at Gemma's house, where she and Rufus were staying, and Caroline looked at them both sheepishly.

"I have something to tell you. I feel stupid saying it."

"He's not cheating on you again?" Gemma almost leapt out of her seat as she said it, and Caroline shook her head.

"I went off birth control when Peter left. I figured I didn't need it, and took a break. He spent New Year's Eve with me, when we got back together. I didn't even think about it. . . . I'm two months pregnant. I'm going to be forty when I have this baby . . . and ninety when it goes to college."

"Oh my God." Gemma laughed at her. "You're a geriatric mother! That's what they call it when you're over forty."

"Oh shut up, you will be too, if you and Rufus decide to have a child. You're older than I am!"

"I don't want babies. And he has two kids already, and I take the pill like a good girl!" Gemma said and Kate smiled at the exchange.

"I think that's good news. It's like a renewal of everything and new life. What did Peter say?" Kate asked her.

"He was shocked. It didn't occur to him either. We haven't told the kids yet. I don't know how happy they'll be about it. Morgan will be seventeen when it's born, and Billy will be thirteen. That's embarrassing for them. But Peter is happy about it now."

"Are you? Never mind them," Kate reminded her.

"I think I am. It's like starting all over again, with nursing and diapers."

"I'm taking two pills tonight," Gemma said fervently.

"I haven't made up my mind yet," Kate said cautiously. "If we have a baby, I'd be forty-four when it's born. That's really old."

"Not if you want it," Caroline said kindly. "What does Thad say?"

"I think he'd like it, but he says he's fine either way. He's leaving it up to me."

"We could start a nursery for elderly mothers," Gemma said, laughing at the thought. "An old age home for unwed pregnant mothers. Well, you two are braver than I am." She hugged Caroline then, and the men arrived a little later. And the whole group went into town for dinner. Rufus was having the time of his life, exploring Santa Ynez and the ranch. He had never imagined his glamorous star on the ranch, riding horses, with cowboys, and a family he liked so much. They were varied and interesting, outspoken, and kind to each other.

He knew that Gemma was coming back for her father's memorial in May when they were on hiatus, and he promised to try and come with her.

And when they flew back to London, Rufus had a whole group of new friends, and understood Gemma better after meeting her family. They were unique and very special people.

A month after they'd been there, Kate called Caroline in a panic on a Tuesday morning. It reminded her of when she'd called to say their father had a heart attack. She sounded terrible.

"What's wrong? Did something happen to Thad?"

"No. I have to talk to you. We've had an offer. I got a call from a realtor in Santa Barbara. There's someone who breeds horses who wants to buy the ranch. They're willing to offer an obscene amount of money."

"How obscene?" Caroline asked her, instantly curious. Kate told her and she gasped. "That's way more than obscene." The buyer was Russian.

"I know. What do you want to do? They want a rapid answer. They're considering another property. But our seven thousand acres is bigger so they prefer ours. Caro, do you want to sell?"

"I don't know. Do you? You're more attached to it than I am, but I like it now that it's ours and we all meet up there."

"I don't want to sell, but it's a lot of money to turn down. Should we think about it?" Kate wasn't sure.

"I guess we have to. We'd both be pretty well fixed with that kind of money."

"Do you want to ask Peter about it?"

"No," Caroline said emphatically. "I don't. This is our decision. We can decide for ourselves." She didn't defer to him now the way she had before. She had her own mind, and had found her own voice.

"Why don't you sleep on it, and I will too," Kate suggested. "I'll call you tomorrow."

It was a long twenty-four hours after that. Caroline turned the numbers around in her mind again and again, and so did Kate. Kate wrote it down, and Caroline thought about all the things she could do with it, a bigger house, especially now with a baby coming, but Peter could provide that. She didn't need that kind of money, no one did, but it would be nice to have. And it would give her independence from Peter, since she and Kate were now land rich and cash poor, as their father had said.

They both fell asleep and woke up early. Kate hardly slept all night, and Caroline got up at four A.M., and sat in the kitchen, thinking about it. She finally called Kate at six.

"What do you think?" Kate asked her, worried about what they'd do if they disagreed.

"I know this sounds crazy, and you may hate me for it," Caroline said cautiously. "I'll probably regret it for the rest of my life, but I love the place, Kate. It's our home, and our roots, and it's part of Dad. I don't want to sell. I don't care how much money they offer us, I want to keep it." She sounded agonized when she said it.

"Oh, thank God, that's what I think too. I thought you'd kill me for spoiling it for you," Kate said.

They were both laughing with relief.

"I'll call the realtor this morning. Thank you, Caro. I think we're doing the right thing. How can we sell this?"

"I hope we never do," Caroline said with feeling, and they hung up, and Peter came in a few minutes later, looking for her.

"What are you doing up so early?" he asked her, looking suspicious, he had heard her laughing.

"I was talking to Kate."

"What about?"

"Ranch business."

"Oh." He nodded and smiled at her. "How are you feeling?" She was three months pregnant and everything was fine. He had gone to the doctor with her and the sonogram looked great. One healthy baby. Not twins, which was a relief, since women her age frequently had multiple births. And from a test she'd had, they knew now it was a girl.

"I feel great," Caroline said, delighted with their decision not to sell the ranch.

"I'm going to be the oldest father at nursery school, and in a wheelchair for her college graduation."

"No, we're not. And even if we are, so what? It's a gift. It was meant to be. It happened when we got back together." She was excited about it now after the initial shock. And they had told Morgan and Billy. They weren't thrilled, but they were okay with it, which was good enough. Morgan would be out of the house and in college when the baby was a year old anyway, and Billy would leave when she was five. It was a sign of hope and renewal. It was the baby of their reconciliation, Caroline couldn't turn that away, and it meant a lot to Peter too. They were both grateful to be back together.

"Are you coming back to bed?" Peter asked with a look of particular interest and she laughed.

"If you make it worth my while," she whispered.

"That's how you got in trouble in the first place," he reminded her, and they both laughed, closed their bedroom door and locked it. They had an hour before she had to wake the kids, and they could do a lot with that.

A few minutes later, they did. And even better than that, Kate and Caroline were keeping the ranch. And that was something to celebrate!

Chapter 18

On Memorial Day weekend, three weeks after the actual anniversary, they unveiled the memorial to their father, James "JT" Tucker, it said with his dates. Founder of Tucker Ranch, beloved father, companion, and grandfather, "We will always love you." It was a gentle sand-colored granite, and looked just right for him. They placed it to one side of the barn where the driveway ended, and people would see it when they drove up. It stood about four feet tall, and the family stood staring at it, still unable to believe that he was gone.

Juliette had flown in from Paris as she had promised, Rufus and Gemma had come from London, Caroline, Peter, Morgan, and Billy had come from San Francisco, and Scarlett and Roberto from Santa Barbara. Caroline was almost six months pregnant and you could see it now. The baby was due at the end of September. Caroline and her family were coming for the summer. Gemma would be off then and was coming, and Rufus had promised to come with her. Kate had offered Juliette her house if she wanted to come back in the summer, and she said she might for a few weeks. She said she missed the ranch terribly. And they all missed JT. So much had happened since he left.

Kate and Thad had taken over the ranch, Gemma had found Rufus and was on new wings in her career. Peter and Caroline almost didn't make it, got back together and were having a baby, and Juliette had gone home to France.

"I'd like to say something," Gemma said, stepping forward to stand next to the handsome stone they had just unveiled. Kate and Thad had approved it, and everyone loved it. "We always used to tease about my being 'Daddy's Girl.' Dad would say it sometimes. I thought it was a compliment. I'm not so sure it was. We fought about a lot of things. We had different opinions, and when I turned eighteen, I ran like hell. So did Caro, and we stayed away, in our own ways, for a long time. Dad wasn't an easy man. He liked to have his way, and he expected everyone to do what he told them to do. Kate, me, Caro, Thad, our mother, Scarlett, Juliette. It was his way or the highway. And some of us took the highway.

"But one thing I do know, and it's taken me a long time to figure it out. He loved us all. Not just me. I wasn't his favorite. I was the one he liked to fight with, because I fought back. And Kate was the one he liked to work with because she didn't fight back. She just waited until now. She and Thad can run the ranch the way they want." She smiled at them. "And Caro was the smart one, and he admired her for it. She just went about her business, wrote her books, and went around him. Our mother gave him three daughters. He couldn't take that away from her in the end. Juliette was the woman who loved him, with all his flaws and faults, she never let him down. We all loved him, and he loved us. As for his daughters, we were *all* Daddy's

Girls, and if he were standing here today, he would say that himself. May his memory, our love for him, and his love for us, shine brightly forever."

She stepped back into the crowd then, and both her sisters thanked her and everyone hugged her. She had said just what needed to be said, and what they needed to hear. And with that, everyone walked to Kate's house, where they were having lunch. On the way there, Thad hung back, and touched Kate's arm. She stopped walking and looked at him.

"It's been a year, Kate. We said we'd give it time. Don't you think it's time we got married? I do. We're going to have a new house soon. We have a life and a ranch. I want a wife. When will you marry me?" He looked worried. She stood looking at him for a moment, and knew he was right. She hadn't meant to wait this long, but so much had happened. They'd been busy.

"What about this summer when everyone's home?" He smiled as soon as she said it and kissed her.

"Can we tell them now?" he asked and she nodded.

"How about July? Everyone will be here then, and Caro will be too pregnant to come after that."

As soon as they walked through the door, Thad picked up a glass and a fork, and rang for everyone's attention.

"We have an announcement," he said, beaming. "Kate and I are getting married in July. You're all invited." Everyone cheered and applauded and kissed them both, and as so often happened on the ranch, a serious occasion had become a joyful one, and now they had something to celebrate. Many things, a wedding in July, a baby in September, and Rufus and Gemma's new show.

Chapter 19

The wedding turned out to be a lot bigger than they thought it would be. But Kate and Thad knew so many people, and so many people in the Valley liked them, that even trying to keep it small, there were two hundred guests at the ranch for their wedding day.

Caroline, Gemma, and Morgan were Kate's attendants. Thad asked Peter and Rufus to be his, and Billy was the ring bearer. And Scarlett walked her daughter down the aisle. They were married under an arch of white flowers in a pasture they cleared and mowed specially. A dance floor was brought in. They had a dance band from Santa Barbara. Juliette had come back from France again for the wedding, and brought her brother.

The wedding was at six P.M. Dinner was served at eight with some of the best barbecue Thad said he had ever eaten. The bride and groom on the cake were on horseback, and the guests danced until three A.M., and the last stragglers left at four. Kate and Thad had agreed to a honeymoon in France and Italy in the fall, with a stop in

England to see Gemma and Rufus on the way home. They were going to be away for three weeks, and the new foreman Thad had hired was going to run things in their absence.

Rufus and Gemma sat at their table after line-dancing for an hour and he said he'd never had so much fun in his life. It was a fantastic wedding. They finally went to bed at four A.M., after hanging out with Peter and Caroline. The bride and groom had gone to bed at three. It was the perfect end to a challenging year full of surprises and changes. But they had all come through them, better than before, stronger and wiser and braver. The errors of the past had been corrected, the transgressions had been forgiven. The ranch was thriving, the family was strong, the heartbreaks of the past had been healed, and love had prevailed in the end.

On a Sunday night in September, Gemma's new show debuted in the U.S. They were waiting in England to hear the ratings. The British ratings had been fantastic a month before. Thad and Kate were sitting in front of their TV in their new house. Caroline was planning to watch it with Peter and her kids. Scarlett was glued to her TV with Roberto. It was an exciting episode. One of the ones they had filmed in Africa. The others were going to be used later in the season. The show opened with a bang and a brilliant performance of Gemma's, and Kate wanted to jump up and down when she saw it, it was so good. Gemma called the minute it finished, even though it was five A.M. in London. They had stayed up to hear what her family thought.

"What did you think? How was it?" Gemma sounded tense.

"It was fantastic! Thad's crying!" Kate told her.

"Don't tell her that!" he said, embarrassed. They were leaving on their belated honeymoon in a few days.

"The show is going to be a huge hit, and you'll be a bigger star than ever," Kate said, excited. "Rufus is a genius!" Gemma was ecstatic that they loved it, they were hearing the same from everyone. And the critics had raved when it aired in the UK.

The next call Kate got was from Peter. She picked it up immediately.

"Wasn't she terrific! She's fantastic!" Kate said into the phone about Gemma.

"She certainly is! They both are! Caro just had the baby. She had her twenty minutes after we got to the hospital. We didn't even have time to call you. She's seven pounds, fourteen ounces, and we're calling her Scarlette, with an 'e' at the end."

"OhmyGod! Is Caro okay? She's a week early."

"She's great. We missed the show. The kids were taping it for us. We're going home tomorrow."

"Congratulations!" Kate said, and he handed the phone to Caroline, who sounded tired but thrilled. "You're fantastic. Is she gorgeous?" Kate said to her.

"She's beautiful. The next one is your turn. You have to do it, Katie." She hadn't called her that since they were kids.

"We'll see what happens on our honeymoon. We're leaving it up to fate. No heroics. Just Mother Nature."

"Good. I don't want to be the only geriatric mother in the family."

"Give her a kiss from me," Kate said, and then spoke tenderly to her sister. "Dad would be proud of you, Caro. For everything."

"Thank you," she said in a soft voice. "That means a lot, coming from you."

They would always be Daddy's Girls, all three of them, because right or wrong, for better or worse, whatever his faults, he had loved them all.

Danielle Steel

Have you liked Danielle Steel on Facebook?

Be the first to know about Danielle's latest books, access exclusive competitions and stay in touch with news about Danielle.

www.facebook.com/DanielleSteelOfficial

SPY

Britain, 1939. At eighteen, Alexandra Wickham seems destined for a privileged life. But a world war and her own quietly rebellious nature lead her down a different path. While her country pays the terrible price of war, Alex learns the art of espionage, leading to life-and-death missions and extraordinary adventures.

Paperback published October 2020

MORAL COMPASS

Saint Ambrose Prep, an esteemed school, has just enrolled its first female students. The day after a Halloween party, a student lies in the hospital and only a few know what happened. As parents, media, students and staff attempt to establish the truth, no-one will escape the fallout.

Paperback published December 2020

THE NUMBERS GAME

Eileen Jackson is forty and desperate to get her life back on track after the collapse of her marriage. Olivia Waters is twenty-seven, and she's swiftly coming to understand an affair brings unwanted baggage. And at ninety-two, Olivia's grandmother, Gabrielle, is an internationally successful sculptor. All three women must navigate their relationships and claim true happiness.

Paperback published January 2021

THE WEDDING DRESS

Eleanor Devereux's wedding would be the highlight
of 1929, and the dress a triumph. But with the advent
of the Great Depression, their dreams came crashing
down. Yet the wedding dress, passed down through
generations, continues to hold a special place
in the family's hearts and legacy.

Paperback published April 2021

NINE LIVES

Sometimes there are risks worth taking . . .

Maggie Kelly became used to losing those who were closest to her when her father and brother were killed in war-time military missions in Vietnam and Iraq. She sadly discovered that luck inevitably runs out for those who put their lives on the line, and after the devastating effect their deaths had on both Maggie and her mother, she vowed never to get involved with thrill-seekers or risk-takers.

But when Maggie re-meets her first love, Paul Gilmore, now a successful entrepreneur and F1 racing driver who has not left the wild and crazy days of his youth behind, she must ask herself whether she's still content to play it safe. Because sometimes you need to take a risk to get the life you want.

Coming soon

PURE STEEL. PURE HEART.